I0593209

LOOKING BACK AT A STRANGER

THE SUMMERS CHRONICLE BOOK THREE

PHILLIP ROSEWARNE

Published in Australia by Sid Harta Books & Print Pty Ltd,

ABN: 34632585293

23 Stirling Crescent, Glen Waverley, Victoria 3150 Australia

Telephone: +61 3 9560 9920, Facsimile: +61 3 9545 1742

E-mail: author@sidharta.com.au

First published in Australia 2022

This edition published 2022

Copyright © Phillip Rosewarne 2022

Cover design, typesetting: WorkingType (www.workingtype.com.au)

The right of Phillip Rosewarne to be identified as the Author of the Work
has been asserted in accordance with the Copyright, Designs and Patents Act 1988.

This book is a work of fiction. Any similarities to that of people living
or dead are purely coincidental.

All rights reserved. No part of this publication may be reproduced,
stored in a retrieval system, or transmitted, in any form or by any means without the prior written
permission of the publisher, nor be otherwise circulated in any form of binding or cover other than
that in which it is published and without a similar condition being imposed on the subsequent
purchaser.

Phillip Rosewarne

Looking Back at a Stranger

Book Three

ISBN: 978-0-9587448-3-6 (pbk)

978-0-6456825-9-5 (ebook)

pp302

ABOUT THE AUTHOR

Phillip Rosewarne has lived and worked in various places on the east coast of Australia, his first job being for a shipping company. After working in New Guinea, Phillip was a project clerk for the Australian government in Canberra and the Northern Territory, where he worked in Katherine and Darwin, initially  for the Commonwealth Department of Works, and then for three years as head storeman for Woolworths in the Darwin area, two years either side of Cyclone Tracy. Phillip bought a cattle property in Queensland, which he operated for four years.

After returning to Canberra, he spent the next twenty-five years at the Commonwealth Department of Primary Industries, as it was then known. During that time, he worked in a science bureau within several primary industry sections. He gained a Certificate of Horticulture from the Tafe College and an Applied Science Degree from the University of Canberra.

Phillip always had a desire to write novels as opposed to scientific papers. He began writing shortly after leaving school, and the passion to write never left him. It was only later in life that he had the opportunity to write fiction on a more permanent basis.

Phillip is currently retired, and lives in the Northern Beaches region of Sydney.

This book is the last of a trilogy of vast disparity and apparent disconnection, but coming together in the third. It is dedicated to my wife Patricia, who inspired so much of what has been written.

CHAPTER ONE

Life is a journey, a rocky road. An interlude. Humans are contrary, perverse and infelicitous, the end product of genes and circumstances. The outcome is unpredictable, especially when burdened with heavy baggage and a potentially unsuited personality. Here are two souls formed by outside influences that have heavily moulded the people they became. When they meet, they have a lot in common but also a lot to cause them sorrow.

The long plume of clay-coloured dust hung suspended in the air, slowly drifting up into the still sky before gradually fading back onto the drab, grassy plains. It was late August out on the flat Barkly Tableland. The blue utility torpedoed through the infinite, almost treeless plains, hurtling in its lonely isolation southward towards the bitumen that passed for a national highway in the remoteness of the vast Queensland outback.

The driver was departing for probably the last time from a short and hectic existence as manager of an enormous outback station. The station was owned by a family friend who lived down south on his smaller property located on the high Monaro plains of southern New South Wales.

Thomas Summers was in his late twenties. He had been hired by the owner of the Barkly property, Ted Guise, while he was still quite young and working on his grandfather's place, Bridgehead, just outside Cooma in the Southern Tablelands of New South Wales. It was not all that far from Bridgehead to Ted Guise's place south of Cooma and, in sparsely populated rural areas, everybody knew everyone else.

Thomas was feeling uneasy at leaving the huge Brinkley Downs Station. He had first arrived there about seven years ago as a raw young man fresh from the close confines of a loving home. He was a competent and capable manager, versed in all the requirements of running a large outback station. He was comfortable and contented in his work and managed the place efficiently and profitably.

Thomas was now returning south in a state of some uncertainty to the country that he had originally departed in a similar frame of mind as he was now experiencing: trepidation and apprehension. This time around, however, the motivation was reversed. He was now returning to manage the newly acquired high-tech sheep enterprise that his grandfather, John Summers, had just purchased, mostly as a means of encouraging Thomas's return to the Monaro to be near the family.

Thomas was a wild driver. He drove his Falcon utility as fast as he could safely do so on the long dusty roads in the flat open country of the Barkly. Many of the roads were maintained in good order by governments as developmental roads, mostly for the beef industry but also for tourism. The Barkly Tableland of western Queensland consisted of vast grassy plains that stretched for kilometres in seemingly unending flatness. The curvature of the earth was discernable in the flatness where the earth and the sky melted into one on the cloudless blue days of the tropical Dry.

The Barkly was a huge plateau up to three hundred metres in altitude that stretched from as far away as the mid Northern Territory all the way eastward finishing inside the Queensland border. Although the bulk was in the Northern Territory, there was an extensive area in north-western Queensland. This was where Ted Guise had his property, northwest of Mt Isa but south of the Gulf of Carpentaria flood plains.

It was wonderful cattle country. The quality and resilience of the native Mitchell grasses were such that extensive grazing enterprises could be conducted with little input from the owners. There was a marked lack of surface water, but this was overcome by strategic placement of bores extracting water from the enormous artesian basin that underpinned most of inland Queensland. Thus, despite being located essentially in the semi-arid belt of Australia, vast areas could be utilised that may have otherwise gone on unattended by farming practices. Ted's place was located in the exclusively cattle region, but further east and south was an extensive region that also supported sheep grazing enterprises on the drier inland plains, which gradually emerged into the saltbush country as they fused southwards into the arid zone.

Vast distances between places encouraged locals to hurtle across the usually dry gravel in order to arrive somewhere in as short a time as possible, with destinations not being measured in distance but time. As Thomas approached the junction of the well-maintained gravel road with the bitumen of the Barkly Highway, he slowed a little at the last moment before sliding out onto the highway in a trail of dust and scattering stones. He headed further west for Camooweal, about two hours up the road.

Thomas Summers was born in 1987 to Audrey Summers. Audrey was the first born and elder daughter of John and Livinia Summers, who owned, among other things, a successful grazing enterprise near Cooma in New South Wales. Audrey was only eighteen when she gave birth to Thomas in Sydney while at university, much to the dismay of her devout and conservative parents. Audrey defied her parents at every turn when it came to her morals, and she refused to divulge the name of the father, if indeed she knew who he was. In her defiant way, Audrey insisted on naming her child Thomas Summers, carrying on her own name and no one else's.

The problem was that Audrey was not about to let the issue of an unplanned child interfere with her Bohemian lifestyle in the trendy eastern suburb of Randwick. This resulted in Thomas being neglected and often unsupervised. By the time he was fourteen, Thomas was a wild child with a string of petty convictions and a long association with the police.

At his last appearance before the courts, he was facing jail time. However, it was agreed that his grandparents, John and Livinia, would take responsibility for him, and so Thomas joined them on the family farm near Cooma. It was a difficult and traumatic transition for the wayward and carefree young Thomas, but eventually he was straightened out by his grandfather, mostly by working long hours on the farm. This gradually turned to total respect and admiration, but Thomas never forgot the intimidating and menacing demeanour that could emerge from his grandfather if provoked.

Thomas was straight out of the city. He knew nothing about country life, let alone farm work. But John, his grandfather, began to instil in him a deep appreciation of rural living and the grazing industry. By the time Thomas was eighteen, after years of enforced discipline and fixed schedules, he was a competent and capable farmhand and showed real promise.

One of John's acquaintances, Ted Guise, who had purchased cattle from his properties many years previously, noticed how capable Thomas was when he ran into him at various sales around the Cooma district. Ever on the lookout for promising young jackaroos for his Barkly cattle run, he had asked John if he could offer Thomas a job as an overseer on probation, leading onto managerial positions on one of his huge holdings on the Barkly. Thomas had reluctantly agreed to the impressive offer but the wrench from his comfortable existence was difficult, especially in the early days.

Ted Guise not only owned Brinkley Downs on the Barkly but had recently purchased, in partnership with two other Queensland grazing families, a couple of large stations in the Channel Country on the Queensland-New South Wales border. Part of the agreement with the other two families was that he had agreed to supply the managerial expertise to run the newly acquired southern Queensland properties. This meant that he was obliged to transfer his most experienced manager from Brinkley Downs to the Channel Country. Brinkley Downs ran on a minimum of personnel, the manager and three jackaroos. It always proved very difficult to get reliable, sober workers in such an isolated location.

Ted had his eye on Thomas since he first noticed him with his grandfather around the Cooma district. Thomas always appeared to Ted as reliable, sober and, as an associate of John Summers, must be dependable and consistent. Thomas struck Ted as the sort of lad that could replace his manager on Brinkley.

When Thomas first arrived at Brinkley Downs, he was met by the manager and shown to the men's quarters where he was asked to bunk down for the week or so that the handover would require. Then he could move into the manager's homestead and take over.

At this time there were three young jackaroos, one a third-year trainee and the other two were two years on. They were all wild and uncultivated, and it came as a shock to Thomas to see the uncouth character of the men under his control. The third-year boy was not too bad a lad and Thomas had high hopes that at least he would form a firm friendship with him in time.

It was a dramatic and stressful first week trying to learn the ropes. Thomas was shown over the entire property, all the bore sites, the riverine plains and the cattle and former old sheep yards.

On his many long, lonely drives from Brinkley Downs to Mt Isa, or occasionally Townsville, Thomas had ample opportunity to review his life. He was quite resentful of his mother, Audrey. It pained Thomas to recall the lack of parental love that he endured as a child and the endless stream of weird young people that passed for his mother's acquaintances – people who indulged in what he now knew was the drug experimental culture and who misled him in many ways as a child. In his neglect he turned to himself and found solace in the company of similarly unsupervised and freedom-loving youths who had all been informed that one was to do as one pleased in order to achieve Nirvana and avoid the authority of the ruling classes. All possessions were theft; therefore, taking for oneself was challenging the status quo.

Unfortunately, as Thomas gradually realised, the ruling classes also had a set of rules that did not coincide with the philosophy of his mother's push, and Thomas soon discovered that 'enemies of freedom' had a much better system of imposing their regime than the less numerous 'hippies'. This resulted in Thomas's numerous 'indiscretions' and, accordingly, countless encounters with the law. The courts were losing their patience with his ilk, and especially with Thomas.

To compound Thomas's sense of abandonment, his mother moved into a state of co-habitation with an older man and abandoned her communal existence. The product of this union was two offspring who, to Thomas's eyes, received all the benefits that he had so cruelly been denied. Nothing was spared them in a material sense or in affection either.

Thomas turned into a rebellious and bitter youth who expressed his outrage in anti-social and criminal undertakings, especially related to other people's vehicular and electronic property. He cringed at the thought of how his bitterness manifested itself. It shamed him enormously how he had acted. It was also a constant source of latent embarrassment whenever he was in the presence of his grandparents, the two most respected and respectable people with whom he had ever had any association.

Thomas could not express in words the feelings of gratitude and obligation he felt towards his grandparents. As a successful adult, well respected in his field, he knew he owed it all to his devoted grandparents. He understood the sacrifices they must have made to take on a fourteen-year-old, sparing him from a downward spiral to destruction.

His grandmother was obsessed with education and learning, and finally got the support of her husband for Thomas to gain some qualifications in agriculture. In the end, Thomas succeeded very well in that field. Over the intervening years, he lost a lot of his bitterness and reverted to a more reliable and trustworthy young man, such that, by the time he was nineteen, Ted Guise had sought him out to work on his property on the Barkly. As a parting gift from his grandparents, Thomas was given a new Falcon ute, and that same vehicle was now returning him to his home.

Seven years ago, at the age of nineteen, it took Thomas nearly a week in the beginning of this journey to drive from Cooma to Brinkley Downs. At the time he was in no real hurry to get there as it was with some trepidation that he accepted the job. He feared failure and he was wary of unfamiliar surroundings.

Thomas's grandfather was John Summers. He had come by a fortune by devious means as a young man. He had secreted himself away in an isolated and quiet backwater situated near the foothills of the Snowy Mountains not far from the town of Cooma in New South Wales. He purchased a near-virgin block of country and planned to live a life gently disposing of his nefariously gotten gains and passing his time indulging in his passion for bush living and playing at farming.

John knew he had immorally accumulated his comfortable lifestyle and that the price he was prepared to pay was punishment for his sinful misdemeanour. For reasons beyond his understanding, John was seemingly blessed with the exact opposite. Unforeseeable circumstances, and a trait in his character that forbade him from wanton waste, led to John accumulating valuable property assets scattered throughout

Cooma and the Sydney area, which forced him to engage more than he had planned in a 'normal' life. He met Livinia in whom he found a similar soul. Together they embarked on a life that was enabled through his theft of money from his grandmother, of which Livinia was totally unaware. Together they forged a fortunate life, successfully raising four of their five babies.

Along the way, John purchased his neighbour's large but neglected adjoining acreage which comprised many acres of prime grazing country. It was during this testing time that he met his future wife at the Cooma show, usually run in the height of summer in March.

One of the happy results of this union was the arrival of five children. The eldest was Audrey, the mother of Thomas. She was followed by Ethan, the heir-apparent to the management of the diverse and profitable Summers family company. He was followed by Damien, a smart but troubled youth who resigned to living the life of a satisfied artisan of the land.

The last additions to the family were a set of twins, one boy and one girl. The boy, named Brendan, drowned aged ten amidst a thorny family difference of attitude involving education. This single event had more effect on the family cohesion than any other. It brutally affected John and nearly split asunder the relationship with his dearly loved Livinia. The sister of the drowned lad, Hannah, became a retiring and trampled shell, devoid of ambitions beyond a quiet life close to the roots of her genesis.

John Summers was years recovering any sense of deep

purpose, but slowly returned to the absorbing management of his diverse enterprises. His tranquillity was not aided by several family events involving his offspring, culminating in the total disruption caused by the arrival of the troublesome Thomas as a fourteen-year-old. John accepted the challenge eventually as did Thomas, once a few rules were established and it was made clear who was in charge.

Thomas began to use technology in the planning and running of the farm. He rebuilt an entire windmill system as part of a project and found electronic systems admirable for monitoring stock processes about the property. It was these features that finally convinced Ted to offer Thomas the position on his own property in Queensland, where advanced technology was replacing the dwindling availability of staff.

John had little interest in technology. He was continually entreated by Ethan to improve the running of the place but found it beyond his needs to have to master such things at his time of life. He did, however, encourage both Ethan and Thomas to use technology, if it advanced outcomes for the property.

In time, Thomas was accepted into the family as a rightful member. He despised his mother and her new family. Not long before Thomas returned from Queensland to the newly acquired Auvergne Station the other side of Cooma, John admitted him as an accredited member of the family business, with access to all the information and voting rights. It was this event that finally opened Thomas's eyes to the full extent of his grandfather's capabilities and his accumulated wealth.

The family company consisted of several diverse sources of income based on a substantial asset base. There were grazing properties that consisted of over ten thousand acres of reasonably good, fine-wool sheep country at Bridgehead. Then there were two other properties, one bordering the back boundary that John had not that long ago acquired, and the new one, Auvergne, south of Cooma to which Thomas was now heading to take up the management position.

There were several commercial buildings owned by the company in the heart of Sydney that were now worth many millions, but more importantly returned a consistent and reliable income independent of the vagaries of the weather. There were also several rental properties located in the suburb of Harbord that did likewise, plus some commercial interests in Cooma itself.

Auvergne was located about thirty minutes or so the other side of Cooma from Bridgehead on the plain country of the Monaro. John and Thomas inspected the place prior to its purchase with Ethan, John's eldest son, who proved less than supportive as he harboured ambitions of managing just such an enterprise himself. But John was steadfast that Thomas was to manage it. Besides, at Ethan's beckoning, the family had recently purchased John's back neighbour's large, abused property for Ethan to indulge in his chief desire of building up an advanced technologically oriented, fine-wool enterprise.

Auvergne was a large property that was well developed and contained a huge amount of technical infrastructure designed for producing extra-fine, low-micron fibre wool. It required a level of technical expertise. There was a trained bio-technician who remained there after the sale. Thomas had already cultivated a friendship with him throughout the purchase process and he hoped to forge a strong working relationship with him.

There was also a farmhand seconded to the place after the sale who would be able to do most of the hack work. To Thomas the property was strikingly similar to many parts of the Barkly, except for its undulations.

Auvergne was extensively grazed with a commercial flock of sheep. It also ran a small herd of commercial beef cattle numbering about two hundred that were run on the harder hill country towards the rear of the property. It was this beef enterprise that Thomas had hoped to engage an independent person to run, at least initially, while he concentrated on learning and operating the shedded sheep aspect of the business.

Both John and Livinia were taken with the presentation of Auvergne. Livinia was particularly enamoured of the housing facilities. To Thomas, however, these were of little consequence. He viewed the stately two-storey granite homestead as almost an imposition on him due to it being sold empty of furniture. He would leave most of that to Livinia.

Furthermore, the homestead was surrounded by a large, and once well-maintained, formal garden, as well as an orchard and produce beds. These were even lower down on his scale of concern. John and Livinia feared that those assets might deteriorate rapidly once bachelor Thomas took on the reins.

At Brinkley Downs, Thomas had initiated and developed a successful and innovative electronic tracking system based on the data required for the operation of the new National Livestock Identification Scheme or NLIS. Expanding the database to help manage weight gain and feed processes on the Barkly property had filled him with enthusiasm for the possibilities. The problem for Thomas was that Auvergne was a prize sheep property and the cattle were a secondary adjunct to that main enterprise. It would be necessary for him to ensure that the sheep side was progressing satisfactorily before he could devote any time to implementing his grandiose schemes for the cattle. In the meantime, he hoped to employ a satisfactory proxy to maintain the mob and maybe even establish the rudiments of his ideas.

At Auvergne, Thomas had briefly met the two local lads, neighbours from a few kilometres away, who had been employed casually to muster and truck the cattle to market and was unimpressed with both their character and their attitude to the work.

The other employee, Warren Costello, was responsible for the high-tech biological aspects of the sheep component and was a highly trained and competent operator. Warren was a middle-aged man of dour countenance, severe and reserved, but very knowledgeable about his subject. He was married to a hardworking woman who was much more voluble and sociable, and who cultivated her contacts through her association with the local church and the Country Women's Association.

Warren had worked on the property for over ten years

14

before the Summers bought the place and he had mastered the art of artificial and genetic-based breeding. He understood cloning and producing superfine Merino wool. This was chiefly achieved using shedding techniques with controlled nutrition designed to produce clean and contamination-free wool for the high-end market. Warren worked long hours and rarely took time off.

He steadfastly refused to be involved with the mustering of the stock as he did not ride a horse and certainly was never going to attempt to ride a trail bike, especially over dangerous paddocks chasing sheep, let alone cattle. This he had pointed out to Thomas on their first encounter and this added to the problems that Thomas had regarding the mustering issues of the new property. All these matters played on his mind as he contemplated his move south to take over the management of Auvergne.

There was one other employee whom Thomas had briefly met. His name was Samuel. As it turned out, Sammy was a cast-off from Dave Quiggin's old place at the back of John's Bridgehead property.

That was the background to the situation whereby Thomas was now to return to Cooma. All of this would play out in the future. Firstly though, it was now necessary to return to the beginning of Thomas's journey north and the start of life on the Barkly, when Thomas was at the other end of that journey. This was when he first began heading north to begin his life at Brinkley Downs. Thomas would arrive at Brinkley as a raw young man with little experience of this part of Australia.

The transition would be stressful.

The station homestead at Brinkley Downs Station was a rambling wooden structure that was all verandas and green tin roof. It was so isolated that, at first, he was quite homesick for the comforts and camaraderie of his former home. The strange thing for him was the extensive featureless plains that stretched interminably in all directions. There were almost no trees and the country barely even undulated. The rivers were few and far between and often indiscernible in the flat open fields. In fact, unless there was a signpost indicating the existence of the watercourse, one could drive through the large meandering riverbeds and, apart from a minor dip in the terrain, would not even know it was there, except of course when it rained; and when it rained up there it often forgot how to stop.

The cyclones would roar in from the north or the east and usually deteriorate into a cyclonic depression by the time they reached this far inland, dumping metres of water on the coastal floodplains and tablelands, sending flooding waters hundreds of kilometres inland and down through the channel country all the way to Lake Eyre. When this happened, Thomas would be isolated for weeks and the only way in and out was by air.

Thomas worked most of the days of the year at Brinkley Downs. He occasionally attended the Mt Isa rodeo held every August and a couple of the other country shows. It was at the Mt Isa rodeo that Thomas met Becky Alderson, a young woman from a coastal family that he rather fancied, at least at first. Her loose morals and carefree attitude slowly dissuaded him from regarding her as a long-term girlfriend. The other woman he met there, however, was a different story. Her name was Petra Camilleri. She was about eight years older than Thomas and she had a young son about ten. Petra sent her son off to one of the boarding schools in Townsville during the year but could visit him often. She worked in the roadhouse at Camooweal associated with the caravan park owned by her family.

Petra was a sensible and able worker and Thomas found her rather attractive. She had long dark hair that often shone in the sunlight. Her gentleness captivated him. She and Thomas had known each other for about three years and he maintained regular contact with her at the roadhouse. She was sensible enough to understand that, as nice and pleasant as Thomas was, their relationship could probably not go much beyond a casual status.

Mature female company was something he sorely missed and lacked, living as he did out at Brinkley. While she was pleasant and placid, she was poorly educated and knew little about the intricacies of outback rural industries.

The only other female company was with the wives of the property owners or managers. These women always seemed to be younger versions of his highly esteemed grandmother, rather portly ladies, supremely capable, and the mothers of many children, long abandoning any attempts to remain beautiful, as indeed many of them would have once been. Their lives were spent in support of their hardworking spouses. Petra was a pleasant distraction and he valued deeply the times he spent in her company. It was Petra that Thomas was on the way to see as he turned onto the Barkly Highway and headed west towards Camooweal, a few hours up the road. After that he would be turning south towards his new life on the Monaro.

Thomas's life on Brinkley had been demanding. He endured the isolation by busying himself for all the hours of daylight that were available. He also mastered all the modern technologies that sprang up from the innovative Australian farming community.

He was extremely interested in the endless possibilities that solar panels offered to the outback farmers. He acquired and adapted these small panels to operate remotely the many sundry activities that were required to operate the property. He was able to sit in his office in the homestead and monitor things such as gate operations, bore levels, pump timing, windmill maintenance and even stock movements within certain limits. He found that part of his work interesting and absorbing as did his boss, Ted, who visited the place regularly from the south. These operations did not entirely eliminate the necessity to physically monitor fences or watering points, but it did cut down the time and the expense of so doing.

The two younger jackaroos who were there when he first arrived had not found his company so appealing and had both departed within three years. The third-year man, a young fellow named Bruce, however, was made of sterner stuff and proved to be a much better proposition. He was adaptable and open to suggestions about modern techniques and methods, and together they ran the place fairly well. Thomas had to occasionally employ contract musterers if he was too short of staff, but with the judicial use of suitable jackaroos, he and Bruce managed to operate the property admirably.

The things Thomas would miss were the freedom to manage as he pleased and the comforts that isolation brought in connection with family dealings. He had much less reporting responsibilities and he would miss the company of Petra from the roadhouse. Even though their relationship could probably go nowhere, he valued their times together. She was the one woman that he had grown to really like a lot since moving up to Queensland. He was not looking forward to renewing contact with his mother and her associated family.

As Thomas sped onwards to return south, towards his fateful encounter at Camooweal, contemplating his emotions at both leaving what was familiar and heading into the unfamiliar, another party was about to do likewise, but from a totally different part of the outback. Fate had decreed that their paths should cross.

CHAPTER TWO

essie MacIntyre stopped her heavily laden vehicle at the junction of the Gibb River Road and the entrance to Ravymoota Station. She had many times in the past come to this point in her journey but never stopped to think what lay to the east; she had always, without thinking, turned right to head back to Milbark, a few hours further down the rough and dusty track.

For the first time in her life in the remote Kimberley, she had a choice, and was fearful and uneasy with that option. She sat for many minutes in the stillness of the late-August Dry season morning. Above the sound of the idling diesel, she could hear the familiar noises of the Kimberley. She was contemplating all the possible ramifications. She felt queasy and slightly unsure of herself, and not for the first time in her unstable and turbulent existence so far.

Every time in the past when she was forced to make these life-altering decisions, she invariably ran into trouble and heartache. She feared that this time would again prove to be no different. Finally, with a sigh of resignation, she gripped the wheel and firmly shunted the lever into first gear and turned east towards Kununurra, many long hours further up the track.

Jessie was not entirely sure where she was going or when she planned to arrive there. She had tentatively arranged to meet her publishers in Melbourne in the next month or so, a journey she hoped would take most of that time occupied in crossing the arid zone in slow interesting travel. Beyond Melbourne, however, she had no plans at all.

Jessie was now in her mid-forties, having been born in 1967. Her arrival into this world was, to say the least, out of the ordinary, let alone her upbringing. This was a complex story of intrigue and chance, always accompanied by turbulence. This time, however, she was leaving her secure surroundings with a lot more than when she first arrived in the Kimberley.

For a start, she was exceedingly wealthy and had a secure and abundant income. She was an author of repute, acknowledged as a world-renowned writer, and her output was eagerly sought. She had the three lifetimes of the wildly differing experiences and memories of the now departed mentors she first encountered on her arrival at Milbark, and from whom she gleaned all her vast array of inspiration. From her times spent in the company of these early teachers on Milbark, she retained memories that would last forever, and they also filled her with inspiration and comfort well into her dotage.

Jess also respected the Indigenous people who lived near the station homestead and from whom she had built up an enormous store of knowledge, friendship and understanding of this ancient culture.

On the negative side, Jess had a litany of bad experiences associated with authority, notably the police forces of two states. This left her with a disturbing legacy of resentment towards authority and power that stayed with her and prejudiced her future actions.

The three most influential souls in her life so far were buried in the sombre little graveyard of Milbark: one was an absconding aristocrat from an almost vanished cultural heritage of England; another the last of the true overlanders from the cattle-droving days; and the third, the man whose surname she shared and who took her in after being sent to Milbark cattle station by his brother from Sydney when she was only thirteen. The only other person of significance was the Austrian mechanic from whom she gained inspiration for one of her pen names and from whom she polished her German-speaking abilities. She had lost him also to the vagaries of encroaching old age and the lure of a settled life in Darwin.

Jessie's story began in the seedy working-class back streets of eastern Sydney. She was born in Waverley on a cold, windy day in August, with the bitter southerlies blowing in from the distant snow-covered southern alpine regions, often beginning all the way from Antarctica. Her Danish mother,

Herge Eriksson, was a somewhat pretty woman; blonde with wide blue eyes and the fairest skin. She was rather serious and tended to be humourless despite her carefree attitude.

Herge was intelligent but she had no common sense or moral compass. She arrived in Australia at the peak of the hippy craze and fitted in admirably. She lived with many different communal groups and bowed down to the gods of free love and gay abandonment to the fullest. She also spent much of her time high on drugs.

On discovering that she was pregnant, she initially embraced the idea and eased off the drugs considerably, especially during the latter part of her term. She even managed to abstain almost entirely from alcohol, which for her was rather an achievement.

The pregnancy was the result of chance, not design. She had come to the attention of one slightly possessive and jealous young man from the Baltic north of Europe, who fancied her as a companion, but not the mother of his children. His name was Olaf and he also was of pale appearance with a sour demeanour, and was severe in his manner. He seldom smiled but could drink with the best of them. When he did so, he became even more stern and introspective and sometimes would become agitated and quite violent. He was hot-tempered and quick to anger.

Herge was in such a heightened state of depression and anxiety after the birth of their child, at least Olaf assumed it was his, that she more or less abandoned the poor infant. Her discovery that his attitude was less than caring, and the realisation of her own unfavourable predicament, led her immediately into seeking relief in drugs of the mind-numbing assortment. These were able to remove her temporarily from her reality, and she began to take them in increasing amounts to counter her anxieties. Olaf was so disgusted with her lack of attention to the child and her permanent inebriation that he became more morose and violent than ever.

The child was still nameless and only two or three days old when, in her stupor, Herge accused Olaf of infidelity, and an argument ensued in which she was near fatally injured. Olaf saw his chance to eliminate this problem by dropping her gently into the harbour at about 2 am. It was with no small sense of relief that he watched as she floated out of his sight.

This only left the issue of the child, malnourished, uncared for, and barely alive. He seriously considered drowning her as well, but at the last minute remembered the Catholic orphanage up the hill from where he had been to a nearby market. He resolved to drop her there instead. This he did at about four in the morning on a breezy, freezing winter's pre-dawn, knocking on the door as a last gesture before departing with some haste down the hill to the stirring and rumblings of the market men. This he achieved without a backward glance, but with relief at the twin disposal of all his problems.

Of course, the child knew none of this and never would. It would have been most advantageous for her to have at least known something of the character and makeup of her parentage. It would have assisted in explaining to her some of the strange characteristics that she later displayed and from which she herself sometimes resiled in abject aversion at her own behaviour and latent melancholy.

The nuns at the orphanage were early risers to prayers and luckily heard the thudding at the door. There they discovered the cold infant wrapped in a dirty cream-coloured shawl that her mother had used as a cloak. She was taken in and examined, and then cleaned up. They called her Clare de Lune, as Clare was the name of the mother of the nun who found her, and the night of her disposal at the orphanage was accompanied by a near-full wispy moon.

Clare was suffering from neglect and steps were taken to ensure her survival. She became an attractive child, with big blue eyes. Her hair was the blondest they had ever seen, and her skin was soft and pale. She was always a small child.

Clare was from the start an enigma to them. They had no idea who she was or who left her with them. As she grew, she exhibited traits that they found most disturbing. Clare never smiled. No amount of coaxing could evince the slightest glimmer of a smile. She had the most disturbing habit of staring at adults in a disconcerting way that perplexed the most avid and experienced child carers.

She rarely joined in group play, in fact she rarely played; she mostly sat and peered about as if memorising things. She could amuse herself for hours alone with pencils and paper. This led to the horrifying suspicion that she seemed to favour the left-hand, a trait that was anathema to them. It was a long-held belief of their creed that this was an evil manifestation that required immediate correction, by any means. Any attempt to correct this affliction was met with total rejection by Clare and bitter struggles ensued in an attempt to correct it, and all to no avail.

The medical staff of the convent system could not account for this strange behaviour and the advice was that she would probably grow out of it. As time elapsed and serious attempts were made to correct her left-handedness, the harshness of the punishment increased. But the beatings or strapping would not change her left-hand-writing preference. Furthermore, Clare retreated more into her shell and her staring habit increased. She never cried nor yelled when hit. It was almost as if she had no human feelings.

Clare had three mortal sins to overcome in the eyes of her new carers. Firstly, she was obviously conceived in sin and nurtured to birth by the ungodly. Secondly, her appearance was that of a child who would grow to torment men with her attractiveness, a trait that they found unnerving and a source of much evil. Thirdly, and worst of all, was the devil's sign of being strongly left-handed. This combination of factors led the nuns to begin calling her Jezebel, a name that began to stick, and by which she became more familiarly known, the attractive and benign appellation of Clare de Lune soon passing the way of the poor child's mother.

By the time this Jezebel was about five, the animosity between her and the authority of the nuns was at such intensity that she absconded from the establishment on several occasions. She always made for the markets located further down the hill in east Sydney where she felt she could melt into the throng with much ease and remain hidden for days.

On one of these jaunts, Jessie had been noticed by a man who was struck by her aloofness and the enigma of so different a child compared to the usual urchins that frequented the market stalls, the majority of stallholders being New Australians of a much swarthier appearance.

Jess, being so small and blonde stood out in the crowd. She was collected by this caring man, who did not normally work at the markets. He was standing in for his partner who mostly operated the stall. The name of her rescuer was Donald MacIntyre and he discovered the plight of Jessie from the nuns after making enquiries when he saw her there several days running. In a moment of compulsive weakness, he took her home to remove her from danger while he decided what to do.

Donald MacIntyre was a middle-aged man when all this occurred. He was primarily a mechanic, albeit unqualified, but nevertheless owned a successful mechanical workshop in the busy thoroughfare known as Australia Street in the Sydney suburb of Newtown. Here he lived upstairs above the workshop in a pokey and dilapidated old building with his two hired professionals, one a German mechanical engineer and the other a French panel-beater.

It was with Don that Jess found her first real home. She casually adopted his name and began a life of her own, going to school in nearby Australia Street in Newtown. The advantages Jess gained from life with Donald MacIntyre were manifold. The German mechanic taught her impeccable

German, firstly as an amusement, but eventually as an art because of her skill at the language. She also learned to speak French, mostly from the French panel-beater's girlfriend. Jess also showed tremendous aptitude for motor mechanics.

Jess enrolled in the nearby martial arts school, which operated only a few doors down from Don's mechanical workshop. Her aptitude for this skill was such that she quickly developed, way beyond her young years, into quite a formidable exponent.

Don gave her two large foolscap-sized, hard-cover accounting journals for her to scribble in when she was about ten. She was so enamoured with them that she deemed them too valuable simply to deface by being scribbled in. She commenced to write a daily diary, which she religiously continued until they were filled.

The run-in with the New South Wales constabulary occurred when Jess was thirteen. She was unfortunately the witness to the gruesome and calculated murder of two young policemen working for a detective who was investigating corruption in the police force. Don had agreed to assist this investigating detective, Ian Knuckey, in exposing corruption and unlawful dealings within the police by gathering evidence of these deeds from meetings held at his workshop. The trap was about to be sprung when it was discovered by the criminal perpetrators.

Unfortunately, Jess was at the wrong place at the wrong time and was inadvertently a witness to the crime and her life was in serious danger. Don packed her off immediately that night to his estranged brother, who owned the lease on an isolated Kimberley cattle station situated along the remote Gibb River Road. Don had not seen or spoken to Stuart for years, not since he had first departed the property on the death of his stern father many years before. Don, more in hope than in knowledge, sent Jess there on the surety that, come what may, she would be safer with Stuart than in Sydney. All Jess could take with her were a few clothes, a small amount of cash that Don had on him and her two precious childhood diaries.

Her arrival at the age of thirteen at Milbark Station in the remote west Kimberley district of Western Australia was tinged with difficulties and complications. Not only was she not expected, but it was plain that she was not welcome either. It was the Austrian station mechanic, George, who finally broke the ice through her ability to converse with him in his native tongue. This set her life off in a new direction. It was on the long, isolated days spent out camping with George, as he graded the station tracks for access, that they forged a friendship that endured.

Jessie had many adventures during the long years that she lived on Milbark Station. The most significant for her, however, was the slow evolution from childhood diarist to romance novelist and then to more serious writing. The romance novels were lightweight, shallow stories that she was able to write in very short time following a formula she mastered very easily. For these she used the pen name of Jane Ransom.

Developing on from this were her creative masterpieces

that she then published under the name of George Norman Thaler. This culmination resulted in the publication of substantial and very popular authentic novels dealing with her knowledgeable, sympathetic and appealing stories about all aspects of life in the remote Australian outback of northern Western Australia. Finally, to assuage an insatiable urge to write, she also published long and less developed stories under the name of Kimberley West.

It was this unfortunate primal urge to create and express this need that led to Jessie's exposure through the agency of television. Her whereabouts had long been sought by some central characters in the assassination of the two unfortunate young policemen, more out of fear of exposure than any real knowledge or certainty that Jess would ever talk. Her whereabouts were finally revealed inadvertently and completely without her knowledge by a well-meaning television reporter operating under the guise of a travel reporter.

Jess stumbled in on the recording team and her existence was revealed almost as an aside. This event culminated in Jessie's violent arrest at Milbark and her extradition to Sydney to face serious charges. Following a lengthy and controversial trial, the outcome of which was favourable for her, but at some considerable personal and emotional cost, she was finally able to return to Milbark Station. Many aspects of her disturbing childhood were revealed and, worst of all for her, the fact that she was not related in any way to her mentors, Donald MacIntyre in Sydney or Stuart MacIntyre of Milbark. This was the most devastating outcome of the trial for her.

It was never actually confirmed, but suspicions were very strongly aroused that Jessie MacIntyre was also Jane Ransom and George Norman Thaler, identities that had hitherto been kept hidden. The trial ended sensationally and abruptly once her devastating evidence was presented and the alluded-to identities of the two reclusive authors were not able to be confirmed. Nobody ever suspected her of being Kimberley West. That was one secret she managed to keep intact as she departed the trial in Sydney.

It took Jess many years to overcome the trauma of the litigation against her. To compound her hurt and insult was the fact that she was placed on a three-year good behaviour bond by an officious Western Australian female magistrate who was appointed under dubious circumstances. This bond resulted from the manner of her arrest and her violent resistance, coupled with other miscreant acts committed by her while living at Milbark Station that came to light during the trial in Sydney. This bond so enraged Jess that she refused the conciliatory offer of the grossly embarrassed state government, which effectively promised to exonerate her of all charges if she would appeal the judgement. This she steadfastly refused to do and ensured that the judiciary suffered as much adverse notoriety as she could manage.

Slowly she eased her way back into the routine of submitting lightweight romance novels to her Melbourne publishers, using the pen name of Jane Ransom. This was more as a way for her to occupy the increasingly long and disturbing nights when she was unable to sleep or work in the cool Dry season air of the outdoors in the workshop.

About two years after the trial, her now famous and rather large childhood diaries were published under the insatiable demand of an adoring and extremely curious public. Apart from this aspect of course, the diaries contained wonderful descriptive passages about her early life in Sydney and especially about her formative years in the isolated Kimberley. They also contained, mostly as asides, many references to the corrupt people of the judiciary and the police force, which had already led to a serious and devastating Commission of Inquiry into the possibly tainted New South Wales police force. This had resulted in many long-serving and retired pillars of society being sullied with the hint of corrupt and unlawful activities, which resulted in many retrials having to be set.

It took Jess much longer, however, to pluck up the courage to attempt another much more substantial effort as the author known as George Norman Thaler. These were the amazing tomes that had initially brought her to the attention of the public. Her drive and the need for her to excel at this endeavour were such that she felt she lacked the desire and inspiration to attempt such a task for many years after the trial. Any output would of course be highly sought after and probably be very successful. It pained her, however, to produce something that was received solely on reputation and not on its primary merit alone. She began to contemplate the demise of George Norman Thaler.

In this frame of mind, Jess delayed any attempt at producing another novel for some time. Eventually, once the good behaviour bond was completed and she overcame that stigma, Jess thought about writing seriously again. There were several items that needed completing before she was prepared to begin typing, however. These included gaining a legitimate driver's licence, registering her old GMC, and legitimising her tax affairs around the multiple names under which she was variously known.

Life after the trial was tinged with sadness for Jess, as a host of dramatic events followed on from each other. As one gazes at the sea one observes that upon each wave there is another. Her mentor and first real friend at Milbark, George, the Austrian station mechanic who befriended her on her unexpected arrival at the station, departed for a less demanding life in the Territory at Darwin. This was a real wrench for Jess as she missed his insights and understanding of the outback environment around the station, and it had been George who had improved both her German and her mechanical skills. He was also instrumental in inculcating in her a real love and understanding of the remote Kimberley region.

Shortly after the good behaviour bond had expired, Jess reluctantly agreed to an interview on UK BBC television on the explicit understanding that the programme was entirely for British consumption, and she gained assurances that it would in no way be aired in Australia. The British had a longstanding love affair with the novels of George Norman Thaler, with their authentic Australian flavour and exotic and romantic locations and content.

The main reason for her agreeing to this proposal, however,

was the issue of the now dead Englishman on whom she had based one of her main characters in her novels. It transpired that his strange disappearance many years ago from England had involved some rather seedy family scandals that were still popularly followed in appropriate circles. As she had inadvertently exposed him to the light of day so many years later, she felt a mild obligation to justify her knowledge of his story to the British people. She naively believed these assurances of British exclusivity, but was sadly betrayed by commercial and, to some extent, genuine patriotic feelings on behalf of the Australian media, when a few months later they were triumphantly aired by the ABC. She never saw the programmes and was unaware at the time of this event, but it would come back to haunt her years later.

The most devastating event for Jess was the death of Stuart MacIntyre. He was the brother of Donald, the man who first rescued her from the Sydney markets as a five-year-old in 1972. Stuart was the other son of the man whose father had taken up the pastoral lease over Milbark and continued with that lease when his father died. Donald was wise enough to perceive that ultimately the Kimberley cattle industry was probably doomed through lack of access to markets and by sheer isolation. He had moved to Sydney and established a life there for himself that included eventually the young Jessie. Stuart's not totally unexpected death forced Jess to seriously think about her own future.

The years between the devastating court case and the death of Stuart were punctuated by long bouts of solemn refusal to contemplate the reality of a world devoid of all the stabilising masculine influences that Jess had hitherto known in her life at Milbark Station. But inevitably, that moment arrived, and her ability to face it was tempered by the recollections of all the discomforts and heartaches that had accompanied all the other wrenches that seemed to periodically, almost cyclically, reoccur in her disjointed existence. She was astute enough to realise that she was incapable of, or at least unwilling, to take on the enervating and difficult struggle of managing a pastoral lease in the dry tropics of northern Australia. Eventually, the reality of being alone and devoid of family support would render that operation a failure. It was simply too difficult in this pioneering region to succeed without extensive backup.

The problem for her was the alternatives. Jess had so much income that finances were not the issue. No, the problem for her was where to live and how to remain anonymous in so doing. The trouble was that Jess was looking at this issue through the wrong prism. She assumed that the notoriety associated with her through the disastrous criminal trial and the subsequent fall-out was her main threat. She wisely and intuitively realised that there existed some people who would still want to eliminate her for the trouble she had caused, indeed to some extent still did cause, even after all these years. This was one of the reasons she continued using pen names for her various novelistic outputs.

What Jess did not understand, indeed never fully grasped, was that her notoriety was not so much associated with her widely publicised trial and subsequent coverage, but with her untold success as a famous author with a world-wide popularity rarely attained by authors domiciled solely in Australia and writing on such parochial topics. It was her naivety that led to her troubles in the first place. In her innocence, she assumed that the desire that drove her to create would be met with a moderate and limited, if indeed any, success, and she was purely motivated by artistic desires, not mercenary ones. It simply never entered her head that she could achieve huge success. Advice from her publishers that she was highly sought-after was always taken by her to mean that they were desirous of keeping her on-stream in order to maintain their own meagre incomes from a moderately successful writer who happened to live in the outback.

Jessie's ambition was to relinquish all thoughts of remaining on Milbark after Stuart's death. This was for several reasons, one being that she feared the responsibility of control. It was one thing to understand the requirements of running a monster such as Milbark Station, yet another to be responsible for the decisions upon which so much depended. Jess knew from long experience that running a cattle station was like owning a bottomless pit of demand for money, resources and attention. At any given moment someone else could simply pull the rug from under her in a number of ways — government legislation, environmental demands, land claims, falling cattle prices, diseases, natural disasters — on and on it went. Jess craved an easier life, possibly somewhere else.

Jess's uninspiring experiences with the types of workers

with which she was forced to associate compounded her discontent. Long gone were the characters of the calibre of George, the Austrian mechanic, a rough diamond and faithful friend to Jess throughout their long association. Norm Woods, the refined and classically educated aristocratic absconder who instilled into Jess an understanding of the finer aspects of life. He was similar to the remittance men of old, except no income was remitted to him in exchange for remaining in the colonies out of sight. His whereabouts was also a mystery to his baffled family until it was revealed well after his death.

The old drover, Peter, who filled in for Jess all the background connected with the cattle industry from the early days. Lastly, there was Stuart. He was a gentleman and cared for Jess as only family could, despite the horrific discovery later in their association that she was neither a blood relative nor indeed any relative of his.

Nowadays, the younger men who worked on the stations were usually the offspring of station owners who sent their boys off to the wilds of the Kimberley to gain extensive experience in the rough and tumble of the industry where those workers with less experience were more likely to be welcomed because of a lack of labour.

These were the experiences that Jess was leaving behind as she departed the familiar and relative safety of Milbark and the folks she had known there. Of course, the other thing Jess was leaving behind was her youth. Another reason for her reluctance to continue her hibernation in the Kimberley was that she had acquired a taste for the cultural, and that was sadly missing up there. She acknowledged that she enjoyed the success of her writing endeavours, especially the critical acclaim rather than the royalties. It was, after all, the intellectual stimulation that originally drove her to strive for publication rather than the income from it. She could not deny she had an insatiable and voracious need to create, and George Norman Thaler had gone a long way to fulfilling that call. Even her later creation of Kimberley West, another of her pen names, who created enormous tomes of mediocre quality from the dross of her better works, helped to assuage her unlimited desire to create. So far, she had not been discovered as that entity by the literature world. Countering this struggle was her conflicting desire to remain very private, even anonymous, as long as she could continue to produce works that people found acceptable.

Her vague plan was to keep her promised appointment with her publishers in Melbourne, which she had tentatively arranged for late September. She realised that she would need to find a location where she could continue her work but be free from constant harassment, and had formulated a few possibilities from there. She could move to a small country town and hope she could remain relatively undetected. This appealed to her as she was fond of rural living after so long in the outback and could feasibly be anywhere in temperate Australia at this stage. She could choose a coastal town between Sydney and Melbourne so she could stay connected with her publishers, and her associates connected with the aftermath of the trial lived in or near Sydney.

The only other option she had considered was to move into the centre of Sydney itself. She could be anonymous in a big city, right in the middle of millions of people. These were the thoughts that swirled about in her head as she contemplated departing the familiar existence that had been her life on Milbark Station.

While Jess tried to hibernate for as long as possible with what remained of her life in the secure isolation of the Kimberley backwater, fate deemed it time to intervene and she was again cast adrift to face the vicissitudes of life alone.

Jess sat at the intersection on the Gibb River Road. It would take her more than a day to travel along the dusty meandering road that was the Gibb from the Ravymoota turnoff to Kununurra. Once she reached Kununurra, Jess planned to stay a day or two then head off on the long, lonely road that led all the way over to Katherine in the Northern Territory.

She did not plan on travelling all the way to Katherine, but instead she planned to deviate off the Victoria Highway near Timber Creek, taking the Buchanan Highway south-east to Top Springs then continue eastward to connect up with the Stuart Highway near Dunmarra. Jess thought that Buchanan Highway was a rather grandiose term to describe the gravel track that passed for a road in this remote part of the outback. However, there was no need for her to travel long distances for no advantage when a shorter route would achieve the same result with probably better scenery on the way. From there it was a simple journey south on the bitumen all the way to

Three Ways Roadhouse, turn east onto the Barkly and head for Camooweal, just inside the Queensland border. There she planned to turn due south down gravel roads through Urandangi to Bourke in New South Wales.

Jess expected to take at least four days to accomplish this first part of the trip. She had prepared the Land Cruiser thoroughly for an extended outback trip and fully expected to dawdle along those remote roads and take in the country. She would be able to camp most of the time along the way as it was so remote that there was hopefully almost no other traffic. It would remain pretty desolate until she was well into New South Wales, way south of Bourke before she would have to worry about towns appearing and civilisation encroaching on her time.

First, she had to get to Queensland before turning south, hopefully at Camooweal from where she could see some of the old droving tracks that Peter had talked about around the flickering campfires after long days mustering in the Dry. That was her plan at this stage. She had no inkling of the path that life was now preparing to lay out for her as she departed the Kimberley.

CHAPTER THREE

Thomas was now speeding along the Barkly Highway towards his meeting with Petra. He arrived at the roadhouse about ten-thirty and filled the petrol tank at the bowsers. He walked into the shopfront and café to see whether Petra was free for an hour or so before he took off for good. There were several buses about so he thought she could be busy attending to the tourists.

Thomas paid for his petrol, waved at Petra, and said he would be back in about an hour. She acknowledged his wave with a beaming smile and nodded in agreement. Thomas returned to the Falcon ute and drove it to the large gravel parking area off to the side of the buildings to wait for the buses to go.

Thomas had been sitting there for about ten minutes when he noticed the large white Land Cruiser. It was not all that unusual to see such a heavily laden vehicle travelling out this way, but it seemed to be somewhat indicative of the types that spent extended time out in the bush. He wondered who was in it and where they were going. He watched casually as the vehicle turned slowly into the roadhouse and shunted up to the bowsers. He thought little more about it and went back to reading the papers on his lap.

Ten minutes later he was disturbed by the distinctive clattering rattle of a big diesel motor slowly pulling in beside him and the engine left running way beyond necessary. He could feel the heat radiating off the engine after a long drive in the heat of the day as it wafted into his car through the open window. The car parked at a reasonable distance from his ute, but because there were so many cars now stopping at the roadhouse, parking was getting a little more congested.

He watched as the big knobbly bush tyres stopped close to him and he noticed they were very expensive and also had been well used in some obviously rough terrain. His observant eye also picked up that the vehicle had been recently in water up to the top of the tyres. From where he sat in his low-set ute, the tyres practically filled his view. Finally, the engine was turned off with a typical shuddering thud of the big diesel.

Nothing happened for a while and he went back to reading, getting a bit bored with all the waiting, but the buses were still there. Then he heard the driver finally get out of the vehicle and shut the door with a gentle click. He heard the back doors open and, peering in the rear-vision mirror, watched as a slight, well-dressed figure removed three heavy jerry cans and placed them on the ground with a metallic clunk. He noticed that the full-length roof rack had a small permanent metal ladder bolted from the chassis to the rack and wondered if this person was going to place the jerries up there. It was then he noticed that it was a she. She had removed her hat momentarily to wipe her brow and contemplate what she had in mind before replacing it, grabbing one of the cans and heading towards the ladder. In so doing, she revealed a head of short, straight blonde hair just short of her shoulders and free of her face so as to wispily wave gently in the zephyr that danced about the plains.

This will be tricky. Thomas watched in the mirror as she gathered the three jerry cans at the base of the ladder and prepared to climb. She was a slim but shapely woman, and Thomas thought that she would have trouble lifting the cans all that way up onto the roof rack. He watched as she man-handled the first slowly up the ladder. *She's done this before.*

Jess managed to place the first can up into the already prepared spot on the rack and was climbing down again when Thomas got out of the ute and scrambled to the back.

'Here, let me pass them up to you,' he said before she got too far down.

Jess stopped with surprise, peering at the stranger with the pleasant voice and kind offer.

'No. It's all right thanks,' she replied in a soft and gentle voice that he could barely hear above the noise of truck engines nearby.

'No, let me help,' he insisted. With that, Thomas picked up

one of the remaining jerries and passed it up to her. He noticed that it was not quite full. *Cunning,* he thought. *That would reduce the weight for a woman to lift.* He also noticed that they had W D and an arrow inscribed on them, indicating that they were heavy-duty, military-quality cans, not modern tinny ones. She accepted the can and clambered back up to the rack.

This time, Thomas passed the last one up to her while she was still up there, trying to avoid her having to climb in and out of the roof rack. She thanked him profusely from up on high and spent many minutes securing them, tying them down expertly and then reattaching the heavy tarpaulin that covered the entire roof rack. Thomas got back into his ute with a sense of satisfaction and watched in his mirror as she finally clambered down and headed back to the rear of the vehicle to attend to the doors. Then he observed her coming towards him from the back of the cars. Jess leaned over, removed her hat, and said in a very soft and lilting voice, 'Thank you very much for your help. It was very kind.'

'No worries,' said Thomas confidently.

She straightened up, smiled a barely noticeable smile, more a pursing of her thin lips, and turned to head back to the rear of the cars. Thomas watched her as she walked away from his side, a slight dizziness attending the pit of his stomach as he suddenly felt a queasy sensation at the very thought of so delectable a sight presented to him in such an unexpected manner. He was rather taken with her.

Thomas gave it another twenty minutes and watched as the buses began to pull out before going back into the café.

As he passed the rear of the Land Cruiser, he turned his head to read the plate and observed that it was from Western Australia. He raised his eyebrows a little. On the rear window and number plate surround was a small notice that stated that this vehicle was from Broome Toyota. *A government worker,* he thought. *No one of that class would work for anybody else. Probably with the Aborigines.*

Unfortunately for Thomas, Petra was still busy. He looked around the roadhouse and spied the woman from the Land Cruiser sitting alone by the windows reading some maps and sipping a drink. He bought a coffee and headed over to her. 'Hello again,' he said bravely. 'Can I join you?'

Jess just looked at him in silence and then looked at the empty seats. He took that as a yes.

'You're a long way from home then,' he continued.

Jess stared at him, somewhat quizzically. *How would he know that?* Then she realised everybody was a long way from home out here. *Except of course, if you were one of the very few who actually lived here.* She placed the maps on the table and gathered in her things to give him more room at the table.

'Well, I see you're from Broome. By your plates,' he continued, getting slightly agitated at her quietness.

'Yes. More or less,' she finally agreed, nodding her fair head slightly.

'Goin' far then?' he asked.

'Melbourne.'

There was an awkward silence. Then Thomas asked, 'Been travellin' long?'

'No. Not really,' said Jess, looking at him over a cup.

Jess was not good at this sort of thing. She realised that she was inadequate at small talk. Firstly, she was usually not very interested in the lives of others, except if it impacted on her own, or she could glean information pertinent to her art. Secondly, she was so reserved that she understood it took her a long time to get to know anybody, and as these meetings were usually brief or one-offs, she could see no point in chatting about nothing. Besides, Jess could never readily distinguish between being simply interested and prying, and because she was so secretive herself, and with good reason, she could never determine whether she was being intrusive. Better to be silent than regarded as nosey and inquisitive.

Jess looked at the young man sitting opposite her. He was ruggedly handsome, well built and athletic. He was shorter than many of the men she had known but had powerful arms and tanned features. His brown eyes shone with inquisitiveness and intelligence, harbouring a mild reserve and hint of sadness or loss that she could not quite define yet. She assumed he was a local and, she thought, somebody would be proud to call him their son. He was well dressed and quite clean, so he was not at work, not today anyway. She noticed that he was a little nervous and kept looking over to the counter where the tourists were still demanding attention before the long trip to wherever, as it was a long trip in all directions from here. She guessed that he was well under thirty but was not sure.

Finally, Thomas, with a nervous air, saw that Petra was at

last free and made his excuses. Jess watched him as he walked confidently over to the waiting woman. Jess looked at them for some time, thinking, then turned back to her maps and her planning. After some time, Jess gathered her papers and walked out of the roadhouse and over to her vehicle.

It would be a long time before she would be in any real civilisation, so she bought a few things to tide her over and prepared to head off towards Urandangi, directly south and just inside the Queensland border. It would be a much quicker way to go to Melbourne, but off the beaten track as most people would travel via Mt Isa and Townsville, following the highly frequented, bituminised coastal roads than this inland back track. It did not faze her at all, as she had a suitable vehicle and was a very capable mechanic. She also valued the isolation.

It was now about two-thirty in the afternoon so she realised that she would not get more than about one hundred kilometres or so down the track. But according to her maps, this was such an isolated place she hoped to be able to camp practically anywhere, especially near some of the bores that the stations had established for their stock over the years. Anyway, her time was her own. Jess walked over to her Cruiser and eyed the vehicle, checking that all appeared in order. Then she climbed aboard, headed back out onto the highway, and set course for Urandangi, over two hundred kilometres down the track.

Jess took it easy down this road as she was neither in a hurry nor anxious to rush out of the calmness of the outback. About two hours out, she spied the tell-tale signs of a large concrete bore tank several hundred metres off the road. As it was now approaching dusk and there may be no more of these in the next few hours, Jess decided to camp well away from the tank and the windmill but near enough to take advantage of the plentiful water. She pulled up at some distance from the tank so as not to disturb the livestock that used the bore, mostly during the evenings.

Jess was a veteran at bush camping. She had learnt early from George, the station mechanic, that just because you were in the bush did not mean that you had to rough it. Jess set up her camp and lit a fire to prepare for the long night. She was a poor sleeper, but seemed to require little sleep. This created the problem of how to occupy herself during these long, lonely periods of total awareness. This was partly where her talent to write had come to her rescue. She was still able to create stories using a laptop.

Jess was sitting at her small table as the dusk quickly descended upon the stirring outback country. Most of the native animals in Australia were nocturnal, and as the cooler evenings approached, they began to emerge and scurry about. Jess had very good hearing and she detected the emergence of the animals as they increasingly bounded about.

Then Jess suddenly sat upright. She thought she detected the sound of a distant motor. She was more concerned at the prospect of the local landowner objecting to her being there than the thought of passing traffic, as rare as that would be. She strained to listen as the sound of the engine came and went as it travelled over the hills of the dusty arid country. It was definitely getting closer. She hoped it was someone trying to make Urandangi, about an hour further along where there was a hotel. Eventually, she could see in the distance the dust of the fast-moving vehicle rushing along the winding gravel road and speed past her heading south.

But then it came to a sliding gravelly halt well past where the occupants could have seen her, if indeed they had seen her, as she was well hidden among the sparse trees and bushes. She heard the car slam into reverse and, with a whining gearbox and racing engine, reverse up the road in some haste. Then the car stopped and turned into where she was camped and headed for her and the bore.

Jess watched in great disappointment as the vehicle approached her at some speed, bouncing about over the rough terrain and dodging trees and bushes. It was then that she noticed through all the dust and debris it threw up, that it was a blue Falcon ute, similar to the one that the young man at the roadhouse drove. The car slowed a little as it approached Jess and then came to a dusty halt a few metres from her truck. She watched as the young man alighted, banging and slamming the ute door as he made his way over to her camp.

'Hi there!' he yelled in genuine friendliness. 'I saw the wagon camped near the tank and thought it might be you. I'm Thomas, from Camooweal.'

Jess just looked at him. Although he seemed pleasant enough, she did not crave company right now. She remained seated at the small table.

'Are you staying here the night?' he asked enthusiastically.

Jess nodded, still staring at him from her chair.

'Could I stay and chat with you? I was goin' to try for 'Dangi, but this is much nicer.'

Jess slowly stood up from her table and folded away some papers.

'I don't mind, if you like,' she replied, with a soft hint of annoyance. Thomas either ignored her tone or missed the inference. He stood by the table and surveyed the campsite, carefully eyeing off the whole scene and then said, easing back his well-worn brown hat, 'You've been to sea before.'

Jess stared at him in confusion at that comment.

'I mean, you have all the comforts of home here.'

She nodded again. 'Would you like a cuppa?' she asked, forcing herself to be more friendly.

'Well,' he drawled, 'if it's no trouble. I'll get me mug,' he said, and turned back to the ute to retrieve a mug from his swag. Jess expertly poured him a mug full of water for him to make his tea. She collected another small chair and Thomas sat down, still admiring the cosy setup.

'I suppose you'd like some dinner?' asked Jess in mock sarcasm.

'Well,' said Thomas in a conciliatory tone, 'I have a tin or two with me, an' some bread. I could just chuck it in a billy, if that's all right?'

'Go on, get it then.'

Thomas got up to walk over to his tucker box and retrieved a tin out of a large metal trunk, after rummaging noisily for some time. Then he grabbed some wrapped bread and margarine. He plonked it on the table along with a metal plate and some rough old cutlery. Jess poked the fire to enliven it preparatory to arranging her evening meal.

Jess made quite an effort when it came to camp cooking and was no slouch at preparing fine cuisine from whatever was at hand. She always travelled well prepared for dinner preparations as it was one of the things that passed a lot of time and she was fond of fine food after a long hard day in the open. Thomas noticed how expert and familiar she was with this routine.

'You work for the gov'ment?' he asked.

Jess turned and looked at him in silence, slightly disdainful at the accusation. Eventually she replied, 'No! Of course not.'

'Sorry,' said Thomas, slightly chastened by the tone. 'It's just that I thought you must have. What with the set up an' all. I mean, you sure know how to travel in comfort.'

Jess did not answer but left it at that.

Thomas watched in mild fascination as Jess calmly prepared the fire and gathered her implements and cooking gear. He was amazed to watch as she prepared vegetables and toast and some sauces to go with the contents of the tin he had thrown, like a rock, onto the table.

'I'm sorry,' he finally said admiringly, 'I don't even know your name?'

Jess hesitated for a long moment, rather dreading this question, wondering what to say.

'Jessie,' she finally said without looking up at him.

'Hi,' he said, 'I'm Thomas. I live on Brinkley Downs – that

is, I did, until yesterday.'

Jess noticed the hint of sadness at that last remark and wondered. But she dared not ask; it was not in her nature to pry.

'Well, if you don't work for the government then, what is it you do?'

Jess was always astounded by these types of forthright questions, especially when they were directed at her. 'I work on a cattle property in the north,' she finally answered, hoping that would satisfy his curiosity. Thomas was slightly unprepared for that answer. He had noticed her hands were roughish, rather like those who work constantly outdoors, and she seemed to be at home wearing moleskins that were obviously not new. But she had an air about her that reeked of class and breeding, something he rarely saw anywhere, let alone out here. Then he ventured, 'What. In the office or outdoors?'

Finally, after some time and an air of confusion, Jess straightened up and turned her face towards him. She replied, saying in a deliberate tone, 'Mustering on horseback, of course.'

Her tone intimated that he should have observed that as obvious. He had not entirely expected that answer. It confused him a little. He left it at that for now.

The next few hours passed in tranquil pleasantness, especially for Thomas, who had rarely experienced such refinement outside his grandparents' property in Cooma. He found her thoroughly enchanting and such a mystery.

She studiously avoided his intermittent questioning. He did find her a very good listener, however. She seemed very knowledgeable about many things, yet strangely unaware of many others, almost as if she had been locked away in some isolation. During the long evening, Thomas had a beer or two, but Jess did not drink, she never had. He stayed up much later than was normal for him, just drinking in her charms and her stories, while he drifted on about his life and his next move back down south to the high country. Once he got to know her a bit better, she loosened up and became more congenial.

Jess was unsure whether it was the beer or the intoxicating location, but she gleaned from Thomas during the course of the peaceful starry night quite a considerable sum of information. As the dying embers and the comforting glow of the gently crackling fire slowly changed from orange to black, Thomas had alluded to the reasons for his sad departure from the station on the Barkly where he had cut his teeth. He was travelling south to rejoin his loving family on their new property on the Monaro, where he was going to be the manager.

Jess discerned from Thomas that he was not all that enamoured at the prospect of this new venture. He described in some detail his family background and the difficulties that he envisioned encountering once he arrived back in Cooma. Jess could see his frustration and trepidation at the move and felt a tinge of sympathy for the lonely, slightly distressed young man who had somehow crossed her path momentarily in such a strange place and way.

Thomas described in detail the sheep industry and the

system he was returning to manage. Jess knew nothing about sheep but found it fascinating to learn of what he was involved in doing on his return. Thomas in turn, likewise found that she was totally ignorant of the sheep and wool industry, but had gleaned from her by the end of the evening that she was quite familiar with cattle, mechanics, bush living and possessed a road train licence. That was an enigma to him. It was quite late by the time Thomas rolled out his swag beside the ute and crawled in. Jess stayed up much later and spent some time thinking about things and fiddling with the smouldering fire.

Thomas was awakened early by the sounds of someone rummaging about in the camp. He was normally an early riser, but after such a late night and a few beers in such pleasant company he was slightly drowsy this morning. He finally aroused himself and wandered over to the blazing fire with all its attendant implements poking about at the side as Jess was preparing another range of delicacies from the store of items she had stashed somewhere.

'Morning, Tom,' she said in that soft but reassuring voice.

'G'day Jess,' he answered, slightly dull from the long night. Very few people actually called him Tom, except for his gran. It sent a mild tingle through his body at Jess's gentle tone. The reassuring familiarity of the tone was rather comforting to him.

It took Thomas a while to wake properly. He sat in deep contemplation, occasionally glancing up to check on the apparition that had so enchanted him the evening before. Jess was her usual quiet self, basically never speaking except to answer his inane questions. Sometimes it was pleasant just to be in someone's company without the need to talk. Finally, Thomas ventured, 'Listen, Jess. I've been thinking about what you said last night. You know, about not having any plans much.'

'Yes,' she answered in a mildly alarmed manner.

'Well, you say you can ride an' muster an' look after machines an' things. I've been thinking. If you're at a loose end for a while, why don't you come and work for me for a short time. I need someone to manage the cattle on Auvergne while I master all this new technology on the sheep side.' Thomas could see her defences rising and the look of horror on her face at the mere suggestion.

'I'll pay you well for the help. You can stay in the quarters there. They're quite good, you know.'

Jess did not answer, but just looked into the fire. Thomas could see that this suggestion did not seem to go down very well with her. He quickly changed the subject to the pleasantness of the surroundings. She seemed more comfortable there.

Jess cleaned up the camp and prepared to leave by mid-morning. Thomas was ready much sooner and decided to get under way. He thanked her profusely for the wonderful encounter and turned to get into his ute. He reached into the glove box and rummaged around for a few seconds. He returned to her and passed over a card, saying, 'Look, Jess. If you reconsider my offer about the cattle, please give me a ring. I'm serious about the offer. I would really appreciate having someone reliable to help me for awhile, especially at the beginning. Will you at least think about it?'

She put out her left hand and took the card, turning it over and looking briefly at both sides.

'Yes, of course Tom.'

He could do no more, so he put out his hand. He really wanted to give her a gentle peck on the cheek, but that would be a bit forward. After all, the pleasantries of the last evening for him deserved more than a handshake. As there was nothing in between a kiss and a handshake, the latter would have to suffice. Thomas got into his car and drove off rather quickly onto the road and passed on out of Jessie's life, leaving behind quite an impact on her jangled soul.

Jess watched as his ute disappeared over the horizon in a cloud of dust and slowly silence redescended. She sat for many moments thinking about the last day or so, poking the dying fire with a slim bent stick from one of the local trees. *Why did such a nice young man cross my path, only to drive out of it again as suddenly as he had entered?* She sat for some time thinking and studying the card he had passed to her. She read and reread the card, taking in all the details. Then she finished cleaning up the site and packed the Cruiser ready to continue her journey south.

Jess headed off, following the dry dusty track that wound drearily across the mostly featureless plains of the arid inland bush. The further she headed south the drier and more isolated it became. She planned on taking many days of slow travel to cross this desolate and sparsely populated part of the inland.

Once she finally reached Bourke in northern New South Wales, she was beginning to approach country that was more civilised. Once she reached these more settled areas, Jess would have to forgo her preference for camping and begin to use the motels and camping grounds located in every little town. She dreaded the prospect of the large metropolis that was Melbourne.

Jess did not like Melbourne much. It was a huge city with little going for it in the way of scenery. It did, however, have a vibrant cultural side that Jess found quite attractive. Apart from her appointment with the publishers, she had no reason to go to Melbourne.

She finally reached the city towards the end of September. It took her a few days to settle in and arrange to meet her publishers as she had two separate publishing houses to see; even though they were related companies, they did operate separately.

After three more days in Melbourne, Jess wished to leave and head for Sydney. Sydney was a much brasher city with unlimited physical beauty centred on its magnificent harbour and the linked coastal regions from the south right up to Pittwater. There were several ways that Jess could drive up to Sydney. She could follow the long coastal route around and stop at all the small villages that dotted the coast. Then there was the quickest route which followed the Hume Highway almost in a straight line up through the south east of the state. This was fast but boring and was accompanied by a lot of traffic including many trucks. There was, however, a third way Jess could drive to Sydney. It consisted of a small diversion that would take her up near to Kosciuszko. It was a very scenic route with a lot of history along the way. It also went through Cooma.

Jess had found herself thinking regularly about Thomas. Not so much in an amorous or romantic way, but in a sympathetic and compassionate manner. Even though she did find him attractive, she never thought of him in any other way than as a fine young man who had had a tricky start in life but had made good with considerable help from others; a bit like herself in many ways. She had tremendous empathy for anybody in that position. It touched her heart deeply when he spoke of his fears and concerns for the new venture. His almost begging plea after that magical night by the outback fire in Queensland to assist him in his early establishment had somehow pierced her rigid defences. She recalled the pathos and feeling with which he spoke of his fears and dread of returning to Auvergne Station to manage the new property that his family had bought especially for him.

There was also one other slight influence that had played on her mind. Jess regarded herself as having no skills whatsoever, except one. As far as she was concerned, anybody could write novels, after all, she had no trouble, and wrote under three different names. Speaking foreign languages was not unusual either, and most anybody living in the bush could repair an engine. These, she surmised, were mere gifts, bequests from benevolence dispatched at will randomly to the often undeserving. No, the one skill she regarded herself as possessing was her ability to ride and knowing cattle. This ability she acquired by hard work and much pain. It was an alien trade, and for her initially, very hard to master. She had to incessantly hone her capability by unremitting application. She valued and prized this craft, and now she had a pleasant young man struggling to cope with his new life asking her to aid him by utilising the one skill she regarded herself as having. She felt wanted, almost needed. It was a rare feeling for her.

Jess thought that it would have several advantages for her if she took on that task. Firstly, it would overcome the problem of what to do with herself, at least in the beginning while she sorted herself out. She had no idea how she would be treated by strangers once they learned who she really was, and by that she meant her criminal background, not her authorship. It would also give her a base from which to operate as she hunted down the places that she could consider to finally live. Secondly, her horsemanship and cattle knowledge would be helpful.

Jess nervously decided to give Thomas a ring from Mallacoota and see if his offer still stood. Hopefully, he would remember her after the time that had elapsed. If not, it was as easy to follow the coast around to Sydney as head due north to Cooma. She waited until after eight o'clock in the evening to ring him at his new address.

Thomas did not watch much television and was certainly no cook. He spent much of the evening hours ensconced in his office, doodling with notes about his plans for the technical improvements he had in mind for the station. He sat at a huge desk that was slightly dwarfed by the size of the room.

It was an enormous room, especially for an office. Thomas often sat gazing at its extent and thinking about its origins. It was located immediately inside the ornate front entrance doors and to the left. He realised that it was not originally an office but the parlour for a large country house from a bygone age. There was little need for stately country visits these days. Auvergne did not receive many visitors, and those who did come were usually not socialising. So, he had converted the former parlour into his office. As he sat deep in thought, he was interrupted by the telephone.

Jess heard the telephone ring only once and then an answer.

'Hello, Thomas speaking,' was all he said, thinking it was probably his gran or John.

There was a long delay before Jess could speak as she was not prepared for so quick an answer.

'Hello. Thomas?'

'Yes,' he replied. 'Speaking.' There was another short pause.

'Thomas, it's Jessie MacIntyre here. We met at Camooweal and then again at the bore near Urandangi. Remember?'

There was a long silence from Thomas as he drank in the moment. Then he said enthusiastically, 'Jessie. Yes Jess. Bloody hell. I don't believe it. Jessie. How the hell are you?' he said in animated excitement. He certainly remembered her and her name, although he did not quite catch her last name in all his excitement. 'Where are you?' he asked before she could answer. Jess was taken aback by his expressive and vivacious greeting. 'I'm fine thank you,' she replied in her soft voice. 'At the moment I'm in Mallacoota. I am going to

Sydney in a few days and wondered if you still had the need for assistance on your place?'

'I sure do. Can I meet you in Cooma on your way through?' he asked excitedly. Jess could hear the genuine appreciation in his voice that she had bothered to contact him and that she might still be available to work on his property. They arranged to meet in two days at noon in the park that was the centre of the thriving little town of Cooma.

Thomas rarely went to town on other than sale days or for some specific property matters. It was obvious to Costello, the station's genetics manager, that Thomas was on business other than immediate farming matters. Thomas hurried into town in order to be there well before midday. He parked in a good spot around the back of Centennial Park and waited for Jess to drive in from the south. About ten past twelve he recognised the lumbering and laden Land Cruiser slowly drifting along the main street looking for somewhere to park. He watched as she drove around to the back of the park away from the main street and found a parking spot under the trees along Massie Street. He waited until she emerged from the vehicle and then wandered over to meet her.

Jess thought that Thomas was genuinely pleased to see her and welcomed her very warmly. They chattered for several minutes and then Thomas invited her to come with him to one of the local cafés for some lunch. They sat talking for over an hour about this and that, nothing too deep, but Jess found herself more at ease with Thomas this time. *It's amazing how quickly time flies by when there's someone pleasant to share the time.*

Finally, Jess enquired whether Thomas should be getting back to work. He was still keen to secure her services as a station hand working with the cattle, but she advised him that she still needed to go to Gosford and would be about a week. She would return then and inspect the place and they could then decide what to do next. Thomas drew a rough mud map of the directions from Cooma and they left the place together to return to their vehicles.

As it was now nearing 3 pm, Jess decided to stay overnight in one of the local motels and get a feel for the place. She was still a little unsure whether this was the right thing to be doing, both for herself and for Thomas. Thomas advised that he was normally home every day of the week except Sundays, when he was more or less required to attend the family gathering at his grandfather's place the other side of Cooma.

Eight days later, around two in the afternoon while Thomas was in the sheds attending to the feeding and monitoring processes of the penned sheep, he heard above the low din on the boards, the unmistakable sound of a labouring diesel engine making its way along the gently meandering road that was the entrance drive of Auvergne. Thomas was quite excited at the prospect of Jess possibly working for him, both because of her pleasantness and because it would hopefully finally relieve him of the burdensome cattle side of the property, at least in the initial stages while he mastered the sheep.

Jess had found the country from Cooma down to Auvergne rather uninspiring. She was amazed at how featureless and drab it all looked despite being clothed in its spring greenness tinged with the hint of lushness that only occurred in between seasons. Her spirits were lifted a little more by the time she arrived at the Auvergne turnoff as the country had opened up into more pleasant undulating and tree-covered vistas.

The long and well-maintained gravel driveway wound its way gently over heavily grassed basalt paddocks and the island of green trees that formed the compound of the homestead and all its attendant buildings presented rather an imposing sight for her eyes, being unaccustomed to such displays of flaunted rural wealth. The Kimberley station homesteads with which she was so familiar invariably were meagre compared with this sumptuous and generous display of amenities. It gave her a tinge of envy to perceive the relative comfort that the southern barons seemed to enjoy when compared to their northern cohorts.

She drove wide-eyed into the majestic surroundings past the numerous and large farm buildings up to the stately homestead, which was well disguised by a surfeit of green and ancient trees that partly hid from view any of its sharpness. She stopped under a large portico arrangement just as Thomas had directed and sat gazing around at the sights that confronted her. Finally, she alighted from the dust-covered vehicle and awaited the arrival of Thomas.

Thomas had watched the heavily laden Land Cruiser slowly and deliberately negotiate the long meandering track down from the main road across the gentle valley and slowly climb the moderate incline back up to the flat where the massive homestead and outbuildings were all located in a huge conglomerate of trees and gardens. When he saw Jess get out of the car, he asked Warren to take over the feeding and monitoring of the sheep while he welcomed the visitor.

Thomas walked briskly and eagerly over to the house and met Jess on the veranda under the huge portico. After their greetings, Thomas suggested they amble around the homestead while he chattered to her.

CHAPTER FOUR

Thomas and Jess walked around the outside of the large homestead, Thomas trying to indicate to her where some of the buildings were and the layout of the property. When they arrived at the back of the house, Thomas invited Jess in through the back entrance that led straight into an add-on, a rough timber room adjacent to the main building and kitchen. This make-do room was ideal for casual company and a quick bite if visitors were in any way grimy from working outdoors. Thomas left Jess there while he went into the kitchen and prepared a cup of tea. He excused his inability to replicate her fine efforts in the stark Queensland outback, but a brew in more comfortable surroundings would be the compromise and have to suffice. After some general social chitchat, Thomas asked, 'Are you still interested in working for me?'

Jess delayed her response for some time, then replied, looking him straight in the eyes, 'That depends.'

'On what?' he asked, a little unsure.

'Well, on what's involved and how flexible you are to my requirements to travel between here and Sydney and Melbourne.'

'I'm sure we can organise something. How about we go for a quick ride about the place so I can show you the layout and then we can go from there?'

Jess nodded her agreement.

Thomas collected the crockery, placed it in a neat heap at the end of the table, and indicated for her to follow him out. He went to the stables and the attached small set of yards and paddocks where two horses were roaming about untethered. He grabbed two bridles and handed one to Jess. He wanted to be sure she had not been lying to him about her capabilities.

'Pick your mount,' he said with a smile. Jess looked at the two horses, large and reasonably docile, and shrugged her shoulders slightly. She walked over to the nearer horse. It snorted and raised its head at the stranger. Jess stood motionless in front of the beast and stared deeply and unblinkingly into its eyes. It stared back, visibly becoming calmer the longer she stared at it. She raised her arm and it sniffed the air, reassured. She placed the bridle on its head and secured the bit. Thomas did the same, acknowledging inwardly that maybe she was much more experienced with horses than he could ever be. After saddling, they rode out of the yards and Thomas led her along the southern boundary towards the back of the property.

It took about two hours to ride over to where the cattle were mostly located and to ride among them and then to inspect the yards that were established about the property.

On their return, and while they were still on horseback, Thomas asked, 'What'd yer think?'

'Looks simple enough,' she answered.

'Alright. How about I pay you the goin' rate plus a bit and you can stay in the quarters over there and I'll deduct a small amount for the power an' stuff.'

Jess looked at him closely during a short pause. All that could be heard was the constant creaking of the tack leather. Then Jess replied, 'No, Thomas,' she said in a firm and resolute voice.

He looked at her disconcertingly, fearing that this opportunity was not even going to get to first base. Jess continued, 'Here's the deal. I work for you for free.' She paused as usual, but also for effect, then continued again, 'For nothing. In return, I live rent-free in that old cottage over there.' She raised her left arm and pointed at the old place that had seen better days. 'Plus, I come and go as I please when I have to travel to Melbourne or Sydney.'

Thomas sat silently for a few moments. 'I wouldn't recommend staying in that. It's pretty crook yer know. How much time away would you be thinking of?'

'Not that much, but maybe a couple of times every few months.'

Thomas nodded his head, indicating maybe he could live with that. 'Why would you want to work for nothing?'

After another long pause, Jess answered, 'It's complicated. Let's just say it would suit me perfectly and there would be no ties. Besides, I may be totally unsuited to your needs.'

'And you would rather live in the old cottage?'

'Yes.'

'Look,' said Thomas, 'I've neglected that aspect of this enterprise totally. I need someone to run the cattle side without my input. I haven't time right now to be involved. If you can do that, I won't care what else you do. They need mustering, counting, sorting and trucking to market. In effect, management. That's what I need from you. Okay?'

Jess looked at him. For the first time she saw him in his role as boss cocky. He was direct and authoritative and knew what he wanted. She delayed her reply, then said simply, 'Okay then.'

Thomas responded by saying, 'How 'bout we give it a trial period of say, three months, and then check it from there?'

'Perfect,' agreed Jess.

Thomas stretched out his right arm and Jess did likewise, and they shook on it. They dismounted and Thomas led the horses over to the stables. Jess asked if she could start in a day or so and all was agreed. Jess then tenuously requested that Thomas use her preferred and better-known name of Jane Ransom on any written paperwork concerning her, as that way, her affairs would be simpler. He agreed. He had not retained her originally offered surname, simply remembering her as Jess. Jess hoped by using a pseudonym, her real identity would be disguised. It was many years since her infamous trial and she hoped that no one would now associate her on sight with any of that.

As an interim arrangement, Jess thought that this was admirable. She had something to occupy her time as well as a base from which she could study the country between Melbourne and Sydney. The way Thomas was enthusing about her addition to the station, she was also convinced that she was providing a useful contribution to the struggling new manager. If she could remain there for about a year it would be ideal. It was now October and she would have the whole summer to reconnoitre the entire area during her visits to the capitals.

Jess was offered the use of Samuel, the assignee from Quiggin's place to help her at any time she wished it and initially to guide her over the property. Her preliminary task was to complete a thorough inventory of the stock and then a plan of action would be decided.

The time flew by, but gradually Jess mastered the layout of the place and arrived at an accurate count of the cattle on the property. She mustered them completely over time and began the task of drafting out the undesirables and segregating the breeders from the steers and bulls, all with the aid of Sammy, at least in the yards.

Jess had barely been there a fortnight when her abilities were to be tested without warning. Thomas still spent most of his time in the sheds attending to the scientific feeding and managing of the prime sheep. To guide and mentor him, he had Warren Costello. Warren was not particularly old but he was exceedingly taciturn and rather sombre; a very serious man. Life had not been very kind to him, but he was managing well enough now. He was the resident bio-technician on the property and had mastered his trade under the tutelage and guidance of the previous owners who, in some ways were pioneers in this form of advanced technical breeding and production. He had formal qualifications now and was indispensable to Thomas.

The only other worker on the place was Samuel, but he only did the rough, heavy work and any other odds and ends that he was directed to do. Thomas was fully occupied mastering the intricacies of this new experience and found it difficult to cope with some of the extraneous matters. That included anything to do with cattle. It also included, as far as possible, the lucrative and essential aspect of the sales and delivery of both stud and commercial stock.

Thomas was expecting a high-level and important delegation from an overseas group to visit in a few days, plus he had one of the farm's good customers lined up to take delivery of thirty-five head of prime fine-wool sheep. The sheep were yarded ready to go when Thomas received a telephone call from the foreign delegation that they wished to inspect the place that day, two days early. Thomas returned to the sheds in a quandary and told Warren of the situation. Thomas looked at Warren in a questioning way, as much to say, 'Could you do the delivery for me?' Warren pre-empted the possibility by restating categorically that under no circumstances was he interested or even able to drive anything, let alone that great truck. Warren looked at Thomas and asked, 'What about the new lass? Can't she drive?'

'Yes!' exclaimed Thomas. 'Good thinking. Actually, she's supposed to have a road train licence.'

'Ah, good,' said Warren. 'A real Ben Chifley then,' he added sarcastically.

'What?' said Thomas.

'A real Ben Chifley. You know, the train driver.' The pun was lost on Thomas, but he asked Warren if he could locate Jess and send her to him in the office. Warren saw Jess heading for the horse paddocks so he yelled out to her. She stopped mid-stride and waited until he caught up to her.

'Jess, is it?' he asked in a deep and slow voice that resonated with deliberation while he peered at her discerningly.

'Yes, that's right,' she replied coolly.

'I'm Warren Costello. Thomas asked if you could meet him in the office. It is the first on the left as you enter the front door.'

'Sure,' she replied. 'Thanks.' She turned to head for the homestead. Warren was confused by this encounter. Jess was not what he had expected. The woman he spoke to was rather refined and aloof and, even he could tell, she was a bit older than Thomas. She had been employed, he was informed, because of her abilities with cattle. *Maybe that was all there was to it after all*, he concluded.

The exterior of the homestead was hewn local granite, beautifully constructed with wide verandas and two storeys.

It looked very old to Jess, and the garden, which had been neglected of late, was obviously once quite a feature with mature and exotic trees and shrubs, all of which were a mystery to her. She gingerly approached the ornate, heavy wooden doors, knocking gently on the hard wood. She could clearly hear Thomas's voice coming from inside so she entered into the foyer. Jess gazed in awe at the floor, which appeared to her to be marble or slate, and the dark timber walls. It had the aura of Victorian sumptuousness, something straight out of one of her novels, only much better than even she could have imagined. It was deathly quiet and serene.

She slowly wheeled around the sparsely furnished room taking in all the dècor and scattered ornaments. On the wall opposite the door to the office was a large wall-hanging that was, she guessed, an aerial photograph of the property. She wandered over to it and stared at it intently, taking in as much as she could of the layout of the place and the configuration of the boundaries.

Thomas was some time on the telephone, and she could hear him droning on. She tried to sneak a peak into the depths of the house, but that view was mostly prevented by two large wooden folding doors that guarded the entrance to the inner sanctum. Polished wooden flooring seemed to stretch on interminably into its depths. Finally, she heard Thomas replace the receiver. She sidled up to the door and knocked gently, poking her head around at the same time. He looked up and beckoned her to enter.

Jess walked uneasily across the acres of carpet between

the door and the large unadorned desk, reeking to Jess of modernity and improvisation in the otherwise elaborate room. She sat in the chair in front of the desk. The desk was incongruous in the overly large room. Then it dawned on her that this room was probably the parlour in the past. After all, she was familiar enough with elegant living from her long discussions with the absconding former Earl of Bromley, better known to her as Norm from Milbark days. Thomas looked at Jess slightly frazzled and asked, 'You can drive a truck, can't you?'

'Yes.'

'I've got thirty-five ewes in the yards that need to go to Delegate, about two hours away. If I show you where to go, could you deliver them for me?'

After a long pause, Jess replied, 'Sure. What in?'

'The old Inter. It's already set up at the yards.'

'You mean that old green thing?'

'Yes. It's an ugly lookin' beast, but it goes alright.'

'Okay,' she said, slightly shrugging her shoulders.

'Look, here's a map of the way down and here's a plan of the place you're to go to. I'll get Sammy to help you load up. By the way, while you're here, I'll give you that plan of Auvergne that I promised you as well.'

Thomas rummaged on his desk and located a folded plan of the property and gave it to Jess. He gave her a clipboard of papers related to the delivery and indicated that they were already paid for so all she needed from the buyer was a signature. Then he got up out of his seat and led her through the door and back out into the front of the house. He directed her to go down to the yards and he would send Sammy down to help her load up the ewes.

Jess managed to load the animals by herself and closed the crate gates before Samuel arrived. It was not an ideal way to familiarise herself with a strange truck, one that was loaded with valuable sheep. She found it tricky to drive a right-hand drive truck, but soon began to manage. What threw her was that it only had five gears, but the first was so low it was really just a creeper gear, so effectively it started off in second, except when the road was very steep or the truck was heavily loaded.

It was mid-afternoon by the time she arrived at the buyer's place not far out of Delegate. She drove into the property and followed Thomas's instructions to the yards. She backed the truck up to the loading ramp and got out of the vehicle. The buyer was waiting at the ramp and prepared to slide open the truck's sliding gate.

'You're late, mate.' The solidly built and harassed-looking grazier stared at her from under his battered hat. Jess stopped in her tracks and stared at him in silence.

'These were supposed to be here yesterd'y, as agreed. Now I've lost me boys I'll lose another bloody day movin' 'em up the back.'

Thomas had not mentioned anything about being late.

The grazier moved down the race and prepared to shunt the new arrivals into pens. Jess could see he was cranky. 'I'm very sorry Mr Wilson. I guess it's my fault, but I wanted to ensure they arrived in good condition, so couldn't get away yesterday in time.'

That did not seem to assuage Mr Wilson, but it was all Jess could come up with. He leaned on the gate in a huff and waited for her to slide the crate gate open. Jess stared at him.

Finally, he grumpily hissed at her, 'Well? You gonna open that bloody gate or what?'

Jess kept staring at him and then finally said in a conciliatory tone, 'Do you want these here or would you like me to drop them in another paddock?'

Wilson stood up and stared back at her. Then he glanced at his young offsider. Wilson stared blankly for a moment at the ground, stroking his chin with his hand. Then he looked at the young bloke again. The young bloke said to him, 'Why not? It sure would save us tomorrow.'

Wilson turned back to Jess, and standing straight up with both hands on his hips, said, 'Why bloody not? Let's do that.'

Jess got back into the cab and Wilson climbed in beside her. The young bloke stood on the running board next to Wilson, still smoking his cigarette. Jess looked at him disapprovingly. She thought he got the message. Wilson directed her about two kilometres into the property on a rather rough track to a smaller set of yards in a well-fenced paddock with some farm buildings scattered near the yards. She backed up to the rickety ramp and unloaded the ewes for a mellowing Mr Wilson, who was also beginning to be enchanted by the beguiling charms of a disarming truck driver.

He was genuinely appreciative of her unnecessary

assistance. Jess hoped that all the deliveries, if she made any more, would not be this difficult. He realised that by agreeing to deliver them further into the property it would delay her arrival back at Auvergne by quite some time. He appreciated that. One consolation for her was that on the return trip, it gave Jess a chance to practise driving a strange vehicle on the long, lonely return to Auvergne.

In the sale of Auvergne, a very old cab-over prime mover and its trailer were included. The trailer was still lying about the yard but it was slowly deteriorating through lack of use. Jess had never seen the prime mover as it was seconded to Damien's lucerne enterprise. In exchange, John had agreed to a temporary loan of his faithful old International R190 on condition that only Thomas drove it and that he took good care of it. Thomas used it to transport his few sheep that he traded, but mostly to transport the excess cattle that were rapidly building up under so little supervision.

This was a task he was very keen to pass onto Jess but overcoming John's objections would be a problem. *In the meantime, Jess was a much better driver than me and an expert mechanic so she'll be able to maintain it exceptionally well, something John would appreciate when and if he discovered this ruse.*

Before Jess knew it, it was Christmas. She never regarded that season with any significance and was rather surprised how seriously it was taken by the Summers clan. She decided her best option was to absent herself from the region in order to avoid any unnecessary social interactions with people she barely knew. She spent the short time down on the south coast alone.

Jess was a poor sleeper and often wandered into the night to drink in the unfamiliar surroundings of Auvergne. In the cool stillness of one of those Monaro nights, Jess thought she heard the muffled sound of motors that could be trail bikes, in the deep distance. As it was only January, she thought it unusual for there to be any work being done in this downtime. The moon was nearly full and the whole vista was bathed in a soft mellow light. She had very good hearing and was always alert to her surroundings. The zephyr that emanated softly from the high mountains away to the west drifted from the direction of the distant back hills of the property where she knew there were some fire trails and the road that led onto other properties further over the hills. *Maybe it was just coming from there.* She recalled that she heard the same sound last time the moon was full. This time she was a little suspicious. She would check in the daylight.

Next morning, Jess saddled up one of the many stockhorses and headed off in the direction of the back paddocks, crossing the brown crinkly grasses as she made her way over the open paddocks. After leaving the open basalt paddocks comprising the bulk of the property and where the house was located, Jess entered the granite country.

She made her way along the southern boundary fence and followed it all the way to the back boundary, which ran roughly north-south. As Jess followed the fence line, she noticed that the fence Thomas had indicated to her to be the boundary, ran off at a different angle from the one she anticipated from the plan.

Thomas admitted that he had never been any closer. The fence ran off at an angle that did not fit the layout on the wall in the hall of the main homestead. According to the picture on the wall, the fence should run off at ninety degrees, but this one ran at more like forty-five degrees. The fence was relatively new and seemed to cut off a considerable amount of bushy land in the corner.

Jess was convinced that the back boundary should be further over the ridge. She wondered why she had not checked this out more thoroughly at the beginning. She followed it back and forward and dismounted at the junction where she had first met it and opened the metal gate and led in her horse.

Jess remounted and followed what she supposed was the real boundary for some distance up the gentle slope and over the ridge. It ran through sparsely treed, shaly country. She stopped to reconnoitre the scene. This newer fence seemed to enclose many hectares of the back portion of the property with a few sheep and cattle. Some distance over the ridge she encountered what she supposed was the real back boundary fence.

There was a metal gate similar to the other, but much older. Here she turned north and rode the full length until she came to the northern boundary. Jess turned and headed back along the fence towards the homestead in an easterly direction. After some distance, she crested the ridge again and came to what she supposed was the continuation of the newer fence, the one enclosing quite a parcel of land up the back. She came to another cocky gate, this time in the northern boundary fence itself. It had recently been used and there were bike tracks and what looked like truck tyre marks. The tracks led into the property so she followed them.

A short distance in, she found a rough set of small yards that had also been recently used. Then she retraced her steps and opened the boundary gate and followed the rough tracks through the bush hills until they emerged a few hundred metres further out onto the local back road that led to other properties along its route.

According to the map, this road also led off into the distant state forest reserves that existed out in the wilder country to the west. She was a little puzzled. She sat on the horse for some time thinking. She found it inconceivable that someone could possibly be cattle duffing. *Surely not.* She wheeled the horse and retraced her steps again back into the property. Jess spent several hours studying the scene and thinking about the implications. She decided to wait until the next full moon and see if it happened again. Meantime, she would make some discreet enquiries into the fences up the back.

Jess rode home and started up her Land Cruiser. She drove the long and tortuous road that eventually led her to the same point up the back of the property. To her surprise, she discovered that the block of land that was adjoining Auvergne and into which she had ventured, was actually a travelling stock reserve. She thought it a little strange that nobody had mentioned that one of the back neighbours, who partly bounded the property in the granite and shale country, was a government-owned TSR. *That would explain the apparent near-virgin state of its condition, as these days, few drovers existed who actually drove stock by foot and had need of these reserves.*

During the next month, Jess discovered that the boys whom the previous owners had employed to do most of the cattle work and any odd jobs about the place, had erected a lot of new fencing, but she was assured it had all been approved. According to Warren, the previous owners had drifted into financial and mostly personal family trauma and illness that eventually necessitated their need to sell up. The drift had occurred over a period of about five years. *Plenty of time,* Jess thought, *for an unscrupulous employee to engage in shady deeds if unsupervised and with trusting and preoccupied owners.*

Towards the beginning of the next full moon, Jess saddled up her favourite stockhorse and left him ready all night, preparatory to investigating any activities that occurred in the night. Sure enough, on the night before the February full moon at about 2 am, she again heard the sound of bikes in the distance. She quickly mounted her horse and rode off at a canter in the direction of the fenced-off corner.

Jess rode up to the fence and dismounted, tying the horse to the fence with a long rope. She grabbed the stockwhip from across the saddle and hurried up the hill and over towards the yards. The noise was quite near now so she was a little nervous and concerned at what she might encounter. She kept her hat on to shade her eyes from the bright moonlight and then crept up to the action. She could plainly see two men riding the bikes and an old small truck with a stock crate on it set up at the loading ramp of the yards. In the flurry of activity, she was able to dash over to the small truck and turn off the motor and remove the keys. The two bikers were still totally engrossed in funnelling the young cattle into the yards, some distance behind.

Jess was not sure what to do. There were about five head of young cattle in the truck and several still being rounded up. She sat by a log not far from the truck and waited to see what would happen. Some of the young cattle were running off past the truck not far from her. Suddenly one of the bikers rushed past her, quickly followed by the second. As the second went past, Jess swung the stockwhip and struck him a savage blow on the side of his body and legs. He let out a startled shout and swivelled the handles in surprise and pain. Suddenly he was head over heels sideways over the handlebars and under the bike, its motor revving madly as he squeezed the throttle. The back wheel struck the truck and that caused the engine to stop. In his shock and pain, he yelled out, 'Jason! Jason! Come back, I'm hurt. Quick come back!'

The other bloke had already quickly skidded in a turn and doubled back to his mate. He roughly picked him up and dragged him onto the pillion seat, all the time shouting unintelligibly in all the noise. They shot off through the night and out onto the road. Jess tried another crack of the whip but this time they were too quick for her to land a stroke.

Jess heard them disappearing off into the dull light of the night and silence slowly descended upon the scene except for the clatter and bellowing of the startled young calves. Jess was suddenly confronted with several problems. She could easily release the animals and return them to the paddocks, but she was still left with the abandoned bike and the now empty truck. It was about 3 am and getting quite cool. She wanted to ensure that none of the evidence in the form of the vehicles could be moved but was unsure how to go about it. If she left now to retrieve some tools, they might return and remove the vehicles.

Jess decided to return quickly to the horse and ride him back to the truck and maybe wait until first light and see what happened. She let him graze about the bush near the truck while she thought of attempting to remove the injectors in order to render the truck immovable. Although she had the key, she did not know whether they had access to another somewhere and might return to retrieve their property. She secured the bike and turned off its ignition, leaning it up against the side of the truck.

By mid-morning, nothing had happened. Jess decided to return to the house as she was by now feeling hungry. She gathered her horse and rode back to the house. She had a short rest and some breakfast, then, gathering a few tools, drove the Land Cruiser back to the site of the action via the rear road. Everything was as she left it. She removed a couple of injectors and returned to the house.

Jess entered the homestead and examined the large plan of the property that hung on the hallway wall. It was as she thought. That corner of the property was at a ninety-degree angle, not something much greater, as the present fence line indicated.

The next day, Jess approached Warren to enquire about the name she had heard called out that night.

'Morning Warren. Could you tell me the names of the young lads that used to do some of the work on the place?'

He stared at her momentarily before answering, then replied, 'Morning Jess. Yes, their names were Jason and Tim Makepeace.'

'And where do they live?' she asked.

'Over along Briggetts Road,' he said, pointing in the direction of the distant hills.

'Thanks.' As Jess walked off, Warren stared at her bewildered and then returned to his work.

The next afternoon was a Wednesday. Jess drove her Cruiser to try and find where the Makepeace's lived and confront them with the events she had witnessed. It was a long drive all the way around to Briggetts Road and it took her about twenty minutes to locate their property. She drove in across an old grid that rattled and shuddered, then along a short gravel track up to a neat brick house that was surrounded by a presentable garden and tidy treed yard. Jess got out of the vehicle and sauntered up to the front door and knocked. A tall, elderly woman with a surprised look on her face answered the door. She stared at Jess, unnerving her slightly.

'Yes? Can I help you?' she finally said.

'Hello,' said Jess in her soft unassuming manner. 'I'm looking for Mrs Makepeace.'

'Yes. What can I do for you?' said the older lady, still standing in the half-opened doorway.

'My name's Jessie and I work on Auvergne.'

'Oh, yes, alright. Nice to meet you. Please come in.' She talked in a friendly way, shaking her head slightly, an action that bewildered Jess. Mrs Makepeace led Jess into the kitchen where her husband was seated at the table fiddling with some preserving bottles. She introduced him to Jess and indicated for her to sit at the table too.

'Would you like a cuppa?' she asked, to which Jess indicated her agreement by a simple nod. Mrs Makepeace prepared some new cups and saucers and opened a huge cake tin, removing an enormous homemade cake and cutting generous pieces to be placed on a matching cake plate. Jess was now slightly embarrassed at all the trouble. Mrs Makepeace reminded her momentarily of Edna Coniston from Ravymoota.

They chattered away for twenty minutes. During that time, Jess learned that Mr Makepeace had been unable to work for the last dozen years or so. Their two boys did all the work and odd jobs about the district, especially trucking stock about. They really appreciated the assistance offered by the former owners of Auvergne in allowing the two boys to do so much work there. Jess felt genuinely sorry for the old couple and realised that they had no idea what their two boys were possibly up to on the side.

Jess also knew from their conversation and what she had learned from Warren, that the Makepeace's were staunch churchgoers, attending the same little bush church that Warren and his family did. Finally, Jess asked where the boys were now. Mrs Makepeace stated that their elder boy had suddenly departed for the lucrative mining industry in Western Australia only a couple of days ago, following a call from a mate already over there 'making a packet'. Her younger son was sitting in the lounge with a broken leg following an accident a few days ago.

Jess asked if she could meet him. Mr and Mrs Makepeace looked at her quizzically and then nodded. They got up from the table and led her through the doorway into the small and dingy lounge where a slothful lad was watching television draped in a chair with his right leg in plaster. Mrs Makepeace asked him to turn it down, a request he refused; in fact, he refused to acknowledge their presence at all.

'There's someone who wants to meet you, Tim,' she said pleadingly. Jess was embarrassed for the elderly couple. She walked over to the chair and sat next to him.

'Turn it off,' she demanded in a menacing voice, soft but determined. At the same time, she placed her left hand over his wrist, turning it slightly. 'Now!' The lad was startled as she tightened her grip on his wrist. 'Would you like me to rip your elbow away from your arm?' she asked audibly only to him and with a vicious look in her eyes.

Suddenly he sat upright and turned the television off, staring at her in fear.

'That's better,' she said. Jess stood up and walked over to his parents, who were looking on in consternation at the minor drama unfolding.

'How did you hurt your leg?' asked Jess.

'I fell off me bike the other day.'

'And where was that?'

'Over the other side of town. Luckily Jason were with me or I wouldn't of got back,' he said nervously.

'And where's your truck?'

'It's broke down. I have to go an' pick it up when I can drive.'

'That's right,' piped in his mother, simply repeating his own story that he must have already told them both. 'It will be ready soon.'

'So, your bike and truck aren't sitting in my paddock right now then?'

'I don't know what you mean,' he said defiantly.

'Listen, mate. Stop messing me about. Your truck is still in my paddock along with your bike. Right where you fell off it on Monday night. Here's the key,' she said, dangling it in front of him.

'Timmy, what's going on?' asked Mrs Makepeace.

Jess continued, 'On Monday night, two blokes on bikes were poddy dodging on Auvergne. I wager they were you two.'

Mrs Makepeace sat down in an adjacent armchair and held her hand to her head.

'Timmy. You promised. No more you said.'

'How long have you been doing this?' asked Jess.

There was a long silence. Mrs Makepeace started to weep a little. 'Look Jessie, they're good boys really. They just need to be given a go. Jason was arrested for stealing cattle and Tim was on a bond a year ago. But they promised to be good.'

'How long?' asked Jess again, staring at the pathetic lad sternly.

There was a stony silence, except for the sobbing of Mrs Makepeace. 'What're you going to do?' she asked with distraught pleading eyes.

'Tell me how long!' Jess demanded again.

Tim lowered his face and with shaking hands confessed that he and his brother had been stealing both calves and sheep for about five years now. It was easy enough, as Auvergne was understaffed and no one ever checked on them or their work. They were able to get Auvergne to pay for all the fencing and yard building plus much of the diesel for the truck. He explained how they circumvented the National Livestock Identification Scheme requirements and implanted their own tags into the stock. They mostly stole calves as these were cleanskins.

Jess threw the keys at Tim and the two injectors and demanded that the truck and bike be moved by Friday. In the meantime, she would consider what to do about it. With that, she looked at the shattered old couple and her heart was crying for them. She turned and walked out of the house and up to her car. She drove off in a state of confusion and anger at the heartless ingrates with which some people are saddled as children.

The next day, Mrs Makepeace telephoned the Costellos to find out more about the woman who shattered their peace the previous evening. Warren spoke to Mrs Makepeace as his wife knew little about Jess. He told Mrs Makepeace Jessie's full name, although she was also known as Jane, and the little he knew, which was almost nothing, as he told them she was a very private person. Mrs Makepeace replaced the receiver with a look of consternation on her face.

In total disbelief, she rushed into her small stock of books that she kept in a cupboard and rifled through them. She brushed them all aside and held two paperbacks in her hand. She studied them thoroughly. She thought Jess was vaguely familiar but could not be sure. *After all, all blondes look the same.* Mrs Makepeace had followed the life and novels of the famous author for as long as she could remember. She stared at the pictures she had collected from newspapers over the years. *It sure looked like Jess MacIntyre.*

It was soon evident that Tim Makepeace was not going to be able to fulfil Jessie's demand to remove the vehicles by Friday. Moreover, Mrs Makepeace was far more worried about the prospect of the incident being reported to the police and the implication for her two sons. She resolved to approach Jessie and beg her to consider the prospects of her boys.

On Thursday evening at about eight o'clock, a small sedan slowly ambled its way along the darkening Auvergne entrance into the property and pulled up outside the old cottage that Jess was using as quarters. Mrs Makepeace, dressed in her finest Sunday best, sent her husband off to talk to the Costellos while she made her way through the low metal gate and into the house yard. She knocked on the door. Jess never got any visitors and assumed she had heard an extraneous noise of some sort. Again, the knock. Jess, in mild annoyance, left her work and walked over to the door. She was surprised to see Mrs Makepeace standing there in all her finery. Jess just stared at her in bewilderment.

'May I come in and talk to you please, Miss MacIntyre?'

Jess did not recall revealing her full name to her the other evening; in fact, she was sure she did not. After a long delay she replied, 'Sure. Yes, sure,' she stuttered. 'I'm sorry. Yes, please come in.'

Jess led Mrs Makepeace to the sparse rustic kitchen. 'Won't you please sit down?'

Mrs Makepeace sat uncomfortably on the hard wooden chair, placing her arms onto the bare wooden table and arranging her small black handbag neatly to one side. She stared at Jess in some discomfort.

After some moments, Mrs Makepeace began, 'Miss MacIntyre, my husband and I have tried very hard to raise our boys on the straight and narrow. It has not been easy, what with Harold having a bad back for all these years and us having to struggle along with not much money. The boys have not had it easy. But I have come here tonight to ask you please not to go to the police over this matter. There's no way we can move the truck by tomorrow, what with Harold an' all. Not to mention Timmy with his leg in plaster. We will try to arrange something soon, but I am begging you to please consider what it will do to us all if you report it. I can only promise to try to keep them honest in the future. It would kill us both if either of them ended up in jail. Could you find it in your heart to forget this matter if we return whatever stock is yours and stop any more of that?'

Jess sat in resolute silence as the shaking Mrs Makepeace disgorged the contents of her breaking heart. Jess was mortified that this woman would prostrate herself for the benefit of her undeserving sons. She was struck at that moment by the incredible sacrifice she was witnessing, something Norman referred to whenever the seemingly incessant displays of human ingratitude surfaced. Jess was amazed that this connection even occurred to her as she sat there in confused bewilderment.

Mrs Makepeace stared at Jess in expectant anticipation, her sorrowful eyes glistening with suppressed tears, but she had no idea that the last thing on Jessie's mind was to contemplate any involvement with the police. She assumed a good scare would suffice to keep the boys away from her domain; after all, Jess came from a background where you fixed your own troubles and used sufficient force to ensure it occurred.

'Well, can you Miss MacIntyre?' asked an agitated Mrs Makepeace.

Jess was suddenly recalled from her stupor. She stared at Mrs Makepeace and tried to recall the actual question. 'Mrs Makepeace,' said Jess, stalling in an attempt to compose her thoughts. 'Look, I am not asking you to return any stock. I just ask that you keep away from Auvergne paddocks and...' She stopped in mid-sentence, captivated by the struggling woman in front of her. 'Look Mrs Makepeace, what is your name?'

'Jean, Miss MacIntyre, my name's Jean.'

'May I call you Jean?'

'Certainly. Please do.'

'Look Jean, I am not asking you to return stock. And I'm not going to the police if you promise to try and keep your boys in line. I understand Jason has departed for Western Australia?'

'Yes. He left in some haste but I didn't know why he left at the time. You see, Timmy's already on a bond and if he offends again, he'll go to jail. I couldn't cope with that. They're all we've got. Not much to show for a long life, I know.'

'Well, at least you have a family,' pointed out Jess in a mildly sarcastic tone. Jean Makepeace missed the point of that remark entirely. Jess peered over at the troubled lady before her and suddenly asked, 'Would you like a cuppa, Jean?'

'That'd be lovely, thanks,' she replied in a coldish manner, trying to smile.

'I'm afraid I don't have any of your marvellous homemade cakes. I don't get much time for that.'

Jean was quite touched by what she interpreted as a compliment. Jess stepped over to the bench and flicked the switch on the jug. Over the civilising beverage, tensions lessened and a rapport developed that eased into a more garrulous and friendly encounter in which each woman appreciated the position and strong points of the other.

The two ladies chattered away for over an hour; Jean's husband all this time wondering what was happening. It was at last getting a bit late for the visiting Mrs Makepeace, but before departing, she plucked up the courage to ask one more question. 'Miss MacIntyre,' she ventured rather gingerly, 'can I ask you a personal question?'

Jessie's heart sank a little. She hoped it would not be THAT question; the one she always feared would come eventually. She looked into the eyes of her interrogator and replied in a soft, defensive, 'Yes.'

'You are *the* Jessie MacIntyre who wrote all those wonderful books?'

Jess paused, realising that the longer it took her to reply, the more certain Jean Makepeace would be of the answer.

Jean added enthusiastically, 'I have all your wonderful books as the author Mr Thaler and a lot as Jane Ransom, though not all of them, of course, as they are very hard to find now.'

At that moment, Jess had two possibilities. She could lie outright and hopefully end the affair, at least for the present, and in so doing disappoint the elderly woman who peered at her in child-like adoration, so expectantly hoping for the right answer. Jess cocked her head slightly to one side and pursed her lips in sad resignation. Before her sat a strong but slightly disillusioned woman of proud countenance and unbending scruples, who was prepared to humiliate herself to a complete and total stranger at even the slightest hint of a chance to protect her wayward sons. In her pleading eyes, Jess saw more hope than she had seen in anybody. But a simple, 'Yes', the second possibility, would possibly open the doorway to her own potential ruination for the ideal life she so desperately sought and had so far found, no matter how briefly. Jess could delay no longer.

'Yes,' she whispered sadly, her eyes diverting down to the table.

'I knew it,' said Jean in triumph. 'I thought you were so

familiar from the first time I saw you. But what are you doing here?'

'Mrs Makepeace,' said Jess, peering back up at her, 'would you mind if I ask you to keep our little secret. It would be a big favour to me if you could.'

'Certainly, Miss MacIntyre. Certainly. I have so admired you and your books for years. You have no idea what a marvellous pleasure it is to actually meet you. You know, you are just exactly how I imagined you to be. Oh, it's so wonderful to meet you. And you know Jessie ... sorry, can I call you Jessie?'

'Yes,' said Jess dolefully.

'Well, you know Jessie, you are truly as nice a person as I always imagined you to be from your trials and articles that I have read about you.'

Jess was slightly embarrassed at the compliments but doubted her request for anonymity would be honoured. She could only hope.

Jean Makepeace stood up from the table and thanked Jess profusely, proffering a hand in heartfelt appreciation, and beaming with a broad smile.

Finally, Mrs Makepeace departed the cottage a happier person than when she arrived and she strode purposefully over to the house that was the home of the Costellos. She entered in a cheerful manner and asked her bewildered husband to please take her home.

Jessie felt unsettled and wondered, *Is this the beginning of the end of my brief sojourn into society? Time will tell.*

A few weeks later, Tim Makepeace paid a visit to Auvergne. He gingerly stepped out of the car and ventured into the workshop. He could hear the repair work from outside the shed, saw Jess working at the bench and sauntered sheepishly towards her.

'Hello Miss MacIntyre,' he ventured.

Jess was startled by the unexpected intrusion and jumped backwards at the voice.

'Oh, it's you,' she said, replacing the tools on the bench and rubbing her hands down her trousers. 'What do you want?'

'Mum asked me to give you this,' he replied, handing her a porcelain cream-coloured cake tin. Jess stared at the gift and looked back up at him in silence.

'I am also to thank you for your kindness and apologise for what I did. And I promise to never do such things again.'

Jess stared disconcertingly at him as he squirmed in discomfort. Finally, she answered, 'That's alright. How's your leg?'

'It's mending fine.'

They stood in awkward silence. Jess looked at him, a very young man trying to behave civilly to someone he feared.

'I hope you mean it, Tim.'

'Oh, I do, Miss MacIntyre,' he enthused with too much exaggeration.

'You better, mate. You'll never understand what wonderful parents you have. How could you disappoint them so?'

Tim just looked at the ground in shameful embarrassment. 'Follow me and I'll return the tin.' Jess led him out of the shed and over to her cottage. She removed the cake with an admiring sigh and placed it on the bench. 'Wait here a minute.'

She disappeared into a back room and returned with a piece of paper. She placed it in the tin, put the lid back on, and handed it to him. 'Make sure your mum gets the note, will you?'

He nodded. Then he turned and walked to the car, thanking her again for her act of generosity in not reporting the incident. Inside the tin was a short note from Jess to Mrs Makepeace thanking her for the present and a list of all her publications under the name of Jane Ransom. She suggested to Mrs Makepeace that if she marked those books she thought were missing, Jess might be able to supply some for her.

CHAPTER FIVE

J ess was settling in comfortably in her new surroundings. She was now controlling the cattle side of Thomas's property and he was very happy to have someone taking all that responsibility. All this, however, was about to be challenged by her notorious past coming back to threaten her newly gained tranquillity.

One of the consequences for Jess of her discovery and subsequent trial was that she granted to the BBC an interview that was conducted in the lounge room of the Ravymoota Station homestead. She sought, and received, strong assurances that the interview was for British television only and that it would definitely not be screened in Australia. That assurance quickly went by the wayside in light of the high ratings.

Jess, of course, knew nothing of all this, either at the time or at any time afterwards. But that was about to change. The actual interview was conducted by a rising star of the television world, Patrick Main in 1999. But in the year that marked his fortieth birthday, and as a tribute to his phenomenal success and hugely popular interview shows over the years, excerpts from some of his most famous or notorious interviews were to be screened.

Warren Costello, and in particular his wife, were avid TV viewers in the evenings. The tribute programme was scheduled to be screened in prime time on a Saturday evening but there were plenty of advertising slots during the week or so beforehand. Of course, one of his most prized interviews was with Jessie MacIntyre. She had only agreed to the interview because it would focus on one of her most prized chief characters, based on the life of the fourteenth Earl of Bromley, known as Norman Woods to his friends, and the surrounding controversies that attended his mysterious life. The promotions previewing the programme featured her heavily. Jess never watched TV so was unaware of this threat.

Thomas heard Warren discussing a TV programme with the other farmhand, Samuel, but it did not register with him that they were talking about Jess. Thomas tended to watch very little TV. That Saturday afternoon, as he was departing the shed for his house, Warren said to Thomas, 'See you, boss. Check out that interview tonight, mate. You might find it interesting. It's on ABC at 8.30.'

Thomas was baffled but decided to watch it. He sat relaxing with a stubbie and was suddenly struck with a devastating sensation of rising anger as he watched the drama

97

of the interview and realised that he was harbouring such a notorious individual. Thomas was feeling both betrayed and foolish. He turned off the TV in disgust as it finished and sat there fuming about the whole matter. Jess, of course, was blissfully unaware of any of this. Thomas had no inkling that Jessie MacIntyre was *the* famous Jessie MacIntyre of criminal fame. *No wonder she preferred the name Jane Ransom. How come everyone else knew?*

Thomas did not sleep at all that night. He tossed and turned and his anger slowly grew. He was already feeling a little inadequate about his ability to run the property and still depended on Warren to perform most of the functions. He also realised that he totally neglected the cattle, leaving that entirely to Jess. It would not take too much of a jolt to knock him over the edge.

Next morning, being a Sunday, Thomas, still tired and frustrated, was supposed to go to Bridgehead for the weekly family gathering. He was not in any mood to do that and, for the first time since his return, he decided not to attend. Instead, he decided to confront Jess. He marched over to her cottage and walked in through the open door to find Jess in the kitchen.

'And just when did you think you were going to tell me?' he demanded. Jess turned from the bench with a start. She looked at him, but then realised something was seriously wrong. Her face turned slightly sterner, and she looked more quizzically at him, saying nothing.

'Well?' he demanded again. Jess just stared with a pained

look on her face as she fiddled with her hands. She was still unsure what she had done to so upset him.

'I suppose you think it was fun was it, to play with this dinky little farmlet and amuse yourself with the little kids for a while?' he said angrily. 'Well? Answer me, you bastard.'

Jess was so hurt and offended at this sudden turn and his language, that she was speechless. This reticence had always been an endearing trait, but at this moment, it was an irritant to the fuming Thomas. In his wound-up state he demanded instant answers. 'When were you going to tell me then, eh? When you got bored with playing with farming, you would go off and giggle to all your friends about how amusing it all was to dally in the bush?'

By now, Jess understood near enough whàt was happening. Thomas was getting so annoyed at her lack of response, that his face was reddening. Jess tried to apologise but the words would not come out. He spluttered on and turned to leave after giving the table a thorough bashing. He marched out of the room and gave the poor defenceless front door such a slam that Jess cringed in confusion as the shockwave reverberated about the cottage. She feared the entire property would have heard it.

Jess sat at the table, a rising wave of shock beginning to overwhelm her. Tears slowly welled in her eyes and trickled down her cheeks. She wiped them away with her hands and got up from the table. She went to the small bedroom that she used as her study and began to pack her things.

Sadly, she tried to neatly and carefully replace all her treasures into the few small boxes. She gathered them all near the front door and then began to pack them into the Cruiser. The bulk of the books went into trunks on the roof rack. That took her the longest. She had finished loading by midday but would have to return for a few items. She went around for one last look at the rooms to ensure she had not missed anything and, leaving a neat pile of things in the small room, headed for the car. She hoped Thomas, in his fury, would not destroy the few items she left. She placed a small note on them to let him know that she hoped to return quickly to retrieve them.

Jess drove out without a farewell from anyone, and headed off alone and distraught, yet again. She headed for the coast and found a reasonably secure block of units near the ocean at Narooma. All the while she could not remove the image of the angry and contorted face of the man who had been so kind to her. She was able to take out a six-month lease on one of the units and began to unload her things.

The following Sunday, Jess planned on returning to Auvergne about midday to retrieve the last of her few things. She expected Thomas would be at his grandfather's place for the usual family meetings, and hopefully, Warren would be quietly spending the day at his own house after their usual morning attendance at church. Jess pulled up the Cruiser at the side of the cottage out of view and began moving the boxes to the front door.

Jess had put two loads into the Cruiser and was preparing to collect a third when suddenly she was confronted by Thomas. She was visibly startled and jumped back in fright at his appearance. She did not expect him to be there and hoped he was not going to repeat his previous performance as she was in no condition to go through all that again.

Thomas looked haggard and pale, and his clothes were a little dishevelled. She did not fear for her physical safety, even Thomas must know what she was capable of, but she dreaded another outburst of his anger.

In the intervening week, Thomas had time to discover that the Costellos had a vague idea who was living among them, but were not really sure. Just in case though, Mrs Costello refrained from conversing with her and warned her young children to avoid her too.

However, Thomas realised that Jess had not deliberately deceived him, and he missed her immensely. Thomas looked at her almost pleadingly and said in a sad and melancholic low voice, 'Jess, I'm so sorry. I didn't mean all those horrible things I said. I really am so sorry. Please forgive me for that.'

This was even more unexpected than his first performance. Jess had never seen him so conflicted. She looked at him with hardened eyes and a set face. She had steeled herself to be strong during this retrieval, and this strange turn of events was not in her plan. She stared at him again. He continued, 'I really am sorry, Jess. I don't know what came over me to say those terrible things. Please don't go. I really can't make this work without you here to help.'

Jess still did not reply. She did not know what to say, recalling all those pent-up emotions he had poured out on her in his anger. She thought he must have meant some of it at least. She looked at him in his sadness and finally said,

'I'm sorry, Thomas. I've offended you grossly in some manner and I am truly sorry for that. You've been so wonderful to me that I'll never forget you for that. But I think it's time for me to move on out of your life. If I can annoy you so much now, what will it be like when you learn all about me, as no doubt you will? The world will make sure of that.' The sadness in her tone was conspicuous.

'But Jess, I thought you liked it here?'

'I did, Thomas,' she said after a long pause. 'But things have changed now.'

Thomas could feel his world drifting away again. He stepped closer to her and said, 'Jess, please reconsider. I can't make it here without you. I'm truly sorry for what I said.'

'No. You'll have no trouble getting someone to run the cattle for you Thomas, no trouble at all.'

'No Jess, I will. But more than that, I love … love having you here. I love … being around you and knowing someone competent is running that side for me.'

'That will pass, Thomas. Please, let me go now.'

'Jess, please reconsider. I promise it won't happen again. It's just that it was such a shock to me to find out all those things about you from someone else, especially when the others seemed to know already.'

Jess was taken aback by that statement. She tried to keep her identity secret, but that was obviously proving impossible. She wondered if Jean Makepeace was the culprit, or whether people just knew when they met her who she really was. Warren Costello's wife seemed to detest her and overtly ensured her children kept away from her. She felt that it was always going to be an issue, everywhere she tried to go. *Maybe I'm just fooling myself to think I could ever live in peace.*

Thomas went on, 'You liked it here, didn't you?'

She just looked at him.

'Well, didn't you? You know how much I need you, Jess. Promise me you'll at least think about it, eh? Will you? Please Jess?'

'Alright Thomas, I promise. But now I must go.' She went to go, but then realised she had not even thanked him for all his kindness to her. She turned back to face him and said, 'Look Thomas, I did like it here, but more importantly, I'll never forget your kindness to me, so thank you very much for that.' She started to pick up the last of her gear.

'Let me help you with that, at least.'

'No thanks, Thomas. It's okay, thanks.' It suddenly struck her that this was how they met: he offering to help her lift her jerry cans onto the roof rack and she declining that offer. He did it anyway. Now here they were in the same position: he offering to help, she declining. But he helped her anyway again. *Déjà vu*, she thought.

Jess was anxious not to prolong this awkward moment, so she quickly closed the back doors, bade Thomas a terse goodbye and hopped into the driver's seat. In a few seconds she was driving out of his life again. She looked in the rear-view mirror at the bedraggled and dejected figure of the once-robust man who had shown her such trust, and her heart was breaking. Nevertheless, every time Jess recalled those piercing barbs that he hurled at her, she recoiled with feelings of repulsion that she could arouse such venom towards herself from someone she so respected. Her mind was in turmoil; this was no time to be making any decisions.

Jess drove the long and lonely country road back to Cooma. 'Oh Thomas!' she exclaimed in confused anger, thumping the steering wheel. She drove around Cooma for a few minutes and then parked the car in the familiar Centennial Park bays. She sat there thinking. After about twenty minutes, she started up again and headed for the unit at Narooma.

Jess spent the next few days in total turmoil. On the one hand, she found his stinging remarks very hurtful, but on the other, she still missed the paddocks and the freedom, and the respect for her work. *Maybe the price I would have to pay for my secretive and devious life was the occasional hurtful outburst, but the benefits seem to outweigh the detrimental aspects. I might just have to accept that this is how life is going to be from now on. I'm also mindful that Thomas is certainly in need of my assistance for a while longer. I'll think about it.*

Jess found that wandering along the beach had its limits. She thought fondly of the life that she had just driven away from.

'Oh Thomas!' she kept saying. The words of Norm from Milbark came to mind. He called it Norman's Law: everything always interferes with everything else. She sucked in a knowing breath.

Thomas was equally despondent. He had driven away the only woman he had grown to love, other than his grandmother.

He almost told her but could not quite bring himself to say it. He feared she would spurn his announcement, especially under those terrible circumstances. He lied to his family about the first Sunday gathering, but excuses were wearing thin now and he would have to attend the next one. He was not looking forward to that.

Warren Costello also anxiously observed the events unfolding about him. Firstly, he feared Thomas's departure would bring about the appointment of Neil Brody, the leading hand from John's big property at the back of Bridgehead. He had been out a couple of times with Ethan, John's elder son, and Warren found him particularly obnoxious. Neil had hinted at the radical changes he had in mind for Auvergne if he ever got his hands on it. Warren wondered why the Summers employed such a dolt. Secondly, Warren had grown to like Thomas a lot, and he knew that Thomas relied on him. This lifted his self-esteem enormously.

Warren also admired Jess. Her ability to manage the cattle side of the operation meant there was no call on his limited ability to help in that area. Warren did not ride horses and refused to ride a bike. In fact, he was a little scared of cattle. He was bitterly disappointed at the departure of Jess. He even chided his wife for wishing 'that criminal' gone, warning her of the possible consequences for them and hinting that her aloofness and coolness towards Jess would not have helped her in her decision to stay or go.

Thursday morning dawned cool and cloudless on the early autumn day. Thomas was lethargically and disinterestedly attending to the work in the shed accompanied by a worried Warren. There was talk of getting the Makepeace boys back in to attend to the cattle. That was a sure indication to Warren that Thomas had lost all interest in the broad operation of the property. Suddenly, above the moderate commotion of the large shed full of demanding sheep, there was the sound of an approaching vehicle.

Thomas and Warren stopped doing the feeding and ration distribution and awaited the view of the approaching vehicle. It was travelling slowly, so Thomas thought it must be heavily laden. Finally, the familiar sight of Jessie's Land Cruiser with its huge bull bar, two massive spotlights and weird oversized aerial she seemed to adore came into view as it carefully picked its way along the gently rising track. Thomas let out an audible sigh and Warren allowed himself a wry smile.

They watched in increasing anticipation as Jess drove the swaying Cruiser over to the cottage and stopped the car. She jumped out and looked about. Thomas dropped his bags on the floor and began swiftly walking out of the shed.

'Take over, will you Warren?' he announced, more animated than he had been for days.

'No worries,' merrily responded the usually taciturn Warren, smiling broadly now at the happier prospects. He watched as Thomas began to run over to Jess and meet her at the car. He would have given anything to be a fly on the wall at that very moment.

Jess and Thomas conversed for many minutes out on the grassy verge that surrounded the cottage. She informed him that, though things had changed, she was prepared to come back and help him out while he tried to find a replacement and she established herself somewhere else. Thomas was just grateful to have her back. He so wanted to embrace her. He went back to the shed a much happier man.

The next day, Warren made a point of crossing Jess's path as she prepared to venture out on horseback. He touched his battered straw hat and remarked with an unusual broad smile, 'It's good to have you back, lass.'

Jess was momentarily surprised by that comment, but coming from Warren, who was noted for being particularly sparing with words, she took it as a vote in her favour.

More surprisingly, however, was the appearance the following day of Warren's aloof wife near the cottage waving at Jess and commenting on the 'coolness of the days now that autumn was well and truly here'.

Why did it take such traumatic human interaction to evince better relations? Jess wondered.

However, life was never quite the same again for Jess. Thomas's outburst instilled in Jess a constant fear of unpredictable reactions from those around her if they discovered who she was. It increased her unsettledness and paranoia, and also her introspection. She became even less communicative.

Jess wanted to be prepared the next time it happened. To that end, she began to search out a suitable place to buy to call home. She spent many months searching and finally purchased a three-bedroom apartment near the harbour in the Sydney suburb of Rushcutters Bay. The property had undercover security parking and an allocated spot for each apartment plus an outside parking bay behind the security fence where she could park the Cruiser, as she doubted it would negotiate the undercover parking with the roof rack on it. All she needed was the security key and she could arrive any time she wished.

The property was located in a district of high-rise apartments, but close to the city and public transport. She always timed it to arrive in the small hours of the morning, but once there, she had no need to drive anywhere. Jess went up and down to the apartment regularly, especially once the lease on the Narooma flat expired. By then she had moved all her belongings to her own property and kept very little at the cottage. She also thought it had the advantage of introducing her to city attractions and the possibility of her final domestic arrangement if Thomas grew tired of her and erupted in abusive anger.

The incident seemed to break the spell of Jessie's hibernation. She now had a more honest relationship with those around her and she could live life as the person she really was, with all her abilities in the open. It also set in motion a series of events that followed on in quick succession. The first involved the master of the entire enterprise, John Wesley Summers.

The stock sales were well and truly under way for the autumn season shortly after the harrowing events and ramifications of the TV revelations. John decided to check out the sales at the saleyards as Auvergne had started shipping a few steers and weaners in again. He knew that Thomas would be delivering, so he wanted to catch up with him there. John arrived early in order to survey the stock on offer and talk to a couple of the vendors and traders.

Early in the morning, John saw his old cattle truck, the big green International R190, enter the wide saleyard entrance area and carefully drive up near to the yards and then slowly reverse up to the ramp. He thought it was unlike Thomas to be this early and to be driving quite so carefully. John was about to walk over to him when he noticed that the person alighting from the vehicle was not Thomas, but a much shorter person, indeed, a woman. He was confused for a minute. He checked himself and then confirmed that this was his old truck. He walked over casually but gingerly and thoroughly looked it over. It was indeed his truck; they were his plates, but the dent in the left-hand mudguard was missing; someone had repaired it. Also, he noticed it had two new tyres, but it was definitely his truck. *So where was Thomas?*

John observed her passing over the paperwork and she seemed to be known to the officials. She took copious notes in a small notebook and jotted down other information. *Who was she?* John went over to the receivals area and asked the fellow if he knew the name of the driver from Auvergne. He replied that her name was Jane Ransom. John was thoroughly confused. He ended up staying for most of the sales and observing Jess until she departed. He noted with some satisfaction that at least she drove very carefully.

John had some other things to do in town, then he rang

Livinia and told her he was driving out to Auvergne to check up on something. *I may be late home.*

John was about two hours later than Jess heading back out to Auvergne, so he figured she should be there by the time he arrived. He rolled up to the sheep shed and approached Thomas. 'Who was that driving my truck?' John asked.

Thomas was stymied for a response.

'And I thought we agreed that only you were to drive it. No strangers.'

'Um,' stammered Thomas. He could see that his grandfather was a little riled.

'Um's right, Thomas.'

'Look Pop, she's working with me on the cattle side of things. Just while I master this sheep side.'

'How long's she been here?'

'Not long really. She's been a huge help to me. Probably wouldn't have made it this well so far without her.'

'I don't like strangers drivin' my trucks. Where's she now?'

'Down at the yards still.'

'I'll go down an' introduce myself. Jane, you said?'

'Did I?'

John drove the heavy Holden WB sedan down the rough track to the yards. He was not happy. He arrived at the yards and pulled up close by. He could see Jess sorting some more vealers and steers, putting tail-tags on some and just looking at others. John watched her for a while and then went over to the rail and climbed up so she could see him. Jess got a start at seeing a stranger. She finished sorting and then walked over to him. She had a fair idea who this was.

'G'day, miss,' said John in a slightly bossy and angry tone. Jess just stared at him. She got closer and peered up at him, his height emphasised even more as he stood on the second rail.

'I'm John Summers,' he said.

Jess thought so. She looked at him intently and then responded, 'Hello, Mr Summers.'

She made her way to the gate and John followed. Jess exited the yards and together they walked in silence to the shed where it was a little quieter.

'Nice lot there then,' stated John.

'I think so.'

'How long you been here then?' asked John.

Jess was slow to answer. It was obvious to her from that question that Thomas had told him very little, if anything at all, about her. 'Not long,' she replied.

John tried to continue the conversation but he found her communication disconcerting. For some reason, John did not like her much. He left and drove back to the house. He had an animated conversation with Thomas and then asked, 'Thomas, I don't recall her appearing on the salary sheet of the accounts.'

'No,' he said. 'We have an arrangement.'

John did not like the answer. His unease was rising. 'What sort of arrangement?'

'Well,' he began, 'she stays in the old cottage for free and I don't pay her any wages.'

'I don't like the sound of that at all.'

'It works very well. She runs the cattle side of things single-handedly, and I agreed she can come and go as she pleases.'

'Thomas, no one works for free. What is it that she wants from you?'

'Nothing at all.'

'Don't be silly, Thomas. You know what I feel about these weird live-in arrangements. After six months she can claim half your assets. Haven't I warned you all enough about this?'

Thomas was starting to get annoyed with his grandfather. He replied in a terse voice, 'I don't like your suggestion there, Pop. I'll thank you to mind your tongue. Jessie is a thorough lady. There is nothing going on here. You have no idea who she is, do you?'

'I thought her name was Jane?' said John. 'And no, I don't know who she is.'

'Have you ever heard of Jessie MacIntyre?'

'You mean the cop killer?'

'Pop, that's a horrible thing to say. She was thirteen at the time and was proven totally innocent of any crime. You really are uninformed sometimes, aren't you? As for wanting half our assets, she can probably buy and sell you fifty times. You don't understand anything but money, do you? She is a world-famous writer, one of the best. She doesn't need your money and I'm very lucky to have such an expert working for me for free. That should count for something in your book. Now, I'm going back to work.'

John had never seen Thomas quite so angry, but he

was uneasy about this strange woman who seemed to be contributing to his own wealth for no apparent reason. As Thomas turned to go, he asked, 'Alright, I better be off for now. Would you mind giving your grandmother a ring and tell her I'm on my way?'

'Sure, Pop. I'll see you later,' he answered tersely.

On arriving home, Livinia could see John was occupied, but no more than he often was. John was quiet all evening and went to bed early.

Next morning, Livinia was preparing to go to a CWA meeting in town. As John sat at the table, he asked her, 'Liv, have you ever heard of a Jessie or Jessica MacIntyre?'

'Of course, dear. Why do you ask?'

'Well, according to Thomas, she's working for him over at Auvergne.'

'Don't be ridiculous. She lives in the Kimberleys. Has done so for years. Besides, she's a famous writer, what would she be doing working on a sheep station in Cooma?' Her tone was condescending.

Was she disdainful of our lifestyle or was she unfavourably comparing it to Jessie's? John answered coolly, 'Well, that's what Thomas told me … I met her yesterday, but I wouldn't know one sheila from another, as you know.'

'There must be some mistake, dear. She must be another woman with the same name.'

'Well, that's what he told me.'

'I'll ring him now and find out.'

That annoyed John too, as if he did not know what he was

talking about and she was checking up on him. She usually relied totally on his judgement. Then Livinia had a thought. She suddenly recalled that several months ago, Thomas had asked exactly the same question. At the time it was straight after the television programme so Livinia did not think it particularly odd. She even remembered lending Thomas her small collection of books written by Jess.

Livinia just had time to ring Thomas before she headed off to the meeting. She dialled his number, but he did not answer. She told John that she would 'phone Thomas that night and that she had most of Jessie MacIntyre's novels, except for those early ones as Jane Ransom.

John thought, *There's that name again, the one used at the delivery sheds.*

Livinia led John to the bookcase in the lounge that was reserved for her books, and amid many cookbooks, some novels and books of general interest to women, Livinia pointed to a neat row of hard-cover books written by Jess, including a large volume that was her diary.

John carefully extracted a volume or two and fingered through them. He found the diary the most interesting but nothing really grabbed him. He was not noted for being a reader. Instead, he decided of far greater interest to him would be Auvergne's financial statements. He carefully replaced the unread books back on the shelf and headed for the study with a little more purpose.

John removed the box-files from his huge antique bookcases and began to open the boxes that contained the papers he had accumulated from Auvergne. He flipped studiously through them, jotting down on a pad the bits that he wished to note. It became evident that the cattle side of the enterprise was certainly successful and profitable, but nothing to indicate anything untoward. He would, however, keep an eye on proceedings from now on.

That evening, about eight, Livinia rang Thomas. To her disbelief, she discovered that John was not mistaken. She still did not believe it herself, despite Thomas's assurances.

John was more than a little disturbed by this turn of events. Not the least of his worries was the reason for his discontent. He could not put his finger on it exactly, but he was uneasy about several aspects of this discovery. There was the serious consideration, as he saw it, of the issue he had already raised so indelicately with Thomas about couples suing each other for the assets of the wealthier. He had already seen evidence of that occurring in other families, and as Thomas was a shareholder, by implication it could affect all of them.

Then there was the unsettling idea that someone would simply work for free. This was a concept John found difficult to fathom. He could see all the ramifications of such an endeavour and his distrusting nature was surfacing again. He was disturbed by the novel sensations of relative inadequacy when comparing himself to Jessie MacIntyre. John had always been the undisputed kingpin in his little world; the man who ran the show and made all the important decisions. This was based on the twin strengths of his undisputed personal wealth and his unwavering ability to make the right professional decisions. Now, suddenly there arrived on the scene someone else with even more undisputed wealth, power, charisma, and carrying the extra burden of fame – *or was that infamy?* John was in his twilight years and confronted with a strange situation that he thought he would never confront as he tailed off to a respectable old age in peace.

Next sale day, John announced to Livinia that he was going in again to observe Jess, and would she be interested in accompanying him. Livinia was indeed of such a mind, and together they departed early enough to arrive at the sales in time to hopefully see Jess. Livinia rarely attended any sales, but this time she would be there to discover if this woman was who Thomas claimed her to be.

John parked in the shade, quite a way from the action, and together they walked over to the sales area where the familiar cry of the auctioneers was already well under way. John spied Jess following the throng and pointed her out to Livinia. Jess was wearing moleskins with riding boots and a large akubra. Together they observed her for a while and finally, when a small break in proceedings occurred, John led Livinia over to meet her.

'Morning Miss MacIntyre,' greeted John in a cool voice to the back of Jess. She turned around, slightly startled as she was jotting down notes in her pad.

'Hello again, Mr Summers.' Jess turned her gaze onto Livinia standing beside him. Jess guessed immediately who she was, but said nothing.

'May I introduce my wife, Livinia.' With that Livinia

extended a friendly hand towards Jess and smiled beguilingly at her, saying, 'Pleased to meet you, Miss MacIntyre.'

Jess passed the pad into her left hand and reached for the proffered hand, looking Livinia in the eye. There was a slight pause, then uncharacteristically for Jess, she expanded her usual responses and said in a soft and genuinely caring voice, though a little nervously, 'Lovely to meet you, Mrs Summers. Thomas has told me a lot about you – about you both. He thinks the world of you, but I guess you know that.'

Livinia was not expecting such an elegant and graceful person. She recalled all the descriptions of Jess during the years of her trial and the police investigations. Livinia was rather taken with her and said finally, 'Likewise, my dear. I was a bit doubtful that such a person would venture into the wilds of downtown Cooma but it is certainly a pleasure to meet you here.' With that, she hinted that they walk out of the centre of the hubbub of the auctions and retire to somewhere a little quieter. They slowly drifted towards the parked car located away from the action and in the shade, chatting amiably. Again, in some ways, Livinia reminded Jess of Edna Coniston from Ravymoota, but with more polish and better presented. It seemed to Jess that everybody worthwhile tended to remind her of Edna.

Thomas was right when he had described Livinia as the most enchanting and motherly woman he had ever known, thought Jess. She could see why few other women would measure up to her high standards. All this time, John sauntered along behind, still confused about his feelings. He was assuaged ever so slightly by the obvious camaraderie exhibited by the two in front of him. *Mind you,* he reminded himself, *there was almost no one that Livinia could not get on with so that might not be altogether a criterion to use as a marker.*

The two ladies talked for around twenty minutes, then Jess indicated that she should be going as she needed to return to Auvergne, but had a couple of things to do in town first. They bade farewell and she left John and Livinia alone again standing by the car.

John looked at his wife and she said, 'What a lovely girl. I'm pretty sure that's her, but she's such a darling and so very pleasant.'

John was a little relieved so far, but still harboured some doubts. He was yet to be convinced that Jess was on the level altogether.

CHAPTER SIX

ohn's old International R190 was a sentimental favourite, dating back to his earliest days at Bridgehead. He had purchased it from a clearing sale in the 1960s. It had a few quirks, but as with all old characters, was worthy of his loyalty. It was tricky to drive in that it had a long nose and high bonnet, so visibility was reduced, but it was powerful and could carry a lot of stock on the stock crate that had come with it. He had only loaned it to Thomas on the understanding that Thomas looked after it for the year or so.

There was an unregistered old cab-over Kenworth K127 prime mover with a semi-trailer stock crate bought with the purchase of the Auvergne property. It was not a bogie drive, having only one rear axle, but it did operate. Thomas had agreed to exchange this prime mover for John's International so his son, Damien, could use it on his property opposite

Bridgehead to cart his lucerne.

Jess was aware of this arrangement, but was happy to drive the truck after she mastered its intricacies. For a start, she had never driven a normal right-hand drive truck. Old 'Jimmy', her GMC war-surplus American vehicle back on Milbark, was a left-hand drive. It took her a while to be able to smoothly change the gears, as she had to use opposite hands to operate the gear stick, and co-ordinating her double shuffle using the other foot was also a bit of a challenge for her. However, given time, she mastered these small difficulties and became as proficient at its operation as she was with her old truck back at Milbark.

A year after her arrival, an incident involving the trucking arrangements had far-reaching consequences. Jess knew that Neil Brody, the leading hand at Bridgehead, was keen to stymie Thomas's efforts at Auvergne. She had learnt more about this from Samuel than anybody else. Neil had cast covetous eyes on the role of manager of Auvergne, and she had overheard Ethan and him discussing it at one of the Cooma sales before they knew Thomas had anybody else doing his driving.

Neil Brody and Ethan came over to Auvergne one afternoon while Jess was away and removed John's old International, leaving Thomas and Jess stranded without a truck. This was not entirely suitable, as Jess made deliveries when stock was either sold on site or needed to be transported to market. Jess was annoyed and suspected that the truck was not needed at Bridgehead but had been removed as part of the plan to destabilise Thomas's efforts and hinder his output.

Jess clearly recalled that Damien had the Kenworth prime mover at his place, and as they had removed the International for his use as well, they decided that they would not need all the trucks over there and asked Thomas to arrange for her to pick it up on Sunday while he was at the meeting. Thomas arranged this through Damien, who was not aware of the machinations of the others and agreed willingly.

On the Sunday, while Thomas attended the usual family gathering, Jess got him to drop her off at the gate to Damien's and she walked down to the trucks and drove the unregistered old Kenworth K127 back to Auvergne. It was a risk, but on a quiet Sunday she expected no trouble.

Over the next week or so, she arranged for the old truck to be registered and made roadworthy for use as a stock vehicle. However, there were two issues involved in this. One was that it now left Damien with a trailer at his place but no prime mover to tow it with. The other was that Jess now had a prime mover but no suitable stock-semi to tow behind it. She planned to overcome both these problems by buying a small single-axle, semi-trailer stock crate and a single-axle dolly so Damien could tow the flat-bed on his place for the lucerne.

On the following Sunday, Jess planned to leave Auvergne early and make her way over to Temora where she had arranged the purchase. She would collect the trailer and the dolly and transport them both back to Cooma. It all seemed so simple.

Unbeknown to Jess, Ethan, and particularly Neil Brody, were annoyed that she had managed to circumvent their plans to stymie Thomas by fixing up the old semi from

Damien. They had connived to fix that unplanned occurrence by appropriating the now-registered vehicle on the pretext that the International was damaged and laid up in one of John's soggy paddocks with a damaged front steering and suspension problem.

The two arrived early Saturday morning, planning to retake the vehicle as it was urgently needed at Bridgehead. Jess was annoyed that they had damaged the old International as she had spent quite a bit of time repairing it. She was doubly annoyed that they felt they could just walk in and take the truck that she had already spent a lot of time and her own money on getting it roadworthy. She normally would have coped with that arrangement, but she had organised to travel to Temora to pick up the equipment she had set aside.

Neil Brody made one fatal error. He was a short man, quite thin but wiry, and also rather elderly, about sixty. He had been a boxer in his younger days and had a rather brusque manner. He was grey-white on top and had a neat white beard. He always carried a surfeit of essential equipment: pocketknives, watches and assorted other leather-clad paraphernalia that he regarded as befitting his occupation. Jess thought it was all for show. He always wore the neatest R M Williams clothes and a matching belt. Jess had heard one of the other farm hands refer to him as having the 'little man syndrome'.

Apparently, he was also rather chauvinistic, having a reputation for mistreating his long-suffering wife. These were not a good combination to present to an already irritated Jess.

Jess was in the workshop on the Saturday morning when

she heard the vehicle pull up outside her cottage next to the truck. Next minute, she heard the truck engine fire up. She wandered outside and headed for the truck, just in time to hear Thomas and the two new arrivals discussing removing the now-registered semi. Thomas was getting agitated and when he saw Jess coming out of the workshop, he knew there was a possibility of trouble. Brody had brought a young farmhand with him to drive the car back while he drove the prime mover. Of course, being a supercilious type, he also possessed a truck licence, and regarded himself as proficient at that skill. The truck was standing outside the cottage for an early getaway next day and Jess planned to travel bob-tail to Temora and tow the gear back from there.

The men were all chatting away oblivious of Jess, so she ambled over to see what was going on. She arrived in time to hear Brody demanding the right to remove the truck. Jess was stunned and a little jittery. As she arrived, they all turned to look at her. Jess just shrugged her shoulders slightly and stared at the strangers. Then she walked on by and prepared to enter the cab of the truck in order to turn the engine off and remove the keys.

'Not so fast, girlie,' said Brody in a curt voice. Jess stopped and turned to face him. Speaking to an agitated Jess in that manner was a fatal error. 'That truck's goin' back wiff me.'

Jess knitted her brows, then she turned and headed for the cab again. Brody leapt over to her and grabbed her left arm, and again said to her as she turned to face him, 'Did you hear me, girlie?'

Jess stared a withering gaze at the short man whose eyes were not far above her own. Then she slowly and deliberately lowered her gaze to the muscular arm firmly holding her own. She slowly lifted her gaze to meet his. 'Let go or I'll break your arm,' she said coolly and softly.

Brody cackled at her but did not release his grip. Jess jerked her arm free and turned to climb the step into the cab. Again, he grabbed her, and in one swift almost imperceptible manoeuvre, she turned and clouted his extended arm fiercely at the wrist. At the same time, she gave him a swift poke in the midriff with her free arm sending him hurtling to the ground in a shattering heap, spreading up the dust and loose grass. Jess just stared at him. The other young bloke prepared to step between her and the idling truck.

Jess gave him a withering stare for a few seconds. He realised that if he did not move, he would suffer the same fate. He quickly slid backwards. Brody was still writhing on the ground clasping his wrist. Jess climbed the steps and entered the cab. She turned off the engine and removed the keys. Then, without a single word, she jumped off the foot rail and walked back to the workshop, leaving the gallery of stunned onlookers in her wake.

Jess planned to travel to Temora via Tumut and Gundagai and estimated the trip would take her about five hours. There she would pick up the two items and return that evening in time for Monday's normal jobs, hoping to be back at Damien's before dark.

The next day, there were a lot of rumours going about the

Summers family gathering once a hint of the rumpus was leaked to those at the meeting. Damien could not tolerate Brody and could not understand why Ethan had employed such a miserable character. Most of the ladies who had met him felt likewise. John did not have an opinion either way, as it was Ethan's job to manage that aspect these days and as long as the job was done, he did not mind that much. Ethan tried to keep the issue under wraps, at least for the present, so indicated that Brody had had a slight accident and damaged his wrist. He had been attended to in the Cooma hospital.

It was late on the Sunday afternoon, and the sky was reddening in the western sky, when Jess arrived at the gate of Damien's place. Damien and his wife were preparing an easy dinner after the big family lunch. Damien could hear a truck engine grinding the short distance from the road to his farmhouse and the clatter of empty stock crates rattling in the quiet evening air. He went outside in time to watch Jess slowly drive along the rough road and stop the vehicle close to his now useless trailer chocked up on blocks awaiting a set of wheels to make it mobile again.

Damien watched as the old familiar semi towing a small stock trailer pulled up and Jess hopped out. She went around to the back and prepared to disconnect the dolly she had towed from Temora. Damien wandered to the back of the trailer and enthusiastically said to her, 'Hi there!'

Jess got a fright from the unexpected voice and jumped a little. She turned and faced a beaming Damien. 'What yer doin'?' he asked, chuckling.

Jess looked Damien up and down, and then said, 'I bought you a dolly so that you can use your trailer again, since I took your truck.'

'That's great. But you didn't have to do that,' he said.

Jess pursed her lips and turned to continue the uncoupling. The dolly uncoupled with a heavy clunk and she dropped the towing eye to the ground. Then she uncoupled the semi and reconnected the dolly so that she could push it in under Damien's trailer. It took her about half an hour in the fast-fading light. Finally, she was ready to reconnect the trailer to the turntable of the truck. Before she could do that, Damien's wife Helen came out of the farmhouse and approached Jess with Damien still looking on. 'You'll stay for some tea, won't you?'

'Oh, no thanks, all the same,' responded a nervous Jess.

'Of course you will,' she insisted.

'I'm sorry,' Jess said, 'I'm a bit dirty, I'm afraid, so I'll give it a miss.'

'Don't be silly,' she countered. 'Of course you'll stay. This is a farmhouse. We're used to dirt.'

Jess did not wish to remain and have a meal with this family, but she could see that they were genuine in their insistence. She wilted and reluctantly agreed.

Jess had heard a little about Damien from Thomas. Thomas described his uncle as a strange and eccentric man, not so much in his appearance and activities, but more in his mind. He had a reputation for being 'different' and thinking in strange ways. Damien was a strong supporter of Thomas, so the two got along quite well. Jess had no idea what to expect from this unconventional person. His wife had struck Jess as simple and lowly educated but very pleasant, much as Thomas had described her. Jess completed her tasks and then, accompanied by a beaming Damien, was escorted to the washroom attached to the rear of the modest little farmhouse and left to clean up.

The meal was simple but adequate and the conversation, at first, was limited. Gradually, however, Damien's true character began to emerge as he wandered over many topics and expressed opinions and ideas about esoteric and controversial issues. Jess observed that he had intelligent eyes and a pleasant smiling face most of the time, indicative of a man content with his lot. Jess sensed there was a towering intellect that possibly was so under-utilised that any opportunity to exercise it was always grabbed enthusiastically. Jess could not always contribute much to some of the issues he covered, but occasionally he wandered into familiar ground where she was more able to contribute. She detected that he was very sharp, for on a couple of occasions he displayed powerful abilities to calculate figures, unless of course he was able to memorise vast numbers and recall them at will.

The evening dragged on into the late hours of the night. Damien's wife and children departed at a sensible hour, but Jess and Damien continued on with animated discussions. Damien had only a very vague idea who Jess really was, but they got on well. He was also mindful that this woman was the one rumoured to have flattened Brody. It was past twelve before Jess could make her excuses and depart the farmhouse, and she still had over an hour's drive to Auvergne.

Thomas heard the rattling and banging of the empty trailer slowly negotiating the gravel road to the homestead. *Even for Jess*, he thought, *this was a late hour to be returning from such a long trip.*

Ethan was beginning to be fixated on removing Thomas from Auvergne simply because he could never seem to get anything to go his way, and on reflection, it always seemed to be down to the woman that Thomas had employed there. Ethan was also constantly comparing his lot on Dave Quiggan's old place behind Bridgehead with the facilities and output from Auvergne that Thomas was managing, and he was determined to try to undermine Thomas in some way, even if this did not gain him the management of that enterprise.

Thomas began to question the reasoning behind the sudden demand for all the trucks at Bridgehead. John was also getting annoyed at the sudden damage to his old International, which was still sitting out in the paddock unprotected and unable to be moved because of the damaged front section and the damp location of its present position. After a few days, he asked Thomas if he and Jess could come over and assist him in finding a solution to this dilemma. He reasoned that, from her record, Jess was good at analysing a problem from her years in the Kimberley. Jess was at first reluctant following all the problems she seemed to engender when around the family.

It was a cool and damp day when Thomas and Jess arrived

at the property and were driven down to the bogged and damaged International. Jess spent time surveying the scene. Half an hour later, Damien arrived in his old Land Rover. Damien asked Jess if she had any ideas. She paused for some time and then surmised slowly that if they could arrange a tripod of stout timber at just the right angle, the weight of the truck, when pulled with a chain, might just enable them to slither the vehicle along the ground enough times to get it to dry ground.

Damien and Jess had an animated conversation involving a few complicated calculations while standing in the cold and damp wind. John was struck by this unknown attribute of his unusual son. He suddenly saw him in a new light. Damien and Jess seemed to play off each other and banter their calculations about as if they were minor computations. John watched in amazement as Damien and Jess, ignoring the others present, wandered around the stricken vehicle and paddled in the muddy quagmire chatting about numerous solutions. Thomas was as awestruck as John.

Together the two of them came up with a simple solution that involved careful placement of logs and judicial pressure from the two tractors. The preparations took considerably longer than Damien anticipated, but he found Jess's thoroughness appealing. It took two days of preparations before Jess was satisfied, and only one full day to have the vehicle out of the mud and chocked up ready for transporting back to John's workshop shed.

Ethan began to enquire inordinately about the running of

Auvergne. He noticed that the wages component of the cattle side seemed to be very low, almost nil in fact. Then he noticed from the statements that the cattle operation was more profitable than the prospectus for the sale of the property would have indicated. He was suspicious how Thomas was managing to achieve this.

John was becoming disturbed by the more overt disagreements that were surfacing between Ethan and Thomas. Jess had warned John, but at the time he dismissed it as a missed message, and Jess was not aware of these inner family squabbles. She had however, proven to be nearer the mark than he wished. Nevertheless, John was intrigued by the greater than anticipated turnover from the cattle side of the business and wished for his own edification to ascertain how they were achieving such numbers when compared with the inventory of the sale prospectus.

To this end, John decided to make a thorough inspection of the Auvergne property on the pretext of familiarising himself with the stock. He arranged for a visit mid-week in the early autumn when the weather was a little cooler but the days were still long enough for a complete assessment. John arrived at about 9 am and Thomas left it to Jess to lead them around the property. She followed her customary route of heading out along the southern boundary up into the shaly western ridges then easterly back along the northern boundary. It was when they reached the newer fence line that enclosed the back rugged country that Jess sprang her first surprise.

Thomas and John thought this fence was the back boundary,

which they knew was bounded by a Travelling Stock Reserve, but neither had thought to mention it to Jess in the beginning. They were rather surprised, to say the least, when informed that it was not a TSR but in fact their own property.

Jess opened the metal gate and John and Thomas rode in. She remounted her horse and they rode off over the ridge and onto the real boundary. The rest of the ride was uneventful until they approached the now dysfunctional array of scattered wood that was the remains of the duffer's yards. Jess said nothing as they approached but listened intently to their conversation. She was unsure whether to tell them about the cattle stealing for several reasons. Firstly, there was the issue of trying to keep secret the names of the culprits. Secondly, she was unsure whether John would inform the police or the previous owners, or both. Thirdly, they might just think less of her for achieving such a discovery over and above the capabilities of better qualified people to manage it.

Unfortunately, John, ever observant, questioned the need for such poor facilities in such an isolated location and why there seemed to be so much recent vehicular traffic evident at this remote point of the property. *What was more, he questioned, it all seemed to depart the property via the unused back road which led into the TSR.* To save him a lot of angst and wasted effort, Jess decided to tell him the entire story.

Jess explained that on her arrival, she heard the noises up the back and investigated. Suffice it to say, she caught the culprits red-handed and meted out her own brand of retribution entailing some minor actions on her part that ensured the perpetrators understood never to do it again, at least not to this property. John sat silently on his horse for many minutes deep in thought. Then he realised that this woman was more than capable of dealing with miscreants. *Had she not swiftly and efficiently disposed of Brody?* Thomas was thinking much the same.

After a couple of questions, John and Thomas agreed to drop the subject, and rode off with a slight smile on their faces. It occurred to John that this would explain the apparent excessive profitability of the cattle component of this enterprise. She was not only working for no remuneration, which was a saving, but she had eliminated any more stock stealing. *What was her motivation for all this and why was she so good at what she did? Was it simply good luck that Thomas had stumbled upon her in Queensland, or was there more to her than he knew?* It certainly gave John food for thought. Thomas too was rather dumbstruck by the unveiling of these hitherto unknown events. Jess hoped that that was an end to the subject as the person uppermost in her thoughts at that moment was Jean Makepeace.

A few weeks after this visit to Auvergne, Jess was asked to deliver the truck to Bridgehead so they could make a few deliveries. Thomas drove over in the ute so he could return Jess to Auvergne. Jess delivered the truck to the big work shed and walked back to the ute to wait for Thomas. There was another car under the portico but Jess paid little attention to it. She leaned idly by the ute with her back to the bonnet and surveyed the pleasant rural scene of prosperity laid out before her. She rather envied the Summers and their contentment, which she had been denied in life. She was deep in thought when she was disturbed by the sound of Thomas clomping across the wooden veranda floor and then onto the gravel under the portico where she was waiting.

'I'm terribly sorry,' he said to her apologetically. 'Look, my damn family is here an' Nan wants me to stay for lunch with them.'

Jess was nonplussed. She could see no problem. She would just wait and walk about the property for as long as he wanted.

'It's not that simple,' he said sadly, looking at her pleadingly.

'I'm afraid Nan wants you to join us. In fact, she insists.'

'Tell her thanks, but no thanks.'

'I know this is a bit of an imposition, but would you mind joining us? It would be easier all round for Nan and me, and I would appreciate the support with those pigs of people in there.'

'But I have no desire to meet that lot, Thomas. Besides, I'm not dressed to be inside.'

'Don't be silly,' he admonished. 'This is a farmhouse and people expect you to be dusty. Besides, you're a queen compared to their attire,' he said with a sarcastic sneer.

'I'd really rather not, Tom.'

'I know, Jess, but please, for me, would you be my backup in there? It's unpleasant enough.' Thomas had no idea just how much Jess actually knew about his disreputable in-laws. Jess feared she might not contain herself once confronted by that Bales person, knowing as she did his horrible saga beginning with his miscreant father, Judge Bales, going back to the Knuckey days.

Just then, Livinia came out of the front door and called them both in, insisting that Jess join them. Jess felt trapped. She could not remove from her racing mind all the unpleasant details she had gathered from Ian Knuckey on learning that Thomas's mother was married to the famous judicial family of Bales.

Jess reluctantly agreed to accompany Livinia to the front door. She was nervous and not able to take in the full majesty of the grand entrance hall. She just had time to peek at herself in the enormous full-length wall mirror that adorned the far wall as she was ushered into the dining room where Thomas's parents were already seated. Jess was slightly concerned about what she was wearing, but she need not have worried.

Audrey was basically wearing a tent and Geoffrey was in shorts and sandals. Their two teenage daughters were in casual colourful wear that resembled beach attire. Jess then remembered that she had heard Audrey referred to as 'that hippy' which explained her garments. Livinia simply introduced her quietly to the gathering as Jane, the driver who delivered the truck here from Auvergne.

Jess found Audrey to be a most peculiar person with weird opinions on many subjects. After a short period, Jess found the room of much more interest to her than the guests. She peered in wonderment at the elaborate and elegant decorations that gave the room an aura of magnificence, transfixing her attention on the seamless refinement and effort that must have gone into its design. She had not seen anything so outstanding and it caused her to pay scant attention to the conversation.

The dialogue was no match for the surroundings and was indeed stilted. Jess could see why Thomas would want somebody else there. Even the normally unflappable John was ill at ease with the high-tone barrister in his presence. Jess was deep in her own thoughts when she heard the tail end of an inane and long dissertation proffered by Audrey, culminating in a question directed at Jess herself, '... in fact, all ownership is theft and an insult to the greater good of all communal existence. It robs individuals of their rightful share, don't you agree, Jane?'

Jess looked directly at the inquisitor, giving her a furrowed calculating stare. She said nothing.

'Do you not think so, Jane?' Audrey asked again, not to be put off.

Jess had hoped to avoid conversing with the Bales, but with the request renewed, she proffered a curt and deliberate response, saying in a soft slow retort, 'It is a non-issue, I would have thought, as ultimately the earth is the Lord's, and the fullness thereof.'

That was a conversation stopper. John looked at Livinia then back to Audrey. Livinia did the same. All the time Jess just stared at Audrey with a piercing gaze. There was a long silence.

John looked a little sheepishly at the gathering and an apologetic air surrounded his demeanour. *Where did she get that idea from?* he thought.

There was a long awkward silence. Finally, Jess continued, 'Funny how possessions of substance engender a change of attitude in the end.'

'Oh, we never value possessions as such. Just as a means to achieve a better outcome for the group. We never changed our mind,' replied Audrey with a superior tone.

There was another long pause, nobody wishing to speak. Jess looked at the family opposite her with a rather severe gaze, knitting her brows slightly. 'But you own your property now?' she asked, almost in amazement.

'Of course not,' answered Audrey imperiously. 'We rent, as all good earth citizens should. Custodians of the planet for our duration, to pass on to the group in all good health.'

Jess stared at her incredulously. *You hypocrite.* Then she replied, 'Is your stand for our benefit or do you genuinely and honestly believe that?'

'I beg your pardon?' asked an affronted Audrey.

'You mean to tell me you own the house you live in but pay rent to someone to assuage your guilt?'

'I don't know what you mean?'

'Come off the grass,' said Jess, looking her firmly in the eyes. 'The house you live in is owned by a family company, of which your husband is the director, and you claim to be paying rent. If that is so, you are paying to yourself.'

Geoffrey was suddenly all attention. 'Our affairs are none of your business. How we manage our domestic arrangements is a private matter. We certainly do pay rent and I certainly do not own that house.'

Jess could feel all the old animosities slowly rising in her. 'But,' she blurted, 'not only do you own that house, Bales, but you still own the first one your father bought for you in 1977. The one you asked Thomas's mother to move into with you if you could have a word to your father to arrange for Thomas to be leniently dealt with by the courts.'

There was silence as Jess spoke in a soft and menacing tone to the family that she had grown to despise, despite never having met them until now. All her pent-up anger and loathing was welling up in her and she feared she might go too far. She continued, 'The very house that your father bought for you in 1977 with corrupt money laundered through the system that he was supposed to be upholding.'

'I'd be very careful what you're saying, young woman. You could find yourself in court very quickly saying things like that,' said Geoffrey with a menacing tone in his now rising voice.

'I doubt that very much, Bales. You would not want your mother's property seized under the proceeds of the Crimes Act. And I doubt you'd want your father's undeserved good name sullied and dragged through the mud dredging up all that controversy about his assets from crime. Not to mention of course his paedophilic activity.'

'That's quite enough,' said Bales.

'What's she talking about?' asked a now confused Audrey. 'Who the hell are you anyway, and how could you possibly know any of this?'

Jess glared at them, unblinking and with a seriously

threatening posture. John and Livinia stared at each other in amazement and then back at their son-in-law, who was visibly shaking with a rare outburst of defeated rage.

Thomas sat in stunned silence at these revelations. He knew that it was possible that Jess could know some background involving the police inquiry but had no inkling that his in-laws might be involved. The two young girls were visibly confused, looking around at their parents for reassurance, which was not forthcoming.

'What's she talking about, Daddy?' asked one of the girls, who usually called her father by his given name.

Geoffrey was glowing red with subdued rage. 'We had better be going,' he said, fuming.

'I won't be spoken to like that by a truck driver,' announced Audrey. 'A mere farm hand.'

'No, you won't,' agreed Jess.

As Bales got up abruptly and noisily from the chair, scraping it violently across the wooden floor, he glared down at Jess and announced that she better watch herself.

Jess hissed, 'One word from me, Bales, and your career is over. And remember, if anything happens to me, you are squarely in the frame.' She continued staring at him without blinking.

He stormed out of the room muttering and headed for the car parked outside under the portico next to Thomas's.

The Bales packed up in abject silence and departed as quickly as possible, leaving Jess and Thomas alone in the dining room. Once they had gone, Thomas suggested that they go as well, leaving John and Livinia alone in the portico to review the day's events. John was rather pleased with the outcome. He made no secret of the fact that he detested Bales, his arrogance and superior airs that enraged him at times. He had long ago given up on ever trying to understand his wayward daughter. All in all, even though John did not fully comprehend all that had just transpired, he viewed it as rather a suitable occurrence. Not so Livinia. She was much troubled by what had been revealed as she thought the ramifications could be enormous.

On the drive home, Thomas was deep in thought and drove in silence. Jess could see she had upset him and hoped she had not offended him as well.

'I'm sorry, Thomas,' she said finally. 'I hope I didn't embarrass you too much with my outburst.'

'No, no,' he said in a non-committal way. 'Not at all. How come you know so much about that ratbag?'

'I'm sorry, Thomas. It's none of my business. Except when they run you down,' she said, looking up at him in a caring way that rather touched his heart.

'I couldn't believe my ears when you told me the name of your mother's husband. The Bales are an infamously corrupt and devious family. We just can't get enough evidence to prove his father was corrupt. I guess Donald would have known,' she said, almost to herself.

'What did you mean "if something happens to you"?' asked Thomas.

'Nothing's going to happen. Just forget it. It's all too late now anyway.'

139

It would be a long, long time before Jess would see the Bales again, and that was all to the good.

One other thing this unsavoury episode did to Jess was to reawaken the animosities she felt towards those who had contributed to the demise of her first happy home with Donald MacIntyre in Newtown. It sowed the seeds of an idea whereby she might be able to vent her frustrations and exhume some of the wrongs about which she knew from conversations with Don and Ian Knuckey. In Geoffrey Bales, Jess saw the personification in a tangible way of all that was corrupt and threatening to her life, to her previous existence with Donald, and to destroying her life at Milbark. It set her mind to the possibility of a new venture, one that would utilise her main weapon in achieving retribution and maybe even some revenge. Her mind was a whirl of the excitement of all the possibilities.

Jessie came from a background where, if someone crossed you, you simply dropped them and kicked them yourself. Not in her world did the niceties and gentlemanly endeavours of endless intellectual legalities exist to draw out incessantly the pain of the unresolved. No, one dealt with the miscreant oneself. And if unable to so deal, one did not survive. She had to remind herself that in reality she no longer lived in that world but on the margins where she now was, and the line sometimes became blurred.

The raw excitement of possibly raising another devious creation to anonymously fight her battles was beginning to enchant her. After all, half the excitement of her writings was the secret battles she engaged in, trying to carry her creation through to completion and not be revealed as the creator. She had done it three times now, another would be a fine achievement and give her life some challenging meaning, some mischievous sense of triumph. She would begin immediately to formulate the equation.

That happened in October. Jess tried to find out more information about the Bales' companies. In the meantime, Christmas was rolling around again. Jess was still expecting to spend that alone as usual, so had agreed to deliver some stock a day or so before and then maybe visit the coast or her apartment at Rushcutters Bay.

The truck was returned to Auvergne by early December. Following the unexpected delays, however, that were caused by some minor mechanical faults, Jess was now ready to recommence deliveries of the sold cattle.

Christmas was now only a day away. The buyer had requested that all stock be delivered before Christmas as he wished to join his family at the coast for Christmas Day. Consequently, Jess also agreed to make the final delivery very early Christmas morning, as Christmas was basically just another day to her and she had no plans for spending that day any differently from any other.

Jess had the last few remaining stock in the yards and loaded up the stock crate in the earliest morning light. It would take her about two hours to arrive at her destination so she left as soon as possible. It all seemed so simple. What Jess did not know was that there had been many reports of stock theft occurring in the district and the duty police were requested to keep an eye out for suspicious movements. This request had emanated from the local stock-squad contingent, which consisted of only two overworked but conscientious officers. One was Sergeant Berry, a long-serving and diligent officer who had a family history of rural living and understood the industry inside out. Moving stock early Christmas morning qualified for just such a suspicious occurrence.

Jess drove slowly along the back roads of the district heading for her destination via the shortest route. She was barely half an hour from her destination when she was shaken from her idyll by the sight of an approaching police car clearly indicating for her to stop. She was deeply annoyed and fearful, as was her want when confronted by the police. Two young officers alighted from the vehicle, both donning their caps as they headed for her truck. Jess noted that one of them was a shortish female. They beckoned for her to turn off the engine and to get out of the vehicle. Her annoyance level was quickly rising. Their request to show her driving licence presented Jess with a dilemma. She concocted a story that she did not have it on her right now but that she did have one. They were not entirely convinced.

They closely inspected all her paperwork, then examined the animals and finally did a thorough vehicle check. They conducted this investigation in silence. When they had finished, the policeman sternly warned her that it was an offence to drive without a licence and would she mind presenting it at the local station on the first working day after Christmas. Jess was furious; her sedately anonymous life might be threatened by a seemingly innocent desire to comply with the wishes of a local buyer.

'Is that it then?' she asked as they turned to go.

'Yes, madam. All else is in order, all excepting your licence.'

'Then why was I stopped?'

'Routine, madam,' the other replied, and they walked off to their vehicle.

It was several hours before Jess overcame her annoyance. She was cranky the rest of the morning.

The next day, Jess rang her contact in the Integrity Commission to ask if this was normal, and if the two young officers were within their rights. Her contact there arranged to speak to the Cooma station. He ascertained the background and passed on to Jess the reason she was stopped. He asked the local police to drop the requirement that she present her driving licence. At first, they refused. But he indicated that higher matters were at stake here.

Jess was grateful for the licence request to be voided, but she was still nervous about being stopped by marauding police vehicles as she desperately wished to retain her anonymity.

The upshot of this encounter was not so much felt by Jess but indirectly by Sergeant Berry. The commander wanted to know who had been inadvertently intercepted and had the ear of the Integrity Commission and why they would be checking up on him. Neither question was accommodated with a satisfactory answer; indeed, any answer, but Sergeant Berry was so intrigued by this turn of events that he intended to pursue it quietly for his own satisfaction. He was the butt of internal, but friendly, teasing at the idea that he was being investigated. It was highly unusual for the top brass to interfere with local jurisdictions when it came to routine policing matters, such as the requirement to carry one's licence.

The thing was, for him, that there had been a number of reported cases of cattle duffing and some sheep stealing occurring in the district. He was having no success at all in clearing up the cases and he was being pressed to try to cut it down. It suddenly struck him as possibly a little odd that, of all the known cases, none had been reported from Auvergne, the alleged source of the driver and the stock then being moved, a large and well-known property in the district and one he thought of as a prime target for stock theft. That might give him an in to investigate who was living there and why they appeared to be bypassed by the problem. After all it was still suspicious to him that anybody would move stock on Christmas Day, despite the whole thing appearing legitimate. The tricky part for Sergeant Berry was to gain access to the property without incurring the wrath of those who had demanded that place be left alone. He would work on a solution. In the meantime, he could possibly try and sight the woman described as the driver by frequenting the cattle sales. He could also visit the well-known troublesome duo, the Makepeace boys, who lived at the back end of that district and nearby to Auvergne.

Sergeant Berry and his offsider paid a visit to the Makepeace place two days later. Jean Makepeace was devastated that this issue was raising its ugly head yet again. She interrogated Timmy thoroughly and then decided to seek the help of Jess in trying to dissuade the police from the notion that her boys were again into that disreputable trade. Jason had now returned from Western Australia as the mining boom had collapsed momentarily and he was laid off.

Jean Makepeace ventured over to Auvergne again in her finery to see Jess and try to obtain her good word for her boys. Jess was surprised to see Mrs Makepeace standing on her doorway that evening. After a short talk, Jess suggested that she drive herself over to see Timmy at home and discuss the matter. Jess was at a loss to know what Mrs Makepeace thought she could do about it but seemed convinced that she was able to carry some weight on the subject. She little realised that Jess wanted even less to get involved, but Jess was concerned that the issue had again arisen, so agreed to attend, especially as she may have inadvertently been the cause of the suspicion with her Christmas Day delivery.

Tim assured Jess that he was definitely not involved in any such thing and neither was Jason. What Jess insisted on getting out of him, however, was the *modus operandi* of the scheme as previously operated by the boys. Tim was quite concerned that his name continually cropped up when anything such as this happened in the local area, so he was prepared to explain how the system as he knew it was operated, but on strict conditions that the source of the information never be divulged. Jess took careful note of the names he mentioned and the way they operated the system.

After a few days, Jess rang her contacts in the Integrity Commission and asked about the character of Sergeant Berry. It went against all her instincts and better judgement to do so, but she was contemplating contacting the sergeant and passing on some of the information that she had gained from Tim. She firstly, however, had to be assured that the sergeant was a worthy recipient of her hard-won facts. She was considering doing this to safeguard Auvergne stock, but also as a favour to the distraught and ever-worried Mrs Makepeace. Jess admired the struggling woman who fought endlessly to help her often undeserving offspring. How to impart her knowledge, however, was her dilemma.

Jess learned that Sergeant Berry was regarded as a particularly honest and hardworking cop who had had only moderate success in tracking down the felons involved in stock stealing.

Sergeant Berry was well known to the saleyard people and had no trouble getting Jess's name from them. He thought he was on his way now to learning a bit more about her. The name he was offered was Jane Ransom. She did not appear on any police databases but strangely she appeared as a successful author of Romantis publications, something of course he never read. She was listed as living in the far north of Western Australia. Fortunately for Jess, the entries were brief and unaccompanied by any pictures. He dismissed that line of research. He was therefore still left with a mystifying blank about her, but he would persevere.

Three days later, he received a terse telephone call from a

woman requesting that he meet her at next week's sales. He suspected it was Jess but was not positive. On the appointed day, he and his offsider were at the sales early and watched as the now familiar old semi entered the yards to disgorge its load. Jess did not attempt to meet them until all the stock had been unloaded, yarded and sold. Then she walked past Sergeant Berry and simply requested that he meet her at her truck in about five minutes. This he did, accompanied by his offsider.

They were standing together at her truck awaiting her arrival for about seven minutes. Finally, they could see her making her way over to the vehicle. She was carrying a small notebook into which she continually jotted down notes during the course of the sales. As she walked towards them, he observed her removing the pair of fingerless mitts she regularly wore, which he assumed were to protect her delicate and very pale skin from the sun, as well as protection against the damages dealt out daily while working with animals and in yards. She placed the notebook and mitts on the front passenger's seat after opening the door and then climbed back down and went around to the side of the vehicle where the two men were standing in somewhat of a confused state.

Jess removed her battered hat and placed it in her left hand. She stood looking at the pair with a slightly knitted brow, just staring at them and saying nothing. They found it most unsettling. Sergeant Berry was unsure how to kick off the conversation because he was still not positive that this was the woman who had requested his presence there. He was also unsure of this woman's name and the motives behind the request to meet. He stood uncomfortably while she gazed at them with an unsettling and, almost piercing stare. Finally, she took a small breath and asked in a soft and low voice, 'Sergeant Berry?'

'Yes, Miss, I mean Mrs. Sorry I don't even know your name,' he responded nervously.

Jess ignored that remark entirely. Then she continued after a minor pause. 'About the stock stealing that is occurring. Firstly, Tim Makepeace is totally innocent of that undertaking.' There was another slight pause, and Jess was about to continue, when she was interrupted by Berry's offsider, who blurted out, 'I wouldn't be so sure about that.'

Jess turned a little to face the conversational interloper, staring at him with a blank and expressionless face. She simply turned her head back to face Sergeant Berry, her big blue eyes giving no hint of acknowledgement of the other man's comments. After a long pause in which no one spoke she continued, 'Here are some names that you may wish to pursue.' Then she listed five names. She noted that no one was writing them down. She looked annoyed and puzzled.

Berry noted her annoyance and simply responded, 'No need to write any of them down. They are well known to us.'

Jess paused again. Then she continued, pulling out a small notebook from her shirt pocket and reading, occasionally looking up at the two officers. 'Jimmy and Dave do most of the duffing, usually at night. They ship them out by truck to a large mountain property the other side of Jindabyne. It's located twenty-seven miles exactly from the Browns Road turnoff on the Gribbley Road. There they remove the NLIS tags and attach their own. They can be in Victoria within two days.'

She looked him straight in the eye and remained silent, as if to say that's all I've got, you do the rest.

Berry stood there in silence for a few minutes, his mouth moving slightly as he contemplated the information. He then began to rub his chin. His eyes were peering at the ground while he thought.

'Do they muster with bikes or horses?'

'Bikes,' she answered.

'And what sort of vehicles do they use?'

'Single-axle tray-top crated trucks. All pretty modern.'

'Do they always on-sell?'

'No,' she replied, a little more animated. 'That's the cunning bit. Often they keep them for breeding and then sell off the progeny legitimately. That's why they try to steal poddies or unmarked stock'.

'Where next will they strike?'

'I don't know.'

'Why is Auvergne immune then?' he asked, looking at her sideways. There was a long deliberate pause. She stared deeply into his eyes and then said, 'I took care of that problem. It won't happen again.' There was a hint of hidden menace and intent in her soft voice, giving every indication to Sergeant Berry that she was well capable of just such a thing. He raised his eyebrows a little and left it at that. He was unsure what she meant by that remark but could well imagine. She was a mere slip of a woman but she had an air of authority and control, even power, despite her small statue. He felt she was not a woman to be angered. He had observed her rather severe and humourless nature, but she nonetheless had a modicum of softness about her that contradicted the severity of her presented persona. He was still not sure that he even knew her name.

'Can I ask your name please?' he asked in his most conciliatory and humble of voices. She merely stared at him and made no reply.

'Well, thank you very much for this information,' he finally said.

'Will you promise me that you will discount the Makepeace lads?'

Both the policemen stared at her momentarily. Then they looked at each other briefly. Berry turned back to face her and nodded his agreement.

'For the time being,' he said. They turned and departed amid some muffled conversation, most of which Jess could not hear. She climbed into the cab and started the engine.

CHAPTER SEVEN

t was a cool morning for this time of year. Jess had taken the load of steers into the sales as Thomas had requested and, as usual, stayed for almost the entire proceedings in order to inform herself, as well as Thomas, how the market was going. She enjoyed that aspect of the cattle industry as, when living on Milbark, she was totally out of the picture and far removed from the marketing facets of the business. Here she was able to be intimately involved in the final outcome of the production phase. Just before the final sale, Jess walked over to her truck to leave before any rush. She had a couple of small errands to perform in town before heading back to Auvergne.

Jess drove the old truck slowly out of the saleyard parking area and headed back into town. She stopped at two places along the main road where she could manage to park the truck safely away from the traffic. She was about to depart the second place when she noticed a car parked some distance behind her which she had also noticed at the first place. Jess constantly checked for any suspicious occurrences and monitored all the time for anything unusual. She still suffered badly from nervousness following those run-ins with the police in the past. In truth, she also feared for her life and expected retribution was possible at any moment for her contributions to the demise of many a reputation.

Jess sat in the truck for many minutes studying the vehicle. Her observant eye took in all the details: colour, make, model, age and distinguishing features. At this distance she could not discern how many occupants were in it or how loaded up it was. It had no roof rack and appeared to her to have New South Wales plates. *Was it just a local or something more sinister?* She reminded herself again that she still feared for her life despite the time lag since her trial.

Jess started up the truck and headed out of town, but at the turn-off back into Polo Flat she suddenly turned in and headed slowly up the road, constantly peering in the mirrors. Her discomfort increased as she watched the car follow her into the industrial area. She stopped again to observe its reaction. It also stopped some distance behind her. She repeated the manoeuvre once more and then with rising nervousness returned to the highway and turned off on the road that led to Auvergne. The car was still following her at some distance.

The road that led to Auvergne was narrow, but bitumen all the way to the turn-off to the gravel roads that then led off to the property. It traversed the typical Monaro treeless plain country for many kilometres to the south, undulating gently over the dry and rather drab-looking paddocks. The distant hills were covered in scattered trees and there were a few rare turn-offs that led off into unknown outlying vistas. About thirty minutes into her trip with the car still following her, Jess turned off to the left into a small gravel road that was dignified with the rather grandiose title of Lochinvar Lane by a neat sign attached to a post that pointed slightly skyward, but in the general direction of the deviating track. The grandness was then somewhat diminished with a smaller sign underneath informing those prepared enough to read it that it was a no-through road. Jess had never been up this road and hoped it did not peter out into something so difficult that she would be unable to turn her truck around. She had noticed the road many times in her travels into Cooma and had always promised herself that she would explore all these interesting-looking side roads. She just did not plan to do it quite so soon and definitely not in the old stock semi-trailer.

She slowly meandered along the road, trying not to kick up too much dust and trying to keep the road in sight in order to observe if the car followed her. If it did, that would prove in her mind that it was definitely following her. To her consternation it did just that, travelling very slowly at some considerable distance behind her. She was beginning to become quite distraught with the way things were going and now began to regret turning off into so remote and isolated a stretch of countryside.

The road was very narrow and began to enter the treed hilly country to the east of the main road. It was also getting windier and flanked with cuttings and batters in some of the steeper ridges. Suddenly it opened out into a broader area and came to an abrupt halt with two gates leading off into properties that bordered its termination. Luckily for Jess there was a reasonable turning area for her to negotiate that manoeuvre, along with evidence that it was regularly done there, no doubt assisted by the unwelcoming notices attached to each gate informing the reader that this was the end of the road for the uninvited. She carefully turned the semi and parked facing the way back out and waited. She estimated that if the car was still following her, it would be there in about two minutes.

After ten minutes, Jess was unsure what to do as no vehicles had appeared. Her confusion began to rise and she hoped maybe it was all just her imagination that led her to this suspicion. She engaged the gears and slowly moved the old truck off along the narrow gravel track. It was a winding narrow track this far in and there were several small creek crossings with rickety wooden bridges that she had to negotiate, so she was barely moving along. She had been returning for no more than a few minutes when it all happened; suddenly, and without any warning to her, despite her careful and alert state.

She was heading up a small rise that drifted off to the left in a gentle curve that had one buttress of carved-out rock face on one side where the road travelled through a small stony ridge.

It flattened out quickly on the other to slide away to her right down a gentle tree-covered expanse of badly fenced paddock. She was startled to see the same white car heading towards her at a moderate pace and she could clearly see the driver, who was definitely not paying attention as he fiddled with something on the passenger-side dashboard. She was about to blast her horn when she saw him look up and jerk the wheel to his left in an attempt to miss the bulk that was suddenly in front of him. She was able to stop almost immediately, but not so the other vehicle. She watched in disbelief as the driver wrestled with the steering wheel, applying the brakes in a sliding spray of loose gravel and headed straight into the bank on the side of the road. The vehicle shunted up over the small piece of ridge, flipping onto its roof. As she stared open-eyed in the mirror, she clearly saw it hit a rock, flip onto its wheels and bang violently into another large boulder, moving it slightly off its ground. She sat there briefly, unsure what was going to happen next. She turned her engine off and stared at the scene in her mirror. There was total silence except for the hissing of escaping liquids and steam from the wrecked car at her rear. She opened the door, still shocked at what had happened. She calmed herself down and walked gingerly over to the now righted vehicle. She could hear the moaning of the single occupant.

The vehicle had slammed itself front-on, but slightly to the left into the rock, so the driver's door might still be able to be opened. She approached the car carefully and looked in to see a large, dishevelled man groaning in pain and covered in dust and some blood. He was conscious but dazed.

'You okay?' she asked tentatively.

The man grimaced with pain and was about to speak when he checked himself.

'You okay?' she asked again.

'I don't think so. Can you call someone?' he pleaded.

'Why are you following me, and who are you?' she asked, regaining a little of her composure.

'Never mind that now. Please, can you call someone? I'm not feeling too good.'

'As soon as you tell me who you are.'

The man looked at her, still grimacing and holding his chest. Jess noticed that blood began to trickle from his mouth. As she gazed at him in his agonies, she glanced into the recesses of the front. She noticed that there were several cameras and lenses and other paraphernalia scattered about in disarray on the floor and the seat. He tried to reach for his mobile 'phone that was still on the dash, but the seat belt and the discomfort prevented that.

'Were you following me?'

The man looked at her rather sadly and replied finally, 'Yes. That's my job. I photograph celebrities.'

'How did you know about me?' she asked, getting annoyed. There was a long silence, as the man grimaced again.

'Tell me, mate. I'm not going anywhere till you do.'

'Look, a few days ago I got a call from a man telling me about you and that you lived somewhere near Cooma. Way out in the sticks, he said. If I went down there, I might get myself some good pics.'

'Who was that then?'

'I don't know!' he exclaimed. 'He just rang me outa th' blue.'

'Tell me who it was, mate,' she demanded.

He was beginning to doze off in shock and injuries, so Jess continued more earnestly. 'Look, I'm not going anywhere till you tell me.'

'I told you I don't know. Please, can you call someone?'

'Not till I find out.'

'All I know is his number. It's the last one there. He told me to make sure I removed it but I didn't, just in case. It's easy to find. It's the one that ends in 404.'

Jess reached in to try to retrieve the mobile. It was almost out of reach but she managed it, even leaning on him a little, causing him to moan and protest. She was about to remove her driving gloves protecting her hands from the sun when she suddenly realised that it would be better if she kept them on. She fiddled with the mobile and retrieved the last number received. He was right; it was easy to remember as it began 0404 and ended 404. She wrote it down in her notebook. She chucked the mobile back onto the front seat.

'Aren't yer gonna call someone?' he asked.

'Not here mate, there's no reception out here.'

She looked at him with some sympathy as he was obviously in much discomfort, but she was weighing up all her options. Her first thoughts were who had sent him on this mission, and why. The second was that she was fearful of dealings with authority because she always seemed to be the villain. In fact, she was beginning to get pangs of remorse herself as she felt entirely responsible for this predicament. *Is that how the cops would see it?* She already had the worst possible reputation for causing trouble. *Who would believe me here?* She looked at him again. He was beginning to lapse in and out of consciousness. She would have to decide soon what she was going to do.

'What's your name, mate?'

'What?' he stammered, trying to reawaken himself.

'What's your name?'

'Percy Pavilon.'

'And you're a photographer?'

'Yes,' he muttered. His head was drooping now and he was slurring his words. He suddenly gave a louder moan and sat motionless for a second and then slumped slowly forward to rest on the bent steering wheel. Jess was not happy at all about this and she feared the worst. She was right: he was dead.

Jess's first thought was to depart as quickly as possible. Although it was an isolated spot, there was evidence that the traffic was regular enough for someone to come along eventually. She quickly jotted down the number plate of the car and then walked back to her truck and started the engine. She drove out of there slightly faster than her normal pace. Jess passed no one on the road out and hopefully no one saw her there. She decided to turn the truck back to Cooma and ring that number immediately to try to find out who owned it. If she were lucky, she might even be able to ring the number before anyone discovered the accident.

Jess stopped at the first telephone box that she saw. She was not going to use her own mobile, as that could be traced.

She inserted the money and dialled the number. It rang only twice and then the voice of a young girl answered, saying, 'Hello, Zoë speaking.'

Jess was so unexpecting the voice that she hesitated to answer. Finally, in a slow and deeper voice than normal, trying to disguise herself slightly, she replied, 'Sorry, who's speaking?'

'Zoë Bales here. Who's that?'

Jess was flabbergasted. She was unsure what to do. Finally, she replied, 'Zoë Bales. Is your father Judge Bales?'

'That's right.'

'I'm sorry. I must have hit the wrong button. I am sorry. Thank you, bye.'

With that, Jess hung up the receiver and stood in deep confusion and annoyance as she slowly began to understand the situation. She walked smartly back to her truck and sat there thinking it all over. *It's obvious that a teenage girl did not dob me in to the paparazzi. But what possible advantage would her irritating, useless, good-for-nothing ratbag of a father, Judge Bales, gain from exposing me?*

Jess was feeling quite nervous and began to feel shock setting in after such a harrowing incident. She decided the best thing for her to do was to go back to Auvergne and see what eventuated; *after all, there was hopefully nothing to connect me to the death on that lonely road.*

The body was not discovered for over thirty hours, as the few residents that lived that far out travelled in and out of town in the dark and it was not until one of the young adult children was returning home from town in daylight hours that the accident was noticed. Jess still felt quite ill when contemplating the incident and remained at home for a few days. The first repercussions for her occurred three days later when a marked police car turned up at Auvergne carrying two young policemen. They pulled up at the homestead and made for the door. Thomas saw them entering the homestead compound and wandered over to find out what they wanted. The driver of the car saw him approaching and said in an official and procedural manner, 'You Thomas Summers?'

'Yes, that's right. What can I do for you?'

The two policemen beckoned for him to come closer to the vehicle and into the shade.

'Is this your vehicle?' asked the driver rather officiously, thrusting out a large photograph of a cattle truck clearly showing the number plate. Thomas looked at the picture, turning it back and forth and then remarked, 'Yes, that looks like mine.'

'Do you know this man?' he then asked, giving him a picture of the now-dead Percy Pavilon. Thomas looked at it for a while and then replied, 'No. Should I?'

'Do you know this woman?' he asked, handing Thomas another large colour photograph of Jess clearly visible standing beside the truck in the main street of Cooma.

Thomas looked carefully at it and then replied nervously, 'Yes, she works with me here. Why do you ask?'

'What's her name please, sir.'

Thomas looked at the tall and well-built young constable and after a short pause replied, 'Why do you need to know?'

'Just her name please sir, if you don't mind.'

Thomas looked again at the two of them. He was finding their manner of operation a little annoying and feared how such an approach would be greeted by Jess if she were so treated. Thomas was now getting agitated. Finally, he said firmly, 'Why don't you ask her yourself, mate. She's down there about two miles at the cattle yards. Yer can't miss it' He pointed down the track in the direction of the big yards where Jess was sorting cattle for the next sale.

The two young policemen thanked Thomas and drove off. Thomas mumbled to himself, 'And good luck, mate.'

The police car bounced along the rough station track and pulled up near the cattle yards. Donning their caps, they proceeded to the main yard that faced out into the fenced-off paddocks that were used as holding paddocks for the yards. Jess was droving a small mob of steers up the gentle slope from the direction of the creek. She was most of the way up when suddenly the cattle propped, then shied away from the yard gates.

Jess wondered what had caused the sudden spooking, and when she peered up and saw the two officers standing by the gate, she rode up and shouted for them to get away from the gate. She left no doubt in their minds that she was angry. As she wheeled the big and now alarmed horse about to give chase, one of the men yelled out for her to come over. She ignored that command and galloped off in haste after the fast-retreating mob kicking up their heels and frisking about in the paddock. She managed to wheel them by the creek with much cracking of the stockwhip and then headed them back up towards the yards, this time a little quicker as they still thought it was playtime and their energy levels were raised.

As they entered the yards, Jess managed to close the gate before any more harm was done. She dismounted and began to attend to other gates when the driver of the police car again commanded her to come over to them. She looked up disdainfully and completed her task at the gate and then slowly walked over to the two men.

'It's customary to obey a lawful command of a police officer madam,' he began. Not a very wise comment to Jess.

'You should know better than to stand at the gate of a set of cattle yards, dopey.' Her voice dripped with disrespect and contempt.

'And you are?' asked the young officer. There was a particularly long pause on Jess's behalf before she responded, 'I am what?' she scornfully replied.

'What is your name please?' There was a long pause while she peered at them both and ran her eyes up and down them. Finally, she replied, 'And who needs to know?'

'We'll ask the questions here, madam, if you don't mind. Just answer the question please. What is your name?'

'Not until you tell me what this is about.'

The young officer was getting agitated. He was not used to simple country people being so dismissive. He thought he would try another tack. 'We are investigating a certain incident that occurred locally and wish to make inquiries from various people. Now what is your name, please?'

Jess stood there for many minutes before answering. It dawned on her that this must be about Pavilon. What name to give? She finally decided that she still did not wish for her name to be revealed to any locals if at all possible, let alone the police. She remained silent. His offsider wrote that down in his book. She began to get a bad feeling about this. Every time she had an encounter with the police, she seemed to end up wronged.

The young officer could see that this was going to be more difficult than he first thought. Then he began to ask her about the truck, and finally, showing her several pictures of herself by the truck and inside it, as well as various shots of her about town. She looked at them all and then asked, rather annoyed, 'Who is doing this and why?'

'I take it you don't know about these then?'

'I certainly do not.'

'Do you know this man then?' he asked, showing her a picture of Percy. She simply shook her head.

'Why would this man be taking pictures of you?' asked the policeman. Jess just looked at him in silence.

'I ask again, madam. What is your name?'

Jess just stared at him.

'Look, we can continue this down at the station if you refuse to co-operate.'

For Jess it always seemed to come down to this – follow their rules or be dealt with. She looked him squarely in the eyes and said in a slightly menacing tone, 'You still think you can just swan in here to somebody's private property and threaten them with arrest, all for no apparent reason, don't you? I thought they were eliminating that sort of behaviour from the police.'

'Look madam, nobody's threatening anybody here. I have a lawful right to ask you your identity and for you to comply. I am within my rights to arrest you if I so deem obstruction.'

'You and what army, mate?' asked Jess with total contempt. With that, she turned and walked over to the horse, led him to a couple of gates to ensure the cattle were secure and mounted to ride off to the homestead.

'We will need to speak to you again,' shouted the perplexed young officer as they both stood in disbelief watching her as she rode off.

Jess had tolerated their intrusion mostly in continued silence, all the time her blood was boiling at how, yet again, she could be simply accosted even out here in the paddock. She felt intimidated by the police. She watched from horseback as the two men drove off over the dusty paddock track. She arrived back at the house shortly after and found Thomas. He could see she was annoyed so he refrained from questioning her for the moment. She asked to use the telephone in the station office. Thomas nodded his agreement and Jess rang her trusted friend Ian Knuckey. She explained the story of the day to him and asked if he could arrange to have the two officious and unsympathetic officers investigated for treating her so badly. She wished to complain about this harassment.

Next morning, the two young officers were hauled into

the police station commander's office and asked to explain their version of events at Auvergne's cattle yards. They were considerably surprised to be so questioned. The commander demanded to know who it was they had so inadvertently offended and what had transpired. In the end, he felt he could not really fault their investigative techniques, but certainly wished to know who had the ear of the commissioner of police and was living undetected in this quiet backwater of law enforcement. That information was not forthcoming, but he did learn that they had all better be careful in future as they never knew with whom they may be dealing at any given moment.

The two young officers were asked to remain in the room while the commander contacted the commissioner's office as he was instructed to do. The commissioner seemed satisfied with the commander's reply and was at least grateful that the situation had not spiralled out of control, the two young officers showing what turned out to be fortuitous foresight in not escalating the delicate position. At the commander's request to know the identity of the person of interest, he received a forceful and firm 'no'.

Two days later, Jess rang her contact in the Integrity Commission to ascertain the outcome of their inquiries into the affair so far. The commissioner tried to assuage her misplaced anger by acknowledging that she had been forthrightly dealt with, following correct procedure, and they were doing their duty correctly by investigating what she now knew was a serious accident with which she was inadvertently, if innocently connected. He informed her that she was not being persecuted.

That was the second time the local commander had been contacted by an irate commissioner or other very high-ranking officer from headquarters. He now knew there was someone of extreme influence loitering within his jurisdiction whom he not only did not know about but was also not going to be told about.

Jess was becoming obsessed with the other distraction that she had hit upon, which involved the possibility of her writing under yet another pseudonym and revealing anonymously what she knew. These twin occurrences blinded her to the possibility of the following incident unfolding about her.

Jess parked the semi out of the way while she was waiting for the sales to commence. John and Livinia arrived after the sale began but before Thomas's stock was auctioned. They deliberately kept out of Jessie's way as John knew how professionally she attended to all the details involved with the sales process, recording results diligently and passing on information to Thomas. Once John was satisfied all was completed as far as Jess was concerned, he and Livinia proceeded over to Jess as she headed back to the truck.

'Morning Jess,' said John as they approached her from behind. Jess was still writing notes in a pad. She looked up and wheeled about, acknowledging their presence in the fashion that they had now come to accept as her reserved and quiet manner. She nodded her head slightly.

'How's it going?' asked John.

'Pretty well,' answered Jess softly.

'Liv and I are in Cooma for a few things and we were wondering if you'd like to have some lunch with us in town. If you can spare the time.'

Jess looked at them, deep in thought about the motives of such a seemingly innocent chance meeting.

'Well...' she started to say, delaying her reply as was her usual custom.

John pressed her. 'We'd really love to see you for an hour or so.'

Jess looked at them both. She thought she detected an air of desperate keenness for her to accept but wondered what they really wanted. Jess reluctantly accepted the invitation. John said to leave the truck at the saleyards and he would drive them the kilometre or so into town for lunch. They went to a café that John regularly frequented and where he was well known.

Finally, John said to her, 'Look Jess, we really appreciate all you've done for us at Auvergne. I'm not entirely sure what you've been spending out there but I feel you should be reimbursed for all your trouble.'

Jess turned and stared up at him across the table. She stared for a long minute, while both John and Livinia waited for her response.

'It's nothing,' she said softly. 'It's been so wonderful for me that Thomas has allowed me to fill in some time while I sort out myself and what to do.'

'And what do you think you might do in the future?' asked

John with a hint of concern.

After a longer than usual delay, Jess answered by saying, 'I'm not entirely sure. I can't keep on annoying Thomas forever, you know. He will want me to move on sooner or later.'

Both John and Livinia looked at each other in an air of mild confusion. Livinia was suddenly quite horrified at the prospect that this sophisticated and worldly international author, noted for her romantic novels among other things, seemed to be totally unconscious and unaware of any deep feelings that Thomas had for her. *Was it possible that she could be so naive and innocent or was she bunging on an act?* Livinia swallowed in anxiety at the implications. There was a long silence.

'Why do you ask? Have I embarrassed you in some way with my antics?' Jess asked with self-effacing concern.

'No, no!' yelled John and Livinia, almost in unison.

'Quite the opposite,' said John quickly.

'You seem to have been a very big help to him,' said Livinia, reaching out and touching Jess on the arm. Jess was a little perplexed at the turn of the conversation. She looked at them both in a slightly sad-eyed manner, which they both observed.

John hurriedly tried to ease her concern by changing tack a little. 'What are your plans for the future?' He asked more out of concern for Thomas.

Jess sat in silence, thinking how to answer such a question. Finally, she looked at them and replied, 'Well. It depends a bit on how much longer Thomas wants me to hang around, but I am looking at Sydney as one option.'

A heavy silence descended on the trio as they each sat in their own little world momentarily. In the background was the low, incessant clinking sounds of people eating and drinking in a crowded and confined café space.

'And you've not given any thought to staying longer then?' they heard Livinia asking, breaking the other two out of their deep-thinking stupor.

'No, not really. I suppose it's not something that has arisen in any serious way for a while,' said Jess.

'Well, Thomas has certainly appreciated your efforts for him. He has told me so,' said Livinia encouragingly.

'I hope so. He's a very nice boy,' said Jess. There was a long and penetrating silence. Jess took the opportunity to continue in the absence of anybody else speaking, 'You know, Livinia, what Thomas needs is a good wife to help him with all the work. You must know plenty of suitable young girls that would suit him.'

John and Livinia looked at each other in amazement. They thought that Jess would have some inkling that Thomas was very fond of her, even though they knew she was probably much older than he was.

'Well, it's not that simple, you know,' said Livinia stammering a little. 'Thomas has not been around here for a long time. He hasn't had the opportunity to meet many women, I guess.'

'No, I guess not,' agreed Jess. 'Well, I wish he'd find a nice young woman to help him.'

John looked at his watch in fake interest and indicated

that it was about time to go. He dropped Jess back off at the saleyards next to the truck and said goodbye, then he and Livinia departed for Bridgehead. Along the way, there was a certain level of melancholy as they drove in almost total silence trying to digest the ramifications of the strange conversation. It was clear to both of them that Jess had absolutely no idea of Thomas's feelings for her, and worse, possibly she had no feelings for him. John could understand why Thomas, indeed any man, would find her physically attractive. Combined with her talent, her aura of mystique, her exotic background, and the hint of danger that exuded from her persona and reputation, John could easily see why any man would desire her. He clearly recalled how much unease he felt on first seeing her and his disquiet had been born out.

Jess drove home in the old truck unaware of the machinations occurring about her. She was deep in thought on totally another matter, one that was beginning to excite her mind enormously. Jess had other deep burning desires stirring within her active and imaginative mind; cravings that did not involve Thomas or his family at all. She had, for some time now been feeling unsettled about an entirely different topic altogether. It had to do with Thomas, but in a completely different aspect.

The episode with the Bales clan so mortified the sensitivities of Jess that she tormented herself with a desire to wreak revenge, or at least expose the hypocrisy of it all in some way. In her mind, Geoffrey Bales was the personification of all that had destroyed her ideal life that Don had provided for her from the age of five. She lumped him and his kind in with cops and the rest of the legal profession that had betrayed their positions of trust and responsibility to feather their own nests at the expense of innocent people.

Jess stewed over the possibilities, and the longing to expose them all and see them squirm as she had had to do for years now. She realised deep down that that desire was really only that – just a desire that would probably remain unfulfilled: or would it? All the evidence that she had been able to provide to the corruption commissions and the police integrity investigations was either too spurious or circumstantial for any real action to occur; besides, they were up against very powerful opponents. However, slowly her vivid and overactive imagination began to dream of possibilities. To use the only real and effective power she had at her disposal—her writing.

Jess sat contemplating ideas for many hours. She had absolutely no shortage of material, any number of stories she recalled from the days when Don ran the small workshop in Newtown, and even many more from the conversations with Ian Knuckey. Slowly the germ of an idea materialised in her fevered mind. *Why not create a new pen name and write crime stories using all the sources I've accumulated over many years of listening to Don and the others?* This was one form of literature that she had never attempted, indeed never thought about at all. She was thinking about it now.

Her only enterprise that she was able to maintain in any anonymity was that of Kimberley West. She had slowly developed that authorship into a success, not of the calibre of George Norman Thaler, but nevertheless, a solid and now well-respected author who was regarded as mediocre but a developing talent of prodigious output. She did not wish to arouse suspicions or comparisons to Thaler for fear of exposure.

The literary agency for that enterprise was located in Sydney, so she decided to attempt to arrange her new venture through that medium. All her old excitement and enthusiasm slowly began to re-emerge as she contemplated the one thing that seemed to arouse her creativity and drive: the thought of another clandestine publishing challenge. She considered all the angles and finally came up with a combination that she thought would succeed. Crime fiction was a common and crowded market; she would need an angle that would distinguish her efforts sufficiently to thrive.

Finally, she decided on the pen name of Joe Scacci. She thought that sounded sufficiently seedy. She had not written anything for years now as Jane Ransom, which allowed her to utilise that name locally without any fear of being uncovered. She also had not written anything as George Norman Thaler since long before departing the Kimberleys. She had, however, been occasionally publishing large un-noteworthy tomes as Kimberley West. This she did as somewhat of a labour but it did continue to bring in a steady stream of finances. It also kept her desire to create flickering, albeit with no enthusiasm now.

Unlike her former works, Joe Scacci wrote insightful, fast-moving, action-packed crime thrillers with a twist. Joe wrote in the first person. His character was a politically incorrect, chauvinistic, misogynistic, somewhat bawdy and uncouth but humorous detective with a latent sense of empathy and feelings. This gave Jess vent to a rather unseen side of her character wherein she displayed considerable dry and subtle humour combined with a raucous and coarse foul-mouthed character who was nevertheless observant and at times sensitive. Despite his name, he was not actually Italian. His grandfather was Italian but had married an English girl in London before the war. His father had migrated to Australia and Joe had been born here. He was more ocker than Italian any day.

Joe Scacci lived alone in a squalid rented unit close to the city and was a rather unprepossessing shabbily dressed man. This was not particularly by design but rather through sheer lack of knowledge and desire. He was solid and rotund, and rather short. His demeanour and attitudes were based on a composite of the characters Jess had known in this line of work, particularly Ian Knuckey, and some of the more unsavoury men she had come across in the outback.

Jess would eventually realise enormous pleasure in writing these novels, as she gave vent to her pent-up anger at the injustices meted out by the system and the unfairness of life. She developed Joe into a likeable knock-about bloke.

All this was fine, but the main aim of this output was to express her knowledge of the underworld in thinly disguised narrative form. From the content and Joe's mannerisms, it was evident that the author knew what he was talking about thoroughly. It was apparent that Joe had considerable knowledge of the law and the criminal mind. It was also evident from the nature of the text that Joe Scacci was either associated with the underworld or involved with it in some depth. Jess tried to indicate obliquely that Joe had formed an association with a long line of criminal dons, aided and abetted by his deceptively Italian name.

Over time, Jess was able to publish half a dozen novels using this pseudonym. While it assuaged to some extent her pent-up frustrations at the lack of any real progress in the fields of retribution and accountability for the corrupt members of the judiciary, it also opened much public debate. This centred on the twin topics of who Joe Scacci really was, and what exactly he knew. More to the point – what was he going to reveal? It was a two-edged sword for Jess, as time would reveal.

CHAPTER EIGHT

O nce Jess had purchased the unit in Rushcutters Bay and visited it a few times, she felt more secure in herself if anything untoward ever happened again to threaten her tranquillity. However, one of the side-effects of this purchase was the realisation that she was not entirely enamoured of the bustling city life, not yet anyway. It had its attractions, especially the vibrancy and the total anonymity. Nearly a lifetime of rural living had engendered in her a passion for the country and its people and the sense of authenticity about its place in the design of things. It seemed valid. Furthermore, she realised that, in the event of further ructions ever occurring, she might be safer, and prefer to have a hideout that was more remote than her unit.

It took Jess many months to locate a suitable property, and surprisingly, it was not that far from her new home.

The whole of the Southern Tablelands and the Monaro in particular were still rather remote and wild country. The high country around the Snowy was in many places still grossly undeveloped and sparsely populated. Jess managed to find a very isolated backwater that was so rugged it was virtually unsuitable for anything.

The block she finally found was located in mountainous terrain on a difficult and rough gravel road that petered out many kilometres past her place into a large wilderness area that bordered the escarpment. The block was very cheap, not that that was any consideration for her, and not just because it was so isolated and rugged but also because the entrance was very difficult. The road ran along a valley between steep mountain ridges, and a steeply gullied creek flowed for many kilometres beside the road, including the front boundary, causing the entrance into the block to be impassable for conventional vehicles. Once the chasm-like gully was traversed, the track in from this creek was exceptionally steep and rough, strewn with boulders and ragged shaly gravel. The attraction for Jess was not only its isolation, its difficult terrain and the steepness of the ingress, but also that once negotiated, the winding and jagged track led up the steep mountains and down a ridge to an isolated valley with pasture that had rarely, if ever, seen domestic animals.

There was a semi-permanent creek running through the meadow-like paddock of about five hundred hectares, and it was mostly level and well grassed. Jess fell in love with the naturalness of the area and bought it at once. She used the name Jane Ransom.

Jess was a competent driver and owned a vehicle that was capable of negotiating the terrain, but the track was so difficult she concluded that she would need a more suitable vehicle if she wished to haul any items of weight out to the place. Momentarily, Jess found herself thinking about her old GMC back at Milbark in the Kimberley. *How handy that would be right now.* After much thought and searching, Jess found an ex-army International ACCO six-by-six diesel truck that had the ground clearance and carrying capacity to negotiate the steep and slippery track. Again, she registered it in the name of Jane Ransom and garaged it at the property, ensuring no one ever saw her in it at Auvergne.

Jess began to frequent the place on weekends and always informed those at Auvergne that she would be away and she was going down to the coast. Jess would drive out in the Land Cruiser and then use the ACCO to head back into Cooma if she needed anything heavy. Over the next few months, Jess reconnoitred the area and spent many hours driving the fire trails and the back roads around her new purchase. The road out to her property was a council road but poorly maintained as few people lived out that way. She followed it around to where it turned off several kilometres past her entrance and found there were more tracks around there that led to a couple of large grazing properties and to an abandoned mine not far from her back fence line. She could access the back of her property from there, and despite the track being very rough, it did afford her another entry point to access her place if she needed that backup.

Over the next year or two, Jess bought a tag-along trailer to float out more equipment to her bush block. This included a tractor with a blade on the front to grade out the tracks better for her to access and traverse the place. She also bought an old four-wheel-drive ute to carry things about the property and a small dozer to attack the difficult track work and some drainage. In order to protect them, she somehow managed to arrange for a large shed to be constructed in the valley and she stored her possessions there. She used her own equipment to facilitate the builders accessing the site and transporting in all the materials.

Jess liked the old ACCO and it was fun for her to drive along the rugged bush tracks that surrounded her property. These tracks wandered in long winding trails about the virgin mountainous country. She was even finding the cold winters agreeable and coped with the occasional snowfalls. However, all this wild country driving re-awakened within her the fondness for her old GMC that hopefully was still sitting in the shed back at Milbark in the Kimberley. It had played such a large part in that chapter of her life that she really wanted to be reunited with it again. To that end, she finally conspired to attempt to retrieve it from the Kimberley late in the Dry.

It was a difficult task, but she managed to abscond for a month in late October, driving the ACCO with the tag-along trailer to Milbark and retrieving her old GMC from the family that had purchased the lease from her years ago. That had proved a daunting enterprise. She told Thomas she was involved with her publishers in both Melbourne and Sydney in order to get the month off. It had been quite a challenge to drive up through the back roads of the outback to Milbark, load up an inoperative 'Jimmy', and drag it all the way back to her bush block near Cooma. The track was so difficult into her tranquil paddock shed that, in the end she had to start up old 'Jimmy' and drive it into the place up the steep ridges.

Jess spent vast amounts of time alone, exploring the immense network of rough, isolated fire trails within the mountainous region that she now so loved. She did most of this in the ACCO, but occasionally took the GMC, although that was not registered. It was so isolated she hoped that would never be a problem. During these enormous periods of time alone, Jess gained a lot of inspiration to write her scathing and controversial novels as Joe Scacci. She formulated wildly speculative accounts of criminal life based on her knowledge garnered mostly from conversations she had heard from Don and Ian, and also from some of the accounts and notes she had read from the commissions set up following her trial.

Jess sometimes became quite agitated, recalling the devious accounts of criminal activity that she encountered. As well, her imagination often ran away with her and she could become quite worked up. This was reflected in the tone of the narrative that she released as Joe. Jess realised that this was aggravating her, so to counter this, she began spending large amounts of time and energy honing her skills in the novels of Kimberley West. She no longer cared what people thought of this effort, so she no longer deliberately scaled down the quality of these works.

Jess began to write more as Kimberley West and to set her novels further back in time to a more elegant and refined period, basing her stories on the endless information and recollections of the now long-dead Norman Woods. She was gaining much satisfaction and success from these endeavours.

Jess spent all her free time either at Rushcutters Bay or out at the bush block. Apart from interruptions driving stock trucks occasionally for the Guises, or unavoidable requirements at Auvergne, she was able to spend most weekends there and any other holidays that came along. There was only one other commitment, and that involved her aged and good friends, the Knuckeys, both surprisingly spritely for a couple pushing eighty.

Jess felt obliged to stay overnight on occasions with Ian and Beryl Knuckey. They had repeatedly and persistently tried to persuade her to spend some time with them in an attempt to express their gratitude. Ian Knuckey was finally beginning to feel a redemptive power late in his life after being set up and pilloried from his days with Don and the workshops.

Late in the evening, on one of these visits, Jess and Ian went for a stroll along the waterfront. The air was cool and the dying sun was setting in the west in a dazzling hue of grey and pink. The gentle zephyr blew with a mild salty tang from the mirror-like, placid bay waters. Jess found Ian pleasant company as they both had so much in common with regards to their shared background. She disliked his almost continual smoking, but after her associations with stockmen, she had come to accept it as normal for that generation of men. As they wandered in the pleasant evening air, Ian turned to Jess, looking at her with steely grey eyes. He asked in a low and soft voice, 'Jess, what do you know about John Summers?'

There was a long silence. Jess turned to stare at Ian and asked, 'Nothing. Nothing at all. Should I? You're not investigating him, are you?'

'No, not at all. It's just that, surprisingly, his name has arisen in connection with an unrelated matter.'

'How do you mean?' she asked quizzically.

'Well, after we began investigating Bales as you requested, we came across his daughter's association with him, and his connection with Thomas, who still appears in some of the juvenile records. We also came across John Summer's father.'

'Tell me he wasn't a crook too?'

'Well,' said Ian, pausing to choose his words, 'it seems John's father was, if not a bit of a crook, then at least possibly a con man. His name was Wesley Thomas Summers, and he was implicated in some racing scandals that to this day remain unsolved. It seems he was either involved in race fixing and other shenanigans with the AJC, or an exceptionally successful and lucky punter.'

'What's that?' she asked.

'What's what?'

'The AJC.'

'The AJC was, and still is, the controlling body for the racing industry in New South Wales and has had a chequered career as far as running a clean industry is concerned in the past. The commissions have been interested in them as a possible front for money laundering. More in the past rather than now. You see, John's father had an application in to become a bookmaker. You need a lot of money, cash, to be a bookmaker. We wondered what happened to it all. Unless John somehow got hold of it. His family that raised him seems not to have got any of it and there's no record of a will leaving it to John.'

'And you think John Summers was involved in that too?'

'No, not him. Only his father. You see, as far as we can tell, John Summers was raised by relatives near Bathurst or Parkes as he was orphaned at a few months old. That family went broke on their property years ago so they never got hold of Summers' money as far as we can tell. That's if he had any to get hold of. But the interesting thing is that the police suspected there must have been a lot of loot when he died and they have never found it, not yet anyway. But John appears to have left home at a very early age and has somehow managed to accumulate a lot of wealth. I'd just be interested in knowing how he managed it, that's all.'

After a long pause with only the sound of the lapping shore and their shuffling feet, he continued, 'You know he paid cash for Auvergne, don't you?'

Jessie kept walking slowly, staring down at the wide footpath, deep in thought. Finally, she replied, shaking her head slightly, 'No, I wouldn't know that.' There was another pause, then she continued, 'I don't know that I'm really very interested in all that, actually.'

'No, fair enough,' said Ian. 'Did you know that he also owns a pile of buildings in the centre of Sydney city?'

'No,' she murmered.

Ian continued, 'Thomas is involved only in as much as he is a shareholder in the private company that John Summers owns and runs. It's pretty darn profitable too.'

All this information was news to Jess. She could see a wonderful story in the rise to riches for the man she knew as Thomas's grandfather. After all, it was John's wealth and decision to buy Auvergne that brought Jess to the happiness she now enjoyed. *Does everyone have to have dark secrets?* she wondered.

'But Ian,' she found herself saying, 'John is a pillar of the church and seems to be so straightlaced. And so is his wife.'

'There's no reason to suspect John of anything untoward,' he said. 'We can't find a thing on him at all. Just curious how he managed to achieve so much.'

It was a long drive from Woy Woy back to Auvergne. Jess spent an enormous amount of time alone, either driving between Cooma, Sydney and Melbourne with occasional trips to the Central Coast. She also spent vast amounts of time walking around her bush block and delivering stock about the local district. It was during these times that Jess exercised her fertile and imaginative mind. She was never really alone but living in a world populated by her fantasies and characters always busily occupied in their respective spheres. These were the times that her stories gelled and the rudiments of new ones germinated. She rarely listened to the radio while driving because she preferred her own thoughts, and she was often out of range. These were the times she created and conspired. Now, on the long drive back to Auvergne alone again, and after her conversation with Ian, she had a completely new subject to think about and ponder—John Wesley Summers.

About eight months after purchasing her bush block, the adjoining five-hundred-hectare block fronting the road was on the market. While her place was exceedingly rugged and possessed a difficult access, the neighbouring place was set further forward of the hills and consequently had more open flats in the front. She had no interest in running stock, but this place included a small, if old, farmhouse that had power. The creek that ran alongside the road by the property had flats that allowed for an easier crossing and drive in. The attraction for her, however, apart from all this, was the fact that she could grade a connecting track up the back into her original place, which would be much less difficult for vehicular access into her secluded valley.

Jess made enquiries about the neighbouring place and managed to buy it under the name of Jane Ransom. She kept her postal address at the original place, however, further up the road. During the course of her investigations into the new place, she also asked about the huge area of virgin bush along the back of the new place, which seemed to run off to the east for kilometres towards the coastal escarpments. There was a huge twenty-thousand-hectare parcel of freehold land owned by the original family who had been in the area since the 1840s.

Jess chased them up one afternoon and enquired if they

would be interested in selling that to her. It was completely useless for anything other than leaving alone as it was very rugged and mountainous bush with little access. It was high mountainous ridge country, often clouded in and covered in drizzly mist. With the new acquisition, she could run tracks through the big block with her dozer and have kilometres of private bush for her own enjoyment.

The price for such a large tract was very low, as it had no commercial value other than some timber. Here she was able to indulge her passion for bushwalking, and bulldozing tracks up into the high peaks, establishing a campsite high up in the tree-clad ranges from where she felt totally at ease and safe. It also allowed her to utilise to the fullest her old GMC's capabilities in the wild and rough tracks.

As the time seemed to drift aimlessly by, Thomas grew more enamoured with the presence of Jessie about the property. He readily acknowledged that, but for her, he would have had much difficulty and probably less income from the cattle side of the enterprise. He found her an enigma of no small proportions and had quickly learned that she was exceedingly intelligent, despite her apparent lack of education. She was very capable and competent at all the property tasks and he was only too aware of her ability to look after herself against any threats.

He did not discuss her much with his grandparents as he suspected that John was less than enthusiastic at her presence there. Thomas followed her past history to an increasing extent and marvelled at her writing ability. This was the aspect of her life that he found the most intriguing. He was mildly aware of her early existence as the writer Jane Ransom, but totally cognisant of her as George Norman Thaler. What came as a bit of a shock to him, however, was the discovery of her potentially existing in other guises, about which she had maintained total secrecy.

This revelation came about quite late in their strange relationship and rather inadvertently. It occurred after she had removed most of her personal effects out to her new acquisition, which he thought was down on the south coast. He had rarely ventured into the old cottage that Jess called home since she first moved into it. On the one occasion that he had blundered in, he almost lost her due to his rage and performance over that television incident. He was aware that she had spent some considerable outlay on improvements in the cottage and upgraded many of the facilities, all at her own expense.

On one of her many trips away from Auvergne, Thomas decided to explore inside the cottage for several reasons, the main one being his own nosey interest in her and her surroundings. It was a rare Sunday that John and Livinia were absent from Bridgehead and the family gathering was postponed. Thomas felt guilty at prying into her space without her consent and knowledge, but he found part of his attraction to Jess was the air of danger that surrounded her life.

He noted that she was a neat and tidy person who methodically and carefully placed items where they belonged.

So, when he entered the small back room that she kept as a store for surplus items of her vocation, he was intrigued by a small but rough wooden bookcase that neatly contained sets of publications all placed in certain order. The room was a little dark, so he put on the light, went over to the bookcase and tried to read the titles. He did not recall ever hearing of Kimberley West and he certainly had never heard of someone called Joe Scacci. He surmised they must be authors whom Jess was particularly fond of; or they covered topics that she identified with for her craft. Strangely though, there were six old novels by Thaler and quite a few by Jane Ransom, mostly very old and dust covered. There were also some computing and printing equipment, and a stack of A4 paper neatly piled up in various heaps on the floor.

He scurried out of the cottage for fear of her returning unexpectedly and made his way back to his office. He was at a loose end so he fired up his computer and typed in Kimberley West. Kimberley West had a huge number of hits and he read with deepening interest about this secretive and moderately successful author whose persona and location very little was known about. *Intriguing*, he thought.

Let's type in Joe Scacci. This entry also brought up a large number of hits, but this time the subject was much more controversial. Not unlike Kimberley West, Joe Scacci was little known and very secretive. This time though, no one seemed to know anything about him. He had released eight novels that were pacey and raucous. Each one had a main theme that revolved around topics that a criminal or former policeman would know little about. The themes followed a pattern. One was on cattle runs. One was on sheep stations. There were stories heavily centred on mechanics and even one on high-class aristocracy. Each story included thinly disguised revelations of well-known criminal cases or celebrity pillars who had ruffled many a feather. Thomas was intrigued. Surely Jessie was not unburdening herself in this form of output. The reason he came to this startling conclusion was that her trials and cases were specifically mentioned in each and every novel along with others that were regularly introduced. *I must get hold of a copy or two to see for myself.*

While Thomas was amusing himself with investigations into the past and present lives of his peculiar colleague, another person was about to enter into Jess's life in a most unusual manner; a person that would prove a considerable threat to Thomas's future happiness.

As time passed by, Jess was spending more and more time away from regular life and hibernating on her isolated and rugged mountain property. She had been able to persuade Thomas to begin to seriously attempt to replace her on Auvergne by introducing two of his nieces from the Summers family as jillaroos. Thomas viewed this as an adjunct to his smoothly running station as it had a two-fold benefit. Firstly, it increased his on-farm capability and it also eased the employment prospects of two of the ever-increasing Summers progeny, many of whom sought lifestyles that involved the family properties. This was not how Jess viewed it, however.

She perceived the arrangement as a catalyst for her eventual departure, as had always been her plan.

The high country of the Southern Tablelands was a challenging climate and region to work in. It was bitterly cold in winter and could be searingly hot in summer and very dry. When wet weather was forecast for the region, Jess would make her excuses and retreat to her mountain hideaway because she loved the mountains when it was raining.

She had made a comfortable campsite right on top of her land by dozing in a difficult track and obtaining a campervan that she basically abandoned to the vagaries of the bush. It had been so difficult to get into the campsite she regarded it as a lost cause ever to try to extricate it. She would normally load up her Land Cruiser in town, drive out to her shed in the valley and then transfer everything to the GMC.

It was early in the new year when Jess heard about the long line of low-pressure systems rolling in from the west. It had already been a wetter than normal summer, with flooding occurring over much of the east and right down through the centre.

Jess spent wet days ensconced under a rough bush humpy that was weatherproof enough for her to use provided it was not too windy. Here she could indulge her passion for bush cooking, work on her novels on the laptop or just sit and drink in the pleasure that was the bush in soft drizzling rain.

It was on one of these sojourns that Jess encountered Heinrich – Henry to his friends. It was a dull, deeply cloudy and grey morning with gentle swirls of moist misty wisps of fine vapour enveloping her secluded camp. The only sounds to penetrate the constant dripping of the soaking vegetation were the vocalising of the myriad of active small birds that twittered about on the lower branches or on the ground. From the softly crackling radiance of the gentle fire arose the pleasant aroma of damp eucalyptus burning.

Jess was jolted from this familiar idyll by what she thought was the dull, unmistakable sound of clunking metal as it met some immovable object deep within the bush some distance from her camp. The bush was always full of strange noises, most of which Jess could dismiss. But this most distinctive and unambiguous noise was intrusive and uncharacteristic for this site; it was definitely man-made. She instantly dismissed Murray as a possibility as there was no reason for his access this time of year to be retrieving timber.

Jess sat straining her hearing, listening for any aftershocks. She waited many minutes, then donned her still-damp Driza-Bone coat and her hat. She struggled into her heaviest elastic-sided boots and went to one of the old toolboxes at the back of the GMC. Here she grabbed a couple of things and began the long walk down the muddy and slippery track that was the road into her camp.

Jess walked tentatively along the winding and, in places, sodden ribbon of greasy and rocky track, all the time straining to hear any sounds that were untoward. Nothing was heard. After she had travelled about two kilometres, all the time descending, sometimes steeply from the heights where the camp was located, she approached a bend that curved off to the right down a short steep incline to a small gully. She could hear the creek babbling as it gurgled its way over a small channel in the road. The road on the other side curved off again to the left before climbing rather steeply up a long incline that crested the next small ridge before continuing on down the spur to the lower altitudes.

She sensed that she must be close to the source of that sound if it had indeed occurred on the road. She stopped at the top and peered down into the misty silence of the heavily vegetated gully. Almost with relief, Jess spied the source of the noise. There, wedged firmly into the steep batter of the narrow track, was the offending vehicle. She remained quietly surveying the landscape for many minutes. She was a little nervous of the situation. The vehicle was a maroon-coloured Range Rover, modern and almost new. She ventured a closer look.

Slowly feeling her way down the unsteady gravel, trying not to look down, she approached the stricken vehicle. As she approached, she could see what appeared to have happened. Despite the continuing light drizzle, the road had evidence of long, uncontrolled skidding as the car had slid down the soggy clay and inevitably into the rocky, sodden perpendicular bank, much of which Jess had cut out herself when forming the track across this small gully. In many ways it was fortuitous that the Rover had slid into the bank, as on the other side, the gully tumbled down a steep incline for hundreds of metres as the ridge fell away to the valley below. Jess surmised that the driver may be inexperienced, as to avoid sliding down slopes, not using the brakes was preferable, relying on the lowest gear and ensuring the wheels kept turning to maintain control.

Jess looked carefully for any signs of life but there appeared to be no one there. She approached the stricken vehicle, noticing many large boot impressions in the softened gravel. She thought she discerned them heading off back up the slope in the direction from which it had come. She looked all about. Then she ventured a tentative look into the cab. No one was in there so she peered in. The vehicle was set at a precarious angle, having been heavily sunk into the passenger's side and jammed into the high bank. The back of the car was wedged into the wall, disabling the back door of the car that opened from the left-hand side.

Jess went back to the driver's door and opened it. She needed to get up on her tiptoes to get a full view owing to the steep angle of the lean. To her consternation, the front seat and floor were strewn with photographic equipment. This suddenly brought back to her with extreme unease the memories of the late Percy Pavilon, the man who died on the back road after following her from Cooma. She was very uneasy.

Jess stood back and surveyed the scene, trying to think how best to extricate this damaged car. At this point in the road, the track narrowed as it curved over the small gully then veered back up the other side of the rise. As it stood, the trapped vehicle was positioned in such a way as to block the track, especially in its present saturated state. Any attempt to pass could send the other side of the road tumbling down the embankment, especially something heavy, such as 'Jimmy'. The problem was that the road was so slippery with all the rain that it was impossible to drag it out from this low point in the road; the towing vehicle would simply get no purchase.

It appeared to Jess that the Rover possibly had only one occupant, as the front was strewn with equipment, papers, books and maps. She managed to clamber into the driving seat and inspect the inside. The keys were still in the ignition. There were several glossy photographic publications, surprisingly to her, all of them in German. These contained some rather grand photographs of Australian scenery. They were printed in Europe, not in Australia. That might explain the German. She hunted about and tried to inspect the digital cameras to see what contents they contained. Again, all scenery, nothing of people. *Strange*, she thought. Inside the glove box were some personal identification papers. She read them with keen interest. It appeared that the driver was possibly Heinrich Liechtenstein, an Australian citizen with a dual passport and driving licence. She replaced all the items back into the glove box and alighted the cab.

She again surveyed the scene. There was a modicum of urgency to remove the Rover as, in its present position, it would prevent her from driving out of the mountains. She concluded that the GMC would have to winch it from the top of the short but steep rise and drag it to the top. *No doubt*, she thought, *it would have sustained some damage to its drivability*. To winch it alone would probably be impossible – she would need the driver to steer it as she dragged it up the slippery sodden incline, preferably with some assistance from its own power.

The car was thoroughly wedged into the bank and leaning at a great angle into it. *If I could winch from the top of the rise onto the passenger side, it might just budge and extricate itself.* While she was deep in these thoughts, and with the soft gentle dripping of the light misty drizzle, she missed the slow clomping of the owner as he trudged his way back down the long slope to the mishap. She did not spy him until he was halfway down. She was startled to see an unexpected figure almost rambling down the saturated track.

She was too exposed to hide, so manoeuvred herself more behind the front of the Rover to determine what sort of person approached. She was not only nervous but also rather annoyed that someone had entered onto her secluded retreat. She would like him gone as soon as possible.

Jess tried to take in all she could before he got much closer. He was short and, even under his thin loosely fitting raincoat, she could tell he was of slight stature. He had sandshoes on that were thoroughly drenched and a cap that really was a failure at preventing the rain from much of his face. He appeared to be elderly and quite bedraggled. Her fear subsided somewhat.

As he approached the back of the car, he said in a noticeably more animated tone than his appearance would have indicated, 'Oh, hello.'

Jess did not respond. He possessed a cultured, slightly accented, mellow voice that indicated to Jess that he was of

European origin, in keeping with the evidence she had already uncovered.

'I say, I am glad to see someone in this forest wilderness.'

Jess still did not respond to the stranger. By this time, he was almost upon her. She gazed into his tanned and thin face, dripping with rain from the cap. He had fine features and grey eyes, with silvering tassels of hair peaking out from under the cap.

'As you can see, I am afraid I am in some dilemma. Can you help me?' he asked in a hopeful, semi-pleading tone. He stood there peering at her, waiting for some acknowledgement.

Finally, she responded in a cool voice, 'What are you doing here?'

That was an unexpected response. It took him aback a little. He remained gazing sheepishly at her then replied, 'Well, you see, miss …' he said, trying to ingratiate himself early, 'I was looking for the road up to the top there.' He pointed towards the camp.

Jess hesitated, staring at him intently. This unnerved him slightly.

'You realise, mate, you're on private property.'

'No,' he said defensively. 'I assumed this was the road to the top.'

'Didn't you see the signs?'

'No,' he replied, getting confused and agitated.

'Which way did you come in?' she asked, annoyance evident in her tone.

'Well, I was photographing the abandoned mine and

followed the track that I hoped would lead to the ridges up there. I am told the view and scenery there is superb.'

Jess quickly realised that if he managed to somehow get to the abandoned mine site located on the neighbouring property at the rear of her place and he wanted to get to the far ridges, then he would probably assume he could follow the track up into the back of her place. That all sounded feasible. She ignored his comments and turned to look at the stricken Rover.

'You okay?' she finally asked him.

'I am okay,' he replied. 'A bit shaken, and I have concern for auto. I am Henry, by the way.'

Henry, thought Jess. She had seen no Henry in her rummaging, only Heinrich. Jess turned to face him again asked, 'You okay to drive?'

'Well, yes, of course,' he responded, a little more confused. 'But auto, it is immovable, no?'

'At present,' she said, after a pause. 'If I can winch it out, can you steer it up the hill?'

'Ja,' he responded softly. In his distraught state he inadvertently reverted to his native tongue. Jess smiled inwardly, a knowing smile.

'Good.'

With that, Jess returned to the front of the Rover and inspected it thoroughly, looking for anchor points for the cable. She looked up the hill and at the angles and tried to estimate the possible directions of the strain. It would be tricky, but if handled carefully she should be able to winch out the Rover from the top of the rise and drag it all the way up to the top, especially if Henry could drive the car in low range. It would take some time, and effort. Jess made him wait there in the cold and damp while she returned to the camp and retrieved 'Jimmy'. She returned quickly. Henry was waiting in the vehicle shivering slightly.

By the time the Rover was sitting at the top of the rise, it was evident that it would not be going much further, not under its own steam at any rate. The slide into the gutter at the base of the bank had damaged the left-hand front wheel assembly and left it pointing inwards at a weird angle. It was also getting much darker now as the heavy cloud settled in and the light drizzle continued. Jess removed the front wheel and inspected the damage. Half an hour later she had the offending pieces sitting on the ground and the Rover propped up on a handy log.

The problem for Jess was that she was loathe to reveal her encampment to anyone, let alone a complete stranger. Now she faced the predicament of what to do with Henry while his vehicle was immobile and he was kilometres from anywhere. She looked at the bedraggled figure in his drenched state and she felt a pang of sympathy for him. He had been most obliging and courteous despite his obvious deep concern for his predicament. She was struck by the anomaly of this sophisticated European gentleman wandering about in the harshness of the unforgiving Australian bush so far from help.

As the darkness and accompanying chilly evening quickly descended on the two lonely souls, Jess was left with no alternative but to take him back to the safety of her camp. He sat quietly in mild disbelief as the noisy, jolting mass trundled roughly over the slippery track in the cold darkness for the few kilometres back up the range to the campsite.

Finally, with the truck's piercing beam of powerful light shooting off into the blackness of the bush, Jess manoeuvred the lumbering beast up the last incline and onto a flat, more open area. She threaded her way through towering gums, splashing gently through large pools of black water strewn about the well-used tracks that formed the campsite. She drew up to a scene that was surreal to the cold and shivering Henry. There were several vehicles and various lean-tos scattered about, all gleaming in the wet glow of the truck's spotlights.

Jess pulled up in a clatter of clanging metal and left the motor running for some minutes. She motioned to him to alight the truck and get under the leaning structure that possessed only a roof, no sides at all. Henry, still soaking and now getting quite cold, made his way through the light drizzling rain and under the tin roof. There was a rough table with a bench. He sat down on the uneven surface. As the light rain gathered into heavy drops on the leaves and then fell from a great height onto the unyielding metal roof, he was overwhelmingly possessed of a deep melancholia at his predicament.

Jess finally turned off the lumbering machine and came in under the shelter. She immediately poked the near-dead embers of the large fireplace that was constructed of a mixture of a few eclectic bricks and mostly bush rocks. She removed her dripping moleskin coat, then started to reignite the fire from a great stack of kindling and assorted sticks and logs neatly stacked under the shelter. The fire quickly burst into life again and she fed it voraciously as the comforting heat began to emanate from its ever-growing brightness. Henry stared at her and her surroundings and perceived that she actually liked what she was doing.

Jess warmed herself and beckoned an exhausted-looking Henry over to do likewise. She enquired whether he had handy any dry clothes in the small amount of gear he had rescued from the Rover. He retrieved some clothes from under the tarp over the tray of the truck and scurried back in under the dry shelter. As Jess manoeuvred the heavily blackened cooking utensils that had remained unattended and abandoned when she went off in her quest to ascertain the source of the disturbance earlier in the day, Henry managed to get into some dry clothes.

The comforting fire and the pleasant aromas emanating from the primitive facilities slowly reduced his anxiety. Her obvious competence at such tasks reinforced his growing serenity.

Jess suggested that he bunk down in the back of the truck. It would be cool but dry under the heavy tarp that covered the tray and was hung over the metal frame. He was exhausted after his stressful and strenuous day and accepted her offer to clamber into the strange quarters rather early for him. He could hear Jess moving about for some time afterwards. It was a noisy place to sleep, with the dripping onto the canvas as well as the metal roofs around the camp.

Henry had a fitful night. It also seemed to him awfully short. He was awoken in the semi-darkness as Jess was heard to be moving about before daybreak. That was almost anathema to the refined sensibilities of Henry. He was most assuredly not a morning person, especially mornings that still possessed some darkness. In his half stupor, he managed to observe that the proficiency of the previous evening was again in evidence as she fiddled with the cooking arrangements in the dull mist of the bracing mountain air. The rain appeared to have eased off completely but the clouds were still low and the air very moist.

Henry found it very difficult to engage Jess in any conversation. He followed her every move and gathered that she had some plan or other for attending to the damaged vehicle. Early in the morning, Jess fired up the truck again and then spent quite some time rummaging about the camp and in the back of the tray sorting and searching. Then they set off back down the track to the spot where they had left the Rover.

It took Jess the rest of the morning to dismantle the damaged tie rods and connecting braces of the front end. One piece was bent and one piece was broken, snapped in two on impact with the immovable bank. She took them back to the camp to repair them with the equipment and spares she had there. She had a powerful generator and plenty of welding equipment, plus some metal pieces that she saved for a rainy day.

Henry looked on in amazement at the abilities and

confidence of this strange woman as she spent the day mending his damaged gear. Jess allocated to him the task of tending the fire while she did the repairs.

Jess thought Henry an enigma. She acknowledged that she was not the best at judging people, usually ascribing to them motives and expectations that simply were not there. He dressed as if going on board a yacht and appeared to her to be an amateur at bushcraft; evidenced by his choice of vehicle and the fact that it was an automatic. Yet he did proffer a real admiration, indeed love for the natural world and spent many hours in it, observing it, photographing it and wandering about in it. In many ways he struck her as almost childlike in his carefree and casual approach to his surroundings. Despite his most unwelcome intrusion, she found something in his character that she was warming to, a sensation that she found undesirable.

Jess managed to repair the rods sufficiently for Henry to be able to drive the Rover at least back to Cooma or possibly even Sydney in a pinch if he were careful with his driving. She reassembled the front next morning and gave him directions to depart the property the same way he had entered. She hoped he would not detect any of her building sites or facilities. He was demonstrably grateful and attempted to repay her benevolence with a reciprocal offer in kind. If she were ever in Sydney, she would be most welcome to contact him again. Jess declined that offer as she did his request for permission to re-enter the property to get to the ridges atop the range around where her camp was located. She bade him a coolish farewell and watched as he drove up the long incline and over the ridge, and hopefully out of her life.

Jess was now content with her small existence. Her novels were exceedingly successful, but more importantly, fulfilling. Her foray into the seedy world of the uncouth detective Joe Scacci had caused much controversy and no little consternation among those at whom it was aimed. She maintained her total anonymity as regards that undertaking. She had even managed to gain some monetary recompense from that endeavour by clandestinely meeting up with her obliging agency. She now was able to spend hours wandering about her bush block and driving her vehicles about the largely untouched bush; she had never been happier. She slowly began to feel a drifting away from the settled and ordered world of Auvergne Station. Her past was becoming a more distant memory; Jessie MacIntyre was slowly dying; Jane Ransom was rising.

CHAPTER NINE

ess was drifting away from her settled pattern of structured work life with Thomas at Auvergne. She was also easing herself out of involvement with the Guises trucking business of delivering stock about the district. She was confident that the family had replaced her with the two young women who were gradually and competently absorbing more of her responsibilities with the cattle. As she aged, Jess wished for a more secluded and quiet life out on her remote bush block while she still had the health and ability to cope with the arduous conditions. Her life seemed comfortably planned out to accommodate these yearnings and continue with her writing while she maintained her drive and ability.

The successful creation and subsequent clandestine release of the Joe Scacci novels slightly rekindled in Jess a yearning, the meaning of which she was at first unsure. Jess had poured out her heart and soul, and not inconsiderable talent, into the first flush of her original creative surge that manifested itself in the novels of George Norman Thaler in the 1990s. His genesis was in her tawdry little romance novels published as Jane Ransom. She promised herself that George Norman Thaler was dead, killed by the ghastly arrest and destruction of her first peaceful interlude in the Kimberleys.

The flourishing activity of Joe Scacci was replicating a similar path. She now was beginning to develop an urge to once again create at her highest level of competence. If she were to release work of the highest standard, she wanted it to be successful because it was good, not because it was produced by her as an already famous author. Yet again she was thinking that she might try one more time to create at the peak of her powers, whatever that may now be, and clandestinely release it under another name. *How to do this?* She gave it much thought.

As the excitement of attempting another venture grew in her, she slowly realised that this was what gave her life meaning – it underpinned her whole purpose and made her function. She worried that she was this way inclined and contemplated this abnormal defect in her character. It did not, however, deter her from pondering the possibilities.

Jess had written a few paragraphs of her thoughts on a new work by her as Kimberley West and realised that it was of a standard way above what Kimberley West was known for. She discarded it to the trash bin on her computer but did not delete it. *Could I reawaken my ability and desire to achieve novels at a much higher standard again?* Finally, she decided to try once more.

Jess wanted to write novels that were powerful, meaty and large, with robust stories of vast dramatic and significant events that could cover any period of time. She began to type and away she went. The only important detail left for her was to choose a name that was independent of all her others. She finally came up with Catherine Holbrook Seymour. It sounded sophisticated, regal and stylish – classy even.

In her early days of George Norman Thaler, all Jess's ideas and research were what she had at hand, but now she had unfettered access to limitless information available on the internet. She began to research. Her first attempt would go back to the medieval period in Europe and concentrate on life and circumstances of that time. Her sources were endless. She even had the foundations of a second novel going even further back to the Saxon period of Britain. Firstly though, she had to get this published. She decided to try through her publisher in Melbourne.

Jess struck problems from the beginning. The publisher did not receive manuscripts directly from the public so she was recommended to try other avenues. This was not entirely successful either, so finally, Jess decided to use some contacts – she pulled a few strings. She would drop them back to her publisher with a note from Kimberley West. Finally, that got some results, and she was under way. Once she had successfully published one novel and Catherine Holbrook Seymour was now known, she could concentrate on her skill as an author and not on her ability to be devious. It gave her great joy to write at her peak ability with no risk of comparison to any of her former or extant incarnations. She was very happy for the moment and had big plans.

Unknown to Jess, however, and definitely not on her horizon, loomed two unplanned and, for her, distressing and complicated experiences. These two separate but related occurrences would impact dramatically on her life. Both involved men she had given little thought to as disruptive; one an old and treasured friend, one a new unintended meeting.

It seems Heinrich Liechtenstein had been struck by more than the roadside bank when he was searching for the track to the top of the ridges near the coastal escarpment. Henry moved in a more rarefied social atmosphere than most. Being closely related to the ruling royal and hereditary family of a small but influential European principality, he was accustomed to some refinement in his company. As a somewhat relatively lower-order princeling in the line of hereditary personages, Henry, being of a shy and retiring disposition thought he would try his luck in more outlying and adventurous surroundings. Australia appealed to him because it was rather passé in his circle and afforded him some small measure of distinction amongst his peers as a distant and exotic place still developing in the settled, established old world. He had acclimatised well into his new surroundings and found a successful niche publishing scenic books and magazines in his erstwhile homeland for the wider European market. He had ventured out to Australia as a youngish man but had never found his soul mate in his adoptive land.

However, after his experience in the company of the enchanting and enigmatic Jane Ransom, Henry found himself besotted. In that brief encounter, he had perceived her to be moderately well mannered and capable of engagement in any company. With his own inadequacies, real or perceived, in mind, he conceived Jane to be an attractive proposition for himself. If he had met her in the more familiar surroundings of the city environment, he would have somehow felt a little inferior to her and feared the competition of more successful men. However, as it was, out in the mountains, he somehow felt none of those usual inhibitions or inadequacies.

Heinrich spasmodically devoted time to investigating the circumstances of the woman he knew as Jane Ransom. He discovered her correct address out in the bush and researched the properties that surrounded the ridge where he had met her. Over the next six months, he travelled down from Sydney to Cooma and explored the district to the southeast where he knew she lived. He was becoming so enamoured of her that he finally decided to disregard her request to remain off her property and would venture a visit or two back up to the ridges where he had first met her that fateful raining day. He was unsure of the reception he would receive.

Henry ventured two visits back to the ridges, as he called them, where he first met Jane. By now, he had determined that it was possible to enter the mountain ridges by the more conventional route that entailed a totally different direction.

There was a gazetted roadway marked on council plans that entered the ridges from the other side of the property from the abandoned mine site route that Henry had stumbled onto at first. This roadway was necessary and allowed for by the original owners of the property. It was never formed as a road and only existed on plans but was nevertheless there. It was incumbent on the owners of the property to allow access to the public if they requested it. Jess encouraged the owners of the paddocks through which this road supposedly ran to keep a gate across it and hang 'private property' signs on the fence alongside the gate.

Jess had upgraded this track into the mountain block sufficient only to give herself a better all-weather access. It was still rough and traversed flat paddock country before entering the hills. This track reduced the roughness of the entrance to a minimum and was more direct. On the third attempt, Henry struck gold. He struggled up the steep track that led to Jess's camp, past the gully where he had run into the bank and, as he entered the plateau that was her campsite, he saw the old GMC parked by the large campervan that Jess used as a shed.

Jess had heard the approaching vehicle and while the tone was not familiar, she assumed it was Murray. Murray was the only person to whom she had explicitly given permission to enter her property. Murray was a tall, well-built, rather handsome young man, muscular and friendly. He did, however, suffer from a mild form of mental disorder that rendered him unable to concentrate and learn academically.

He was a wiz with motors and anything mechanical. Murray drove an ancient Blitz wagon that was designed to tow a timber jinker. Before Jess bought the property, he had an agreement with the previous owners to extract timber, mostly for fence posts and firewood.

Jess did not wish for this to continue but took pity on the young man when she met him and his rather pleasant young wife. They lived close by with their two young children in a dilapidated little farmhouse surrounded by the trappings of his timberwork – mostly piles of cut-up logs and firewood, plus the saws to go with it. He also had a contract to supply firewood to a couple of wood yards, so Jess came to a compromise. While she was bulldozing tracks through her new bush block, any fallen or removed trees were available to Murray to retrieve with his Blitz.

It was early in the morning when Jess heard the vehicle approaching. She was staggered to see that it was not Murray's Blitz, but instead the familiar maroon Range Rover of Heinrich Liechtenstein. Jess had been sitting at the rough wooden table writing and thinking about a novel plot for her new creation when she was disturbed. She was not used to being interrupted, especially in the early throws of enthusiasm of the newly created Catherine Holbrook Seymour. She was more than a little annoyed. She hoped this man was not going to become a nuisance.

Henry pulled up near the table with the loud V-8 of the revving Rover reverberating through the dappled and hitherto peaceful clear air of the ridge top. He was reluctant to leave the car. Jess stared at him in annoyance. Finally, he turned off the throbbing engine and silence of a sort again descended on the bush. He opened the scrunching door and then closed it with a loud click and headed for Jess. He was again well dressed and very dapper in his smart yacht-club gear, appearing cool and comfortable with short sleeves and a small useless cap.

'Hello again, Jane,' he ventured. 'I do apologise sincerely for the interruption, but I just had to see you again.'

Jess stared at him blankly, saying nothing. His tone was one of deference and, she thought humility.

'May I?' he asked, pointing to the vacant wooden bench that comprised the seating arrangements. Jess looked at the bench and said nothing. He took that as a 'yes' and sidled awkwardly onto the splintery bench, trying to avoid the multitude of papers and gear on the slab. He appeared to Jess to be nervous and apprehensive. He looked at her deeply and appraisingly. Finally, he said in his attractive slightly European accent, tinged with gentleness, 'How have you been, Jane?'

Jess was taken aback by that question. It was most unexpected. She detected a melancholy in his tone that lessened her annoyance slightly. She remained gazing at him intently. His sad pale eyes had a poignancy about them that affected her mood and reminded her of one of her miserable characters in a recent novel. His hands were nervously fidgeting on the tabletop.

Finally, she replied coolly, 'Well, thank you. And you?' Somehow, she could not bring herself to admonish him for this unwelcome intrusion.

He answered immediately, 'I am recovered entirely from my misadventure on your mountain top.' He always had a strange turn of phrase, an endearing little trait common to her acquaintances of foreign extraction. She usually found it amusing.

In the absence of any contribution from her, he continued, 'Jane, I really wanted to see you again. I have been thinking of you a lot since we met.'

Jess was getting uncomfortable with where this conversation was going. His pleading eyes and dulcet saddened voice rendered her spirit in some turmoil. They sat there for many minutes, Henry intrigued by the superfluity of paraphernalia strewn about in such an incongruous setting. He finally managed to come out with the real reason for his visit.

'I feel we parted on unhappy occasion,' he said to her. 'I was not myself after that ordeal.'

Jess assured him it was as she wished it. He intimated that he wished to ensure that she understood how grateful he had been for all her kindness. He continued, 'I would like to see you again, Miss Jane. I wish for you to accept possibly invitation to visit me in city where I can repay your kindness myself. No?'

Jess stared at him again. He fidgeted a bit more. Then he reached into his top shirt pocket and passed her a business card. She automatically stretched out her left arm and accepted it. She looked at it and then at him. She inspected the card thoroughly and read both sides. It did not tell her much more than she had already learned about him – except for an address, and his full name.

He continued, 'Would you allow for me to return your hospitality when next you come to city?'

'That's not necessary at all.'

Even though it was still only mid-morning, Jess was starting to get concerned that Henry was contemplating staying the day. She asked him his plans for the time he was there, hoping he was planning to move on. On the assurance that he was moving further down the coast, she invited him to remain for lunch. This he gladly accepted. She found him jovial company and she thought she detected an air of graceful aristocratic refinement and poise that she somehow missed the first time they met. She put that down to the stressful circumstances surrounding their first encounter.

This time around, Henry had much more sedate and serene conditions in which to observe his host on which he had so ungraciously imposed himself. True to his indications and rather disappointingly for him, he kept his word and prepared to depart after a flavoursome fare prepared under what he thought of as totally primitive conditions. He had observed her as much as he could manage without being disconcertingly rude. As a last gesture before departing, he removed from his top pocket a small colourful card and said to her, 'Jane, as you know, I take scenic photographs professionally and publish some of them. I also occasionally stage exhibitions of some of my work in a gallery. I am running another exhibition in two weeks at this gallery in the eastern suburbs and would love you to come to the opening night. It is by invitation only that night. You would be most welcome.' With that, he handed her the elegantly presented card across the crude table.

Jess stared at the beautiful card, reading the detail intently. She remained silent. Her reserve was one of the traits he found so attractive. He also remained silent, not wishing to end, for him, this precious moment. He stared at her as she read. She looked up and saw his eager expectant eyes piercing hers. She was a little unnerved. She placed the card on the table and said, 'Thank you Henry, or should I call you Heinrich? I'll see what I can do.'

'Henry is fine.'

That is all he could ask. With that, he bade her farewell and walked over to his Range Rover. Again, for a second time Jess watched as Henry drove out of her life, this time she hoped for good.

Except that, life sometimes had a habit of not conforming to Jess's expectations or wishes. She found herself thinking of Henry in a pitying way. Her compassion for him slowly rose as she contemplated the humility with which he conducted himself and his self-effacing conversation. He was to her a gentle and unassuming, almost meek person, who seemed to be travelling a lonely road. She began to contemplate the rare opportunity to be in on the ground floor of the kind of arty-type experience that she had never been afforded before. She rarely read articles pertaining to herself and her place in the world of authorship and, while this was different, it was not all that far removed from the creative existence she exhibited. She could stay in her apartment in Rushcutters Bay. *What harm could it possibly do?*

Jess did not need much of an excuse to travel to Rushcutters Bay. She enjoyed her time there once the arduous travel had been accomplished. Attending functions, however, was a novelty for her. She avoided social occasions, but was rarely invited to anything. Somehow though, she felt a mild attraction to this event and was nervously awaiting its arrival. She usually wore smart casual country-style gear when attending to her publishing requirements. For one of the very few times in her life, she found that she actually cared about her appearance.

The evening before the official opening was quite an elegant affair. Surprisingly, Jess found the attendees much more upmarket than she had anticipated. The idea was that there would be drinks and nibbles at 6.30pm, followed by an hour or so for the guests to inspect the exhibition, which would be followed by an auction of some of the pieces so that guests could purchase some of the photographs before opening to the public the next day. There was a considerable number of expensively framed photographs of scenically striking places from all over Australia. Jess wandered about the gallery after being effusively greeted by Henry, intrigued by the quality of the pieces and the ground he must have covered to achieve them. Then Jess spied one that was unnervingly familiar. She got quite a start at seeing it. It distressed her.

Jess peered at the large gaudy picture that resonated colour, space and a primordial sense in its starkness. It had quite an effect on her. There on the wall was a very familiar representation of a scene that she had observed many times on her travels on the Gibb River Road. It was such a romanticised portrayal of the familiar, but nevertheless it was definitely there. It sent a chill down her spine. An ornate label simply stated 'Sunset on the Gibb'. She both loved it and hated it for the memories it evoked. She looked at the price range suggested on the frame. She would buy it.

Jess was an extremely pragmatic person. She knew nothing of art and cared less. All her creativity was poured into her writing, a task she regarded as a gift, not a skill. For the first time she was confronted with what she regarded as art. It was a familiar image, but the eye of the artist had given it an aura that she somehow might have missed on the many occasions she had seen the scene in reality. She was entranced. She could discern in this representation a nuance of light, the sun's angle, time-of-day exposure, depth of field. There were a lot more technical aspects about which she knew nothing. She loved it.

Jess found the company rather boorish. The pretentious cognoscenti flounced about, espousing opinions on art or scenes that conveyed their total lack of feeling. She found the whole affair mostly distasteful and put that down to a long life spent in total isolation and a modicum of personality defects within herself. There were only two people with whom she found something to talk about. One was a well-known author, an elderly greying man wearing inappropriately garish gear and sporting a cravat. He was full of himself and sipped vast amounts of free champagne while trying to hold a conversation with her. The other was an elderly gentleman sitting alone on a bench, one hand resting on an ornate stick, the other holding a tall glass. He was peering dejectedly around the room trying not to appear deserted. Jess noticed a couple of times that Henry sat beside him and chatted briefly.

Jess sidled slowly along the wall, casually nearing the lonely figure seated on the hard bench. He wore a small brimmed felt hat with a touch of a colourful feather on one side and dull conservative clothes. She sat on the bench beside him. He greeted her politely with a heavy accent. Immediately she deduced a Teutonic influence. She tried to make small talk, but that was not her forté. As he struggled with his English, she casually enquired if it would be easier for him to converse in German. He quickly acquiesced.

For Jess, this proved to be a fortuitous move. It transpired that the old man was one of Henry's many cousins from Europe visiting for the opening. Jess was able to learn much more about Henry, his life and his world. Jess found comfort and camaraderie with the old man. There seemed to be a pattern in her life of engaging with mentor figures. *What was the attraction of all things Germanic?* She pondered that conundrum. It was not that she felt particularly German, or was especially enamoured of the culture, it just seemed that she was destined to be swept into, and influenced by, Teutonic persuasions at every turn.

Late into the evening, after the auction at which she managed to purchase 'Sunset on the Gibb', she spent more time with Henry's elderly cousin. Henry was pleased that the two of them got along so well as it relieved him somewhat of that responsibility. Henry was the last to leave the gallery and Jessie, being a poor sleeper, remained with him.

Henry asked Jess, 'What did you think of that?'

'It was most informative. I purchased an exhibit.'

'Did you?' he asked, surprised. 'I did not notice. I am sorry you did that. I would have given you any one you desired. I did not think...' he tailed off into inaudibility. 'Which one did you buy?'

'Sunset on the Gibb.'

'Ah, yes. A particularly beautiful region – the whole area. I did not know that you had an interest in that composition.'

Jess hoped he thought that she had liked it for its artistic merit, not its personal attachment to herself, of which he knew absolutely nothing.

'I noticed that you and Gerard spoke often,' he ventured.

'Yes. He is a lovely man.'

'Well, I appreciate your kindness in attending him. Look, I was wondering if you are free tomorrow if you would like to have lunch. No?'

Jess was taken aback. That was a development on which she had not planned. She was caught off guard a little. While she found Henry pleasant enough, socialising was a pastime that she abhorred. *How to get out of this?* She started to stammer an excuse when Henry intervened by saying, 'I would really like to see you again without all these distractions. Plus, I really owe you some recompense for buying a photograph from me.'

He sounded genuinely sincere. She thought about it a minute then acquiesced reluctantly. They agreed to meet at Doyles for lunch, at his suggestion.

Jess arrived early and sat on the wall studying the lovely harbour. A bit before twelve, she saw Henry approaching with his elderly cousin in tow. He greeted Jess enthusiastically, hinting with apologies that Gerard insisted on coming along to meet with that 'lovely fräulein from the country'. Jess held out her hand in response and indicated she was delighted he had decided to come too. His presence had relieved her somewhat of any anxiety she initially had of being alone with Henry. It was a pleasant lunch spent in the balmy sunshine overlooking the blue of the harbour and the hazy blue of the sky. Jess assumed that would be the last she would see of Henry and his cousin.

Thomas seemed to be a little unsettled lately. He clearly recalled the first time he met Jess in Camooweal. He did not know exactly when it was that he first realised that his infatuation with her had deepened into something more. He just knew that he felt for her an affection way beyond anything he had ever felt for a woman beyond his grandmother.

He felt he had the blessing of his grandparents for his suggestion that he propose to Jess, even though she was much older, but somehow, he was unable to bring himself to actually propose to her, or even suggest they become more than just acquaintances. He was terrified of her answer. It was just like Christmas. The excitement was in the anticipation, the expectation and uncertainty of what was actually in the presents, not the actuality; that always invariably proved a disappointment. Once opened, the excited anticipation was gone. It was like that with Jess. While he had not asked her, there was always the uncontrollable excitement of the anticipated answer; if she rejected him his disappointment would be immense. Finally, he felt he could delay no longer, as his ever-caring grandmother had hinted that he had better 'get a wriggle on' as Jess might move on. Besides, he noticed she was beginning to spend more time away from Auvergne. He caught her one evening as she was heading for the workshop and asked, 'Jess, I've got to go to town tomorrow and do some paperwork. I also need about an hour's shopping for materials as well. As I don't want to be there any longer than I need, could you spare some time and come in with me to pick up the stuff while I go to the office?'

Jess thought for a moment and then nodded her agreement. *It was arranged*, he thought. *Now all I have to do is rustle up the courage to ask her. Maybe on the way back would be the best time.*

Next morning, a cheerful Thomas, quite spruced up for a trip into Cooma, waited for Jess under the portico in his ute. Jess was wary of travelling with Thomas as he was a fast and rough driver, punishing his vehicles on the rough roads, typical of the farmers that Jess knew. Thomas stopped in the centre of the town and asked Jess to go and pick up a few items. He said he would be about an hour and a half, so for her not to hurry. He would meet her back at the park.

Thomas was quite a while and Jess was already back at the park by the time he returned carrying his small case with his papers. He again drove wildly and mostly in silence on the narrow bitumen road that led back to Auvergne through the uninspiring, undulating flatness of the treeless Monaro plains south of Cooma. Jess thought he appeared a little anxious and moody but put it down to the morning's appointments he had in town. She always felt a pang of guilt as she passed Lochinvar Lane. Thomas slowed down considerably as he approached the elaborate entrance to Auvergne. He checked the mailbox then, more slowly than usual, he drove into the gravel road that led to the homestead.

The road meandered down from the road into a wide shallow valley of prime basalt country and then up the gentle slope of the other side and onto the huge complex that comprised the homestead and the many outbuildings of the established property. Part way down the road, Thomas stopped the ute and turned off the engine. He peered lovingly out of the windscreen at the vista.

'Don't you just love it, Jess? Isn't it magnificent?'

Jess nodded in agreement.

Thomas had given this moment a lot of thought. He had carefully rehearsed the sentence over and over in his mind until he thought he had it right. Then he concluded that it would be best to just blurt it out, just as rehearsed. He sighed inwardly and said to himself, 'let's go'.

'Jess,' he began, 'would you consider living with me forever? I'd like to share all this with someone, and that someone is you. Could you live with me, here, forever?'

Jess was initially dumbstruck. Firstly, she was totally unprepared for such a conversation. Secondly, she had no idea this was on the horizon; it certainly was not on her part. She turned and stared at him in disbelief, thinking maybe she had misheard him; hoping she had misheard him. She said nothing, her mouth slightly parting in confusion. Thomas expected silence, so he continued now that it was finally out.

'I know this is a bit sudden for you, but I've loved you almost from the first time I set eyes on you, Jess. Surely you must have noticed? And every day that goes by I love you more. I want us to share the rest of our time together, as man and wife. What do you say?'

Jess was still staring at him. Just as she feared, she had not misheard at all.

'Thomas!' blurted Jess as she wriggled uncomfortably in the seat, unable to speak properly. She could feel the effects of mild shock creeping over her trembling body.

'But Thomas,' she said again. There was a long difficult silence. Jess did not know what to say. Thomas suggested to her, 'What d'yer say, Jess?'

Jess again said nothing. Then she replied slowly, 'Thomas. Look, I'm terribly flattered by all this. But, surely, you're not serious, Thomas? I mean, you could have anyone, Tom, much more suitable than I am.'

'Don't say that, Jess. There's no one better than you. What about it then, eh?'

Jess looked out the side window and then back at Thomas

and finally replied, 'Can I think about it for a while, please Thomas?'

'Sure,' he said, enthusiastically, 'but not too long.'

Thomas dropped Jess off at the cottage and wildly drove off to the portico. Jess was devastated. She had never contemplated this ever occurring. Suddenly she recalled the couple of weird conversations she had had with John and Livinia in town and at the homestead. *Surely they were not also aware of all this as well.* She wondered what they must think of her. Then she recalled some of the dumb comments she had made to them about Thomas needing a wife.

Jess clearly wished to dispose of this dilemma. She considered herself totally unsuitable for almost any man now, let alone her young friend, Thomas. She was also set in her ways, too independent and free from responsibility. Worst of all was her notorious background. *What would people make of all that and how would Thomas cope with being with such a bad case? No, all in all it was no good.*

Jess spent three days thinking how to let him down gently. Then she got an inspiration. *Why not engage the services of John and Livinia? After all, they detested her from the beginning, especially John, and all their civility of late was a charade, I'm sure, just to be polite while I'm still hanging around.* She clearly recalled that café meeting where it was now obvious to her that they were fishing to find out when she would be going. Yes, she would talk to them. That evening, Jess rang Livinia and, after a short talk, asked if she could visit them in the next day or so. It was agreed that tomorrow would be excellent.

Jess arrived at Bridgehead just before twelve. Livinia ushered her into the lounge rather garrulously, Jess thought, and John was sedately seated in his chair. He arose on her entry and greeted her warmly. There followed a short period of chit chat, but finally Jess could contain her anxiety no longer. She commenced the serious part of the day with a question, 'Um,' she started. That was ominous, as Jess was noted for never umming and ohing. 'What would you say to Thomas asking me to ...' she paused mid-sentence, 'to marry him?'

John and Livinia stared at each other, mostly in mock amazement. Then Livinia got up out of her chair, walked over to Jess, put her arm on Jess's, and said in a very demonstrable fashion, 'That's wonderful, dear. You've agreed, of course?'

Jess was dumbstruck. This was not the response she had desired, at all. She looked at Livinia with a hint of a tear in her eyes and said, 'But Livinia.' Nothing else would come out.

John said, 'Couldn't happen to a nicer bloke.'

Jess stared at them both, fighting back panic tears. This was getting out of hand. Finally, she pulled herself together and said, rather firmly, 'No. This is not good. This is not good at all. I am old enough to be his ... I mean he is young enough ... No, it's just not right.'

'What's not right about it, dear?' asked Livinia happily.

'Well, for a start, I'm far too old for Thomas.' There was a pause. 'And another thing.' There was another pause. 'I'm not suitable for such a nice young man.'

'Quiet,' said Livinia. 'We won't have that sort of talk now.

Now you listen to me, Jessie. Thomas loves you dearly, he has told me often enough. You are admirably suited to him. You have made him so happy just being here. What's more, you can keep him in line better than almost anyone.'

'That's true,' agreed John.

'Yes, that's right. You tell her John,' said Livinia.

John continued, 'Look Jess. I don't know what you are so concerned about. He really does worship you and you'll never know how good you've been for him being out there.'

Livinia added, 'Well, I think it's wonderful. I do hope you will be very happy together. Come on, let me get some lunch.'

Jess sat through the rather sumptuous fare that Livinia had obviously gone to a lot of effort to prepare. She was devastated that her plan appeared to have backfired completely. Instead of agreement that she was unsuited to Thomas, they not only supported his offer but encouraged it wholeheartedly. She looked at her prospective grandparents-in-law carefully, trying to gauge their real feelings towards her. She could find no fault.

Jess decided that if they approved the match, it was entirely up to her to dissuade Thomas from this error. She still had not come to terms with the possible outcome.

Livinia rose to clear some plates and make room for the tea. John sat alone with Jess in the dull light of the heavily curtained and ornately furnished dining room. The table was exceptionally large, able to seat twelve, so Jess felt she was exposed in so much space. It made her more than a little uncomfortable. She was keen to be away and to think about things.

John was taciturn at the best of times and Jess was notorious for her reserve, so the two of them together led to deathly silence. But John was deep in thought. He was always prepared to speak his mind if he believed his family needed advice. He looked over at the sombre young woman seated near him and said softly, 'Jess, you are entitled to a bit of human companionship too, you know.'

She looked at him, half hearing him, deep in her own thoughts. John could see a bit of himself in her predicament. He recalled how he had spurned the company of others, indeed inflicted it upon himself as the price he must pay for his youthful misdemeanour. From her comments, John thought he detected similar feelings emanating from her.

'John,' she finally said to him, 'surely you can see that this is not right. It is not right for Thomas and it is probably not right for me. I'm too old and set in my ways to be doing this. Besides,' she said, carefully choosing her words, 'my reputation is such that you would not impose it willingly upon your good name or be associated with such.'

There was another long silence as the pair sat and thought. Then he replied, 'Look, Jess. I can't make the decision for you, but let me ask you this: do you like being around Thomas?'

'Well, yes,' she responded, thinking how much she loved working on his property.

'And you get on well with him?'

'Yes, mostly.'

'He speaks very fondly of you, Jess, and he defends you at every opportunity. No one agrees one hundred percent with another person all the time. I'm blessed to have Livinia. We probably agree ninety-five percent of the time. That's rare. Most couples we see would be lucky to agree fifty percent. I estimate that you and Thomas must get on at much higher than that, don't you?'

Jess thought about that for a minute. That was a good yardstick to measure compatibility and she was trying to gauge how much they would rate on that scale. Apart from the one serious argument, they had never had words. But then they were not married. That certainly put a different perspective on a relationship.

'Do you see what I mean?' John was asking.

'Yes,' she replied, not with all that much confidence.

'Well, as I see it, you two seem to be made for each other, and I say again, you are entitled to some companionship too.'

'But what about my past,' she said bluntly.

'What about it?'

Jess was now getting confused. She had played what she thought was her trump card, her past life, but it had been instantly dismissed. She had come here to seek their support in dissuading Thomas from making a big mistake. Instead, she was now being lectured on the suitability of their match. They even had a bag full of good reasons why they were so suitable. Jess was relieved when she heard the approaching footsteps of Livinia returning to the room.

CHAPTER TEN

ess had felt deflated after the lunch date with John and Livinia. She departed the property feeling worse than ever. She could clearly see that the Summers were fully supportive of Thomas in his endeavours to marry her. She wondered how much of their thinking involved what was best for her. Jess slowly began to get annoyed about the whole thing. Firstly, she was annoyed that romance should come to her so late in her life and with someone that she looked on as a friend. Then she was disturbed that she seemed to live near to this man totally oblivious to his feelings for her, feelings that seemed to have been evident to everybody else. *How could I be so thick?* She felt slightly embarrassed.

The contrariness of life presented her with something she had so longed for all her youthful days, days dissipated in hard lonely work, physically if not spiritually alone. She had not seen it coming and was not even looking for it but, nevertheless, here it was, gift wrapped for her, and she was fighting it desperately. She no longer had any worries about money. She was, however, mindful that as she got older the results of a hard physical life were beginning to manifest themselves in numerous ways. The worst thing she suffered was her right shoulder, first damaged in a horse fall when she was barely fourteen and then badly re-injured in the violent arrest at Milbark. She had suffered continuously since with varying degrees of discomfort. But there were also other niggles, mostly the result of working accidents. Lastly, she suffered badly from jaw aches following the severe thumping inflicted on her also during her arrest at Milbark. This ailment manifested itself at frequent but unpredictable times and could be triggered simply by talking, or eating hard substances, or just a sudden movement of her mouth. It prevented her from fully enjoying eating out and made her wary at gatherings where any food was offered. She acknowledged that she was simply getting old. She was also mindful that there existed out there, people who still would like her to be dead.

Jess spent many disturbed hours thinking about her predicament. Slowly, however, she began to see things from the standpoint of John and the comments he had made to her about their compatibility. Maybe she could think about herself for once in this situation. Yes, she could even begin to think about personal happiness into her few remaining years. Maybe Thomas actually needed her more than she realised.

Thomas began to drop hints that if she agreed, he would like her to think about moving in with him. That terrified her. That was something she had given absolutely no thought to at all. She felt very uneasy about that idea, worrying about what others would think of her, and for that matter, of Thomas. His suggestion set her back a few days until the idea slowly grew on her.

Thomas eased the guilt she felt and the unease at the prospect by initially suggesting they have their own bedrooms and she retain the complete run of the house. That did ease her concern somewhat. Finally, she agreed to have a serious talk to Thomas about the whole thing and set some boundaries. She still had to contend with her unusual habit of poor sleep, resulting in nocturnal wandering and creative spurts that sent her to her laptop.

Before she gave him any answers, she requested that she be given some time to contemplate the whole thing. Thomas understood completely. She would spend some time out at the bush block and then a week or two in Rushcutters Bay, though he was still unaware of either of them existing – more secrets.

The apartment in Rushcutters Bay held for Jess a lot of promise. She anticipated that one day she would probably end up there permanently. For the moment, however, it was a refuge from the stressful decisions that she had to make.

Henry had contacted her again by mail as he was keen to see her once more when she was next in Sydney. With the anxiety caused by Thomas's proposal, Jess was weakened in her normal aversion to socialising and, thinking it would be a diversion, agreed to a lunchtime meeting with Henry. This time, he insisted Gerard would not be accompanying him.

Henry obviously adored Doyles and arranged to meet Jess there again. It was a genial atmosphere and he seemed to be well known there. After a pleasant two hours, which to Jess seemed to fly by, Henry was about to finish drinking the bottle of wine, when he stared across the bay to the north of the harbour, then, returning his gaze to Jess, asked her pensively, 'Jane, I like you a lot. Would you consent to marrying me?'

Jess froze in a pose of unbridled fear. Surely, she had misheard him. She looked at him in total silence, staring intently with an icy glare at his eyes. She felt the blood drain from her sullen face. She grimaced slightly, suffering inner pain. She heard him ask that question, and at the instant he had completed it she realised with a hint of guilt that, in asking her, he did not even know her real name. She thought so little of him that she concealed her identity from the man who thought enough of her to ask for her hand in marriage. Jess was about to instinctively blurt out a resounding 'no', when she suddenly thought the better of it and remained silent. Deep in thought, she calmed down inside and contemplated the offer.

Jess was embarrassed, both for herself and for Henry, a shy introspective and creative spirit who seemed devoid of any malice at all in his makeup. *Why*, she wondered, *would he traumatise himself so to ask me that?* Evasively, she gazed out at the blue and green scenery of the harbour and its foreshore, unable to answer. Finally, she replied, 'Henry …' A long pause. 'Why would you ask me, of all people, to marry you? You don't even know me, or anything about me.'

'Jane …' he began, pausing to gather his words. Again for her, his calling her Jane reinforced her misleading him about her true identity, let alone her deepest secrets.

'I know you well enough to understand I feel safe and secure in your capable hands. You have an aura of serenity that I rarely see in other women. A calmness and assuredness I find admirable.' He paused to look at her face for some reaction. She gave little away. Her mind was racing, however. She was not aware that she was an exponent of such qualities to others. Henry reached over to touch her arm.

'You exhibit poise and charm along with that certain capability, that …' he paused to look at her deeply, '…that certain *je ne sais quoi.*'

'Henry,' she replied, ignoring his praises, 'I don't know what to say. I might have to think on it for a while?'

'Certainly, my dear. Take all the time you require.' He paused again. Then he asked her, 'Jane, I am invited to a special soirée tomorrow evening in Vaucluse. You would meet the sort of people I associate with. I believe you would fit in admirably. I wish for you to come with me. No?'

Jess looked at his earnest face. She was torn between ending this farce immediately and escaping, or trying to let Henry down gently and without too much pain and disappointment. It would do her no harm to attend as his guest; no strings attached. She made that point clear and reluctantly accepted his invitation. She asked if she might now be excused and return home to contemplate all that had transpired.

Jess did not have anything to wear that was not designed to withstand the rigours of dealing with cattle and sheep or thrashing through the bush. Though her appearance was the least of her concerns, she would, however, have to buy something that was suitable for the evening. At least she could show that much courtesy to Henry. For her, that was a chore, but she managed eventually. Jess waited, as agreed, outside a convenient city building near where she lived, for Henry to pick her up in a small car that he kept for commuting about the city.

Henry introduced her to many of the guests at the evening. Jess found them to be strange. Henry moved in a bizarre world of Bohemian artistic types, foreign personalities, local minor politicians and lesser diplomats and dignitaries. She heard copious communications in German and French. Her German was impeccable and her French passable. The gathering constituted a rag-tag conglomeration of characters attired in all manner of costumes and conveying attitudes as divergent as the multicultural community from which it sprang. Thankfully for Jess, Gerard was also there. She was able to pass more pleasant time with him and try to learn a bit more about Henry.

Jess spent most of the time observing the attendees and listening to their chattering, weighing up whether or not she would, or indeed could, fit into this world. Suddenly, the unworldly, frequently innocent and often uncouth society of the squattocracy in which she daily toiled in the quiet wayside backwaters of far distant and remote Monaro, despite its unsophisticated naivety, seemed somehow slightly more attractive and inviting. She found herself fondly thinking of Thomas. Her mind drifted to the simple assuredness of the John Summers of the world. Their independence and self-sufficiency were somehow more real and dependable than the scene in which she found herself. Jess had severe reservations that she would fit in here or could tolerate the thin veneer of pretence that passed for sophistication. She was used to people who were what you saw them to be and no more.

To compound her confusion, Jess was conscious that her notorious background might not be the kind that was totally acceptable to Henry. Even now, she found herself permanently on guard against some person intruding or stumbling onto her secrets. Matters undisclosed to the world in general she did not wish to have exposed. Worst of all, she realised, her miscreant past was fully available to everyone in the form of her eagerly awaited diary, released shortly after her notorious trial. She wondered what Henry would make of that.

Jess managed to glean from Gerard some of his opinion of Henry. It was wrong of Jess to pry, and against her better nature, but she desired to have Gerard's judgment of his cousin Henry. Gerard did not expose much about Henry's demeanour that she did not already know. He was, however, able to appraise her considerably about his background and his origins in Europe.

Something else suddenly occurred to Jess that, until this

point, had escaped her. Mixing with all these foreign and well-travelled dignitaries, another issue presented itself. Jess avoided authority, indeed, she feared it. If she agreed to marry Henry, he would wish her to accompany him all over the world. She would need papers. The mere thought of having to face all manner of scrutiny in order to apply for goodness knows how many different travel papers she would need, filled her with dread. Her precarious prior existences did not allow for detailed authentication. Even now, she was missing certain necessary documentation that made her simple bucolic life sometimes strangely difficult. Poor Henry was looking decidedly unappealing.

The next day they had agreed to meet again. Jess was struggling with the prospect of having to decline Henry and how to go about that task in the kindest fashion. She liked him despite the fashion in which he had imposed himself on her tranquillity. She could not see how they could be entirely happy together as, despite his protestations, their worlds were simply too divergent. She wondered what his refined sensibilities would make of her if he knew of her as Joe Scacci. *More to the point, what would his cultured companions make of me?*

Jess tried to compromise between stringing it out to keep Henry happy and letting go, but finally, after two more days, she had to tell him of her decision. She could see he was disappointed but philosophical about it. It was almost as if it were not entirely unexpected. He had thrown his hat into the ring in an event that, in reality he had little chance of fluking a win. He was just happy to have had the experience of such a positive character in his rather predictable life. He certainly would never forget her. Jess, for her part, found this unexpected interlude made her focus her mind back onto the world that she really knew; the one that she did find some fulfilment living in.

Jess was perplexed and rather annoyed at life. She recalled that she had ventured up to the city to contemplate Thomas's proposal and to do that in quiet solitude. Instead, she had been confronted with an even bigger trauma. Jess wondered at the perfidious nature of communal interactions and the general human condition. She had squandered her youth in the wilds of the tropical Kimberleys and had only ever desired calm matrimony and domesticity but had been denied. Now, instead of one marriage request, she had had two in the space of a few weeks. Both had been judged by her as far too late. She was still in a quandary whether to accept Thomas so late for her in life or whether to deny herself, or him even, that solace. For Thomas, at least, she judged it to be a sort of 'Tom Thumb' outcome; a longed-for result that was not quite right. She hoped he was not short-changing himself over her.

Jess spent a few more days in Rushcutters Bay. She wanted to convince herself that she really did not wish to live permanently in this sort of atmosphere, and it worked. She headed for the more familiar ambience of the tree-clad and wild southern mountains, and the clear air of the Monaro plains. There awaited another dilemma that now required her attention, that of Thomas.

As urban living had not delivered the outcome that she thought she was looking for, Jess decided to escape to the total isolation of her bush block. She arrived there in the cool of the late evening. She usually spent the first night in the comfort of the little house that came with the second small property that she bought next to the first. Next morning, she ventured deeper into the wilds to her large shed. From there she could advance to the eerie high up on the small plateau that was her sanctuary.

Jess sat in the cool, bright early morning light of her huge shed. Inside this metal frame were all her earthly possessions, all that she loved and treasured, at least physically. The source of her enormous wealth and prestige was purely intellectual; esoteric creativity immeasurable by material standards.

Jess came to the shed to be alone; to think, and to decide. She had not gone up to her eerie way up in the mountains along the narrow steep track that she had carved out through the rugged peaks. She often went up there in her bone-rattling GMC to work and to be alone. This time, however, she would not even venture up there. The trip took her hours and she felt that this decision needed her instant uninterrupted thoughts beginning here and now.

Jess sat in the silence. She thought about her life, the things she missed and the things she missed out on. One of the things Jessie MacIntyre missed out on was a mother. Jess rarely if ever thought about her parents. Right now, however, she was wondering about it. Right now, she thought it would be a good time for her to have a mother to talk to. Jess thought about her mother. She wondered what she would have been like, what happened to her and why she would give up her child. Jess had a romanticised view of her mother, or at least an idealised vision of the absent soul. She never delved too deeply into the possibilities that surrounded that topic. Jess had an overdeveloped sense of morality, a distaste of the crude and crass. She feared intemperance and abhorred profanity and vulgarity. She was, in fact, rather judgemental, a trait she acknowledged within herself and for which she sometimes felt guilty and abnormal. She was ill at ease with transgressors and especially the results of that transgression – namely, the suffering of the innocent product. *Did I not suffer intolerably all my life for someone else's lapse?*

Jess had no way of knowing that her mother died almost at her birth, murdered really, by, of all people, her father. Jess knew absolutely nothing about her parentage, her birth or the place of her birth. The little she knew had been gleaned reluctantly from a couple of shady sources during what was to her a traumatic and embarrassing trial. She knew approximately the date, about August in 1967, but there were no records of her birth at any hospitals within Sydney for that week. She had simply been dumped at the door of the orphanage on that cold August morning before light.

What strange mystic contrivance had arranged for her to be born, abscond from the clutches of the terrible orphanage and to be gathered into the bosom of the caring Donald MacIntyre, never to be missed by the nuns? What had ordained that she must be whisked off to the wilds of the

Kimberleys at thirteen to be nurtured by another MacIntyre for the next fifteen years?

Jess had never had the need for a mother. The mother figures she did have were few and far between, starting with Edna Coniston at Ravymoota Station. There were never any other women available in her fractured life. The nearest she had come lately to a mother was Livinia Summers. Jessie envied in many ways the life of Livinia. She seemed to have everything Jess once aspired to. She was married, had successful children and many grandchildren. She possessed a loving husband who, by all accounts, was also very successful and wealthy. The only item in this list that Jess possessed was wealth. She had no hope of any of the others now, not this late in her life.

Jessie's life had been centred on the one attribute she thought she was born to perform – her writing. It was not planned that way; indeed, it was not even anticipated that this would ever arise. It should not have ever arisen. It came about solely because of her fractured life. It was ironic to her that it had come to this, but she was immensely successful because of her losses. She surveyed her success in amusement. As she sat in the warming morning air inside her shed, she thoughtfully contemplated the course that she had deceitfully navigated.

It all began, she remembered, when, at about ten, Donald gave her two large foolscap accounts books to scribble in. So good were they that she decided to commence a diary, which continued on until she had filled them at sixteen. By then, the writing bug had her and she needed an outlet to assuage her prodigious imagination. This was manifested through a succession of noms-de-plume; she was now at her fifth incarnation. Running through a succession of clandestine and deceitful actions, she managed to utilise Jane Ransom, George Norman Thaler, Kimberley West, Joe Scacci, and now Catherine Holbrook Seymour. Most of the thrill of accomplishment was contained not in the writing and publishing, but in the surreptitious concealment of the author's identity, not once but several times! *Ah,* she thought, *the simple joys of clandestine duplicity. If only human interaction were so enthralling and rewarding.*

Now Jess had one more problem – hence her dilemma. Her quiet life of seclusion, independence and deception had been suddenly under siege from two angles: she had two proposals of marriage within weeks. She had never contemplated this eventuality. Her immediate instinct was to reject them both instantly. However, that was not as simple as it sounded, not for her anyway. As she had already rejected one, it had helped her to compare them. All that remained was the second.

Heinrich Liechtenstein had moved in exalted circles and carried a certain gravitas, circumstances that Jess found unattractive. Somehow, she could not see herself engaging in meaningless small talk with people she did not necessarily wish to engage. *A lifetime of being with people who called a spade a bloody shovel has instilled in me an antipathy towards pretentiousness. Besides, I know my personality is bordering on sociopathic and that I'm getting more intolerant as I get older.*

Thomas Summers, on the other hand, came from her own background, entirely. Their similarities were striking. However, he did not come unencumbered. His family was his strength – except for his mother. Thomas came as a package, which included the formidable John Summers, tempered it seems, however, by the lovely Livinia. Jess was sure John distrusted her; in fact, she thought he disliked her. *Why then had he been so supportive of the suggestion of me marrying Thomas? What is in it for him?* She had tried hard to dissuade them of their support but appeared to fail there. *Besides, Thomas is considerably younger than I am!*

Jess liked Thomas … a lot. But love him? She was not so sure. She was very fond of him and admired his abilities enormously but was that a basis on which to build a marriage at so late a stage of her life? Above all, she valued her independence and her freedom and the accountability to no one. She dearly wished to reject his offer as well.

Jess knew that life was a gift, an interlude, but it had always been very harsh, much more so than for most of her acquaintances, especially in the Kimberleys. She found it difficult to hedonise her existence or place herself in frivolity. Jess knew all about the theory of romance, she wrote extensively about it in many novels. When it came to the practice, it was another matter. She was a failure, and she had no experience at all. *On the other hand, what benefits might accrue for me if I accept Thomas's proposal?*

Finally, after much agonising, Jess returned to Auvergne Station and the problems therein. Livinia and John wished to facilitate the advancement or otherwise of the relationship that had been born of the new paradigm. To this extent, they had invited Thomas and Jessie over a couple of times to socialise within the new boundaries. Jess made more of an effort to ascertain the feelings and characteristics of the relationship she now had with Thomas's important relations. Jess was naturally taciturn and very guarded, John likewise, and both for somewhat similar reasons. Livinia thought she would expand the boundaries on a delicate topic, one dear to her heart but, she knew, probably not so with Jess. 'You know you're welcome to join us at the church any time,' she said, looking intently at Jess.

'Thank you,' said Jess coolly, trying not to sound too disinterested or dismissive. Jessie was deep in her own thoughts about that issue when suddenly one of the younger grandchildren entered the darkened room to request Livinia's attendance elsewhere. That left John and Jessie, two notoriously reticent souls, alone in the silence. Jess was surmising to herself how she must avoid any attendance at the local church, not entirely because she particularly had any deep moral or ethical objections to such a venture, but for other reasons. These mostly revolved around her incessant fear of socialising, and the knowledge that the Makepeaces and the Costellos also attended the same church. She had an inbuilt dread of the routine and the ritual, especially when she was so ignorant of the procedures, unlike everyone else.

She was deep in these thoughts when she was jolted out of

her recluse by the unaccustomed intervention of the usually taciturn John.

'You are not a religious person then Jess?' he asked hesitantly. There was some considerable delay in her reply. They sat alone in the dimmed light of the deathly quiet and sombre lounge, a rare occurrence, and she sensed he was not merely making conversation. The time had come, she felt, that a deeper conversation was now possible with the powerful and respected patriarch of the family of which she was potentially now a part, or soon could be. There was a long pause. All that pervaded the silence was the slow rhythmic ticking of the huge long-case clock.

'Religion is such an emotive issue,' she ventured. He did not reply, just gazed at her expectantly, waiting for her to continue. She did not.

Finally, he continued tentatively, 'I suppose it is, to those of little faith.'

There was another long deathly silence. Jess was not sure what John meant by that. She did know that he was trying to appraise his possibly new granddaughter-in-law. Finally, and uncharacteristically, Jess volunteered, 'You see John, one's faith can be attributed to one of many causes. Firstly, religion can be the refuge of the dispossessed. Those who have failed in worldly attainment, either in having progeny, or attaining material success, or gaining fame may seek solace in the next life, sustained in this one by the promise of it through faith and conviction. There is no assurance that this is so, but we all live in that hope.'

There was a pause, then she continued, as he had made no comment, 'Secondly, there are those who, maybe being of feeble mind, are incapable of questioning the doctrine that has carried them from the cradle, unquestioningly accepting the code of beliefs that has been instilled in them.' Another pause. 'Thirdly, there are those who are truly spiritual souls who genuinely and firmly adhere to a belief system that they have thought through and accept as truth. Often truly humble and meekly unconfident people, permanently searching for someone or something to express gratitude to for their perceived blessings in this life. They constitute a sizeable portion of the followers.'

Silence. Then she continued, 'There is another group that forms part of the association too – those who have committed seriously sinful actions for which they either have not yet atoned or have done so but feel eternal guilt for the actions of the past.'

She stared at him intently, unblinking, with that unnerving and penetrating stare that uneased those at whom it was aimed, not always with that intention. 'Then there are the adherents whose sole purpose in attending is to outwardly and demonstratively display to all the world just how devout they are and how much of the rituals they master and control. Not a pastime, I fear, God would necessarily admire.'

John was looking at her sullenly. He had not anticipated quite a programme of such perception and depth to emanate from such a simple question. Thomas had said she was intelligent and articulate but until now John had not seen the evidence quite so dramatically. There was a lot of detail in that discourse and indications of a much deeper comprehension of this topic than maybe he had the wit to counter or combat, or for that matter, comprehend.

Jess sensed that she might have strayed a little beyond politeness with her considered and profound dialogue. She only espoused such considerations to those on whom she looked with considerable admiration or favour. She certainly held John Wesley Summers in that category. She hoped she had not overstepped the mark in granting to him a higher astuteness for wisdom than she supposed. She hoped his reticence was the result of her uncharacteristic verbosity. As he ventured no more comments on the topic and the church was not again mentioned in the absence of Livinia, Jess felt he was vulnerable to an astute enquiry on another matter if she approached it in the correct manner.

She had not planned it to come to this point, but because it had, she decided to venture into, what was for her, forbidden territory – personal questions. She recalled the conversation with Ian Knuckey about John's father and his association with the questionable AJC management of racing. It was an issue that intrigued her. She ventured quietly, 'Have you heard of the AJC?'

'No,' he said, lying as he nervously recalled that long-hidden ancient message attached to the wad of notes he had taken from the safe back on the farm. He wondered why she would be asking him about that. 'Why do you ask?'

'Was your father Wesley Thomas Summers?'

'Yes. How do you know that?'

'Did you know your father had applied to become a bookmaker?'

'No,' said John, feigning confusion.

'The AJC runs the racing industry in New South Wales and issues the licences for bookmakers. Your father must have been quite a man in his day and have had considerable wealth to apply for a licence. When we were investigating the Bales family, his name cropped up in another matter. It seems his wealth must have been dissipated after you were born or at his death. I thought you might know, that's all. According to the police report into your father's accident, any effects he stored in the safe deposit box were cleared by the family from the farm immediately he died, and before anyone else could secure them.'

John sat in stunned silence as Jess unknowingly divulged more information about the stash of money in the family safe than he had ever been able to ascertain from all the years of living there. He had no idea that his father was so wealthy and that his in-laws might have stolen his inheritance. *Why was it coming to light now, and via this person?*

John, ever alert to the possibility of his wealth accumulation being shady, anxiously and tentatively enquired, 'Am I being investigated for some reason?'

'No. Not at all,' Jess reassured him. 'They have no interest in you at all.'

Livinia returned to the room, bearing a large tea tray. That ended the foray into John's past for the moment. Livinia noticed the pall of melancholic silence that descended on the room as she entered. Her cheerful disposition soon restored some degree of normality, however. As was her want, she soon steered the conversation around to more urgent family matters.

'Have you and Thomas made any decisions yet?'

'No Livinia. We are still working through things.'

It was left there for the moment.

Jess returned home to Auvergne late in the evening. She had a lot to think about. Her unexpected interaction with Henry had forced her to focus her mind on Thomas. She would have to give him a decision soon. She spent a lot of time weighing up the advantages or otherwise of marrying Thomas. She would prefer not to, but there were other considerations that were leaning her towards a favourable answer.

Jess spoke at length to Thomas and their compatibility became more evident to her. If she proceeded, she began to contemplate the issue of his despicable family, the Bales. The interlude with Henry in Sydney had almost convinced her that this union with Thomas might be suitable, even for her. She realised she probably would never get another offer, especially as attractive as this one was to her. Finally, she reluctantly acceded to his request with considerable provisos attached. The major one would have to deal with the Bales. It was put in train.

ivinia rang Audrey in Sydney to ask her to come down to the farm for a discussion about family matters. It involved Thomas. Audrey was not much involved in Thomas's life over the last decade or so and rarely saw him. She wondered whether it finally concerned Thomas getting married, as she thought she had heard rumours through the family. Her only comment was to say she hoped it did not involve that dreadful truck driver woman who had so insulted them once before. Livinia made no comment.

Audrey and Geoffrey Bales, accompanied by their elder daughter Zoë, arrived on the Saturday morning preparatory to a separate family meeting about Thomas. They were in good spirits as they hoped to venture further south into the high country while this far down from Sydney. They rarely attended the family meetings as Audrey was philosophically opposed to the whole setup and Geoffrey was not a member so could not attend the meetings. So, as they were so far south, they decided to get some benefits from the trip. They were both in for a shock.

Jessie and Thomas arrived a little later than planned in her late-model Rover Discovery, a car she had recently purchased to provide more comfort on the long trips to Rushcutters Bay. She parked under the portico next to the Bales' BMW. There she waited for a few minutes, touching Thomas on the hand and apologising for the state she was in and the potential outcome of the following events. He sighed with resignation. He hated his mother and her companion, but still held her in his mind as his mother, not necessarily his real mother, as that honour had been usurped by Livinia. Their meetings were never pleasant.

They alighted the vehicle when Livinia appeared at the front door and told them that they were in the informal dining room and she would see them in there when they were ready. She went in ahead to announce their arrival and Jess and Thomas followed shortly after.

It was with some trepidation that Jess entered the house. Thomas wore soft-soled shoes with his casual gear but Jess wore her RM Williams with the high leather block heel. They echoed ominously throughout the quiet tranquillity of the homestead as she strode reluctantly and slowly across the polished wooden flooring. Jess was conscious of the abnormal portent of her tread. There would be no doubt of her approaching, though she had not planned it to be so.

As they entered the informal dining area, Jess took in who was present – Geoffrey Bales, Audrey and Zoë. At the head of the table sat a smug-looking John, fidgeting on the tabletop, and beside him sat Livinia. Thomas greeted the party coldly, sidled up to be near his grandmother, and sat beside her. He frostily glanced at Zoë, whom he disliked more because of all her privileges that he had been denied. Jess stood motionless, framed in the half-light emanating from the darker hallways. There was a long awkward silence. John, despite his power and position, remained silent, awaiting what he anticipated to be entertaining fireworks from the only person in his experience whom he had seen capable of ruffling Bales. Everybody was waiting for Jess to acknowledge them. This she did not do. It was rare for Livinia to see Jess in other than her working clothes. She had no hat, no customary scarf about her neck and tucked into her shirt, no coat, no working gloves which she habitually wore, and none of the trappings of any sort attached to her belt. In her relative finery she cut quite a figure. Her elegant face was framed by her fine wispy blonde hair. Even in this light her stunning blue eyes pierced out from her face, emphasised by her pale white complexion. She stood in stiff silence, her eyes darting about the gathered assembly broodily surveying the scene. Then she moved.

Jess clomped determinedly over to the nearest available part of the table and stood staring at Bales. She moved her gaze to Zoë and said with authority, 'You can go now.'

Zoë did not move. Again, Jess said, a little firmer, 'Please leave the room.' Zoë looked at her father. Jess whipped in quickly, 'You needn't bother looking at him either. Just go.'

'Now look here,' Bales interrupted.

Jess slammed her open left hand on the bare wooden table with an unexpected rapidity and firmness so the sound reverberated wildly in their ears and several of them jumped. So unexpected and out of character was this action that a stunned assembly stared wide-eyed at the perpetrator in surprised silence.

Slowly Jess rose up, all the time gazing unmoved at a shocked Bales. 'You,' she finally glowered, 'shut up. This is not a debate, nor a discussion, this is an ultimatum. You are not in court now.' Bales rose to object. He was a thinnish man of weedy stature, not enhanced by his inappropriate wearing of shorts and a rather colourful short-sleeved shirt.

Jess glowered at him disapprovingly. 'Sit down, Bales,' she said slowly and with menace. He froze in his half up position. He stared back at her intently, deciding whether to take her on now or acknowledge defeat immediately; after all, his stock-in-trade was to be able to decipher the character of adversaries by merely judging them on appearances or intimidating them with his own demeanour. He knew a serious threat when he saw it. He thought the better of it for the present. She started to walk around to him. He sat down instantly. She stopped walking. Jess again looked at Zoë and simply jerked her left thumb backwards, indicating the door. Zoë got up quietly and walked demurely out of the room.

Jess peered about the room slowly. She moved slightly

away from the table and began to leisurely walk back and forward along the length of the room beside the table, stealing glances at them occasionally. Her heavy dress boots clomped ominously on the smooth wooden floor in the silence. She turned after a couple of times of this and, facing them all, announced in a firm and deliberate voice, with no inflection, 'My name is Jessie MacIntyre.' There was a long pause. 'My *name* is Jessie MacIntyre,' she repeated more firmly, with distinct emphasis on the word 'name'. Then she wheeled about and said quickly, straight at Bales, 'But then you would know that already, wouldn't you?'

There was no reply. There was total silence, except for the tick-tocking of the ubiquitous long-case clock that John seemed to have everywhere. Jess recommenced her deliberate striding about the room while the assembly watched in fascination and dread. During this long recommencement of walking around the room, Jess sank suddenly into a momentary lapse of her own little universe. She had never ever before announced to anyone what her real name was. For years, Jessie MacIntrye was slowly dying, to be replaced with the rising Jane Ransom. She was almost universally known as Jane Ransom. Now, ironically, the safe and anonymous Jane Ransom might peacefully be passing on and Jessie MacIntyre could rise, phoenix-like from the ashes of the past lives that constituted Jessie's infamous history. All this was possible because, undeserving as she felt she was, Thomas had offered her a life she had long ago accepted as vanished. Once she had accepted this new concept, nobody was going to ruin that thought for her again, especially not his family. These thoughts swirled in her fevered brain. Then she was transported back to the present. She savoured those thoughts for a moment longer, keeping the others in suspense while she deliberated. Then she turned to face the expectant table. She stared at them imperiously for a moment, then said, directing her gaze more softly and fondly at Thomas, 'Thomas Summers has asked me to marry him.' She paused. 'We are engaged.' She stared at them unflinchingly. 'I am marrying Thomas, not his repulsive and ghastly family.' She turned to face Bales. 'I don't like you,' she said firmly. 'I don't like anything about you.' She turned to face Audrey. '… or you either.' There was a long pause.

Jess commenced walking slowly again. Then she said, 'Thomas has a mother, of what value is debatable. However, he has a wish for her and her entourage to be present.' There was another long pause. 'I, however, do not.' Another pause. 'Nevertheless, I am going to bow to the wishes of Thomas and Livinia in this matter, but not without my feelings being fully …,' she paused for effect, 'fully understood. If you receive an invitation to our wedding, I wish for you to refuse it. You are not welcome and if you attend you will be placed a long way from me and from Thomas.'

Audrey wriggled in her chair. It was the first she had heard of this, or at least the confirmation of a rumour she had heard. The pronouncement of Jessie's real name had sent a shiver down her whole being. She raised her arm as if to speak. Jess cut her short. 'As for you …,' she said, looking deeply into

Audrey's eyes, 'you long ago dissolved any input to the son you so shamelessly abandoned. You pursued a life of carefree thoughtlessness accompanied by degenerates and thieves. That you find this man ...,' pointing at Geoffrey, 'as a suitable partner tells us more about you, than him. I despise you and what you have done.'

She peered again at a now nervous Bales. 'As for you Bales, I cringe with disgust merely at being in your presence.'

Bales indicated that he wished to speak. She cut him dead. She began again to stride along the floor beside the table. Bales, unaccustomed to being put down, nevertheless was determined to have some input. He began tentatively to speak, saying, 'Ms MacIntyre, I feel...'

Jess cut him again. 'Shut up, Bales. Let me make myself totally clear where we stand.' She stood opposite the table to him, staring unblinking at him. 'I know all about you. I know all about your unbelievably despicable father, the paedophile and corrupt personage that stained the system that he was supposed to uphold. I know about his evil dealings and his associations with corrupt police. You live off the earnings of evil. Your mother lives in a house from the proceeds of crime and you have been educated at the expense of far more worthy victims.' She paused to ensure he was riveted on her alone. 'You have been connected to various crimes, and I...'

She was suddenly interrupted by Bales, who objected by saying, 'Now look here...'

'You deny it?' she said savagely. 'You deny you sent Percy Pavilon here? You deny involvement with his death?'

Bales tried to speak. There was a shuffling in the room as the conversation started to get nasty. Jess continued, 'We have the 'phone records to prove you contacted him, Bales. Or do you deny also using Zoë's mobile to do it, eh?'

He was silent, and slightly shaking. Jess continued, 'There is a lot more, but that will suffice for now.' Then she moved a little closer to the table and bent ever so slightly towards him. In a low and menacing tone, she added, 'And if I ever can prove you or your father were associated with the demise of Donald MacIntyre, or for that matter the destroying of Ian Knuckey, I will personally obliterate you.'

Geoffrey Bales fully understood her intent. Jess stared at him in total silence, unblinking. Then she slowly stood up and backed away from the table.

The room was tomb-like in its hush. Only the large clock in the far corner marched on with its unstoppable progression of time. Jess just stood there peering down at Bales. Then she said, 'As long as we all understand where we are.'

There was another very long silence. Livinia, who had sat motionless throughout the whole performance, swallowed noticeably and then ventured, 'Could I please make us all a cup of tea?'

No one answered. She slowly moved her chair as quietly as she could across the wooden floor and stood up.

'I'll go and get Zoë,' said a nervous Audrey.

'No, don't bother,' replied Jessie. 'I'll go and get her myself.'

With that, Jess looked sadly at Thomas and then at John, and then clomped sedately out of the room. She went to the sleepout and other communal rooms looking for Zoë but she was not there. Jess then went outside into the garden area looking for her. Zoë was strolling under the gums on the grassy area near the stockyards. Jess went up to her and said, 'Hello Zoë, are you okay?'

'Yes, thank you. What's happening?'

Jess explained as best she could and with as much protection as Zoë deserved. Zoë was a refined young girl – reserved, slight and polished, obviously well educated and mannered. Jess could like her under different circumstances. They chatted inconsequently for a few minutes and then Jess asked, 'Do you know Percy Pavilon?'

'No, I don't think so. Who is he?'

'Oh, just someone I thought you might have known. Never mind. Shall we go back inside and see what your grandmother has got for us?' They walked in together making small talk as if bosom buddies.

The afternoon had an ominous and frigid air. Jess spoke to John and Livinia, and to Thomas, but pointedly shunned the company of Audrey and Geoffrey. She conversed with Zoë. The Bales were originally to stay the night but owing to the embarrassing throttling that Geoffrey Bales received from Jess, they decided better of it and moved on to Cooma. Livinia was sad as she had little contact with Zoë.

Jess and Thomas returned to Auvergne.

A call came for Jess to return to see her publishers in Melbourne. On a whim, she made a decision. Just before they organised to drive to Melbourne, Jess sat by Thomas and asked, 'Thomas, would you consider marrying me while we are in Melbourne?'

Thomas looked at her startled.

'But what about our church wedding? I thought you wanted that here?'

'I do,' she insisted. 'But I'd feel much happier if we are going to be living together to be actually married.'

'You mean, cancel the wedding here?'

'No, not at all,' she said. 'I'm sorry, I just don't feel right living with you and not being married. It's just not me Thomas.'

'That's alright. I understand completely,' he replied. 'But what will we tell the family?'

'Tell them nothing, Thomas. We don't have to tell anybody. But we would then be married. That's what you want, isn't it?'

'Sure, yes. You mean, just go on as usual and plan for the wedding, but secretly be married already?'

'Yes.'

'I see,' he said, thinking to himself. Then he asked, 'Would that be legal? I mean to be already married and then to go through the whole thing as if we weren't?'

'Who cares, Thomas?'

'Well, I can't see anything wrong with that idea. You know, I knew living with you was going to be a hoot,' he said, smiling and rubbing her arm gently.

Jess said to him that she had made a few enquiries and told him of the things they would need. He agreed. The clandestine nature of the whole thing appealed to his nature.

After Jess had seen her publishers and taken Thomas in with her to show him her world, they made for the registry office and did the deed. Jess immediately felt a great relief personally that she was not now living in a manner that she found slightly distasteful. On their return to Auvergne, neither let on that anything had changed.

Thomas did not usually accompany Jess into town in the truck on sales days, but he did occasionally. This particular day, they left early to unload the steers at the saleyards and then watch the procedure. Jess often ambled about the sales for some time on her own following all the pens as they sold. Thomas would often socialise with the few cattlemen he knew from the district. As Jess hung back from one of the pens jotting down some notes, she heard a deep voice behind her softly say, 'I have a gun here. I won't hesitate to use it right now, but I'd rather you walk slowly over to the truck.'

She raised her head and was about to turn when he continued, 'And don't turn around.' His voice was menacing and she felt the hard end of the weapon in her back as he jabbed it into her.

Jess weighed up her options quickly. She could die here now quickly and probably painlessly or she could risk a possibly horrible death somewhere in the back streets of town. On the other hand, she might just be able to escape yet again from the clutches of whomever this was. The chances of her continually escaping death were always diminishing. She knew that, but hope sprang eternal. She would at least at this stage walk over to the truck.

'Don't bother to look back,' he said again in a calm and nasty-sounding voice. Jess thought she detected the barest hint of a foreign accent, but was not sure. At the truck, the man stated that she was to get into the driver's seat and he would get in the other side. Once they were both in, his accomplice would get in the car and follow them out of the yards. When he was in the cabin, Jess started the truck and peered at the assailant now sitting so close to her. He was a young man with a severe face and rather humourless countenance, and he calmly pointed a short barrel with a thick surround on it at her.

He then told her to drive off slowly out onto the highway and head east. She replaced the fine leather gloves she always wore when driving and engaged the protesting gears. She had barely moved a few metres when Thomas suddenly appeared from nowhere on the passenger's side step, and puffing slightly, with a broad grin, yelled out, 'Jess, where you going?'

The assailant was so startled at the unexpected interruption that he swung the pistol around in a quick motion. Jess slammed her foot on the brake at the same time and even though the truck was not moving quickly, the suddenness of the jolt, combined with the appearance of Thomas, sent the assailant slamming into the dashboard. In his surprise, he discharged the gun and simultaneously Jess sent a vicious right fist straight into his jaw. The combined assault on him of the dashboard and Jess's fist sent him into unconsciousness.

The empty semi-trailer, coming to such an abrupt halt, slid noisily across the bitumen of the car park. The empty metal stock crate clattered and clanged with so much noise that everyone there was startled into looking in their direction. From behind the truck, a small red BMW sped off through the saleyard car park, spewing gravel and sliding wildly as it negotiated the packed and crowded facility. Jess caught a quick glimpse of it as she simultaneously put the gears into neutral and opened the door to see what had happened to Thomas. She quickly grabbed the gun from the unconscious assailant and placed it in a small cotton bag that was lying on the dash. Momentarily, Jess considered whether to jab the unconscious man beside her one more time to ensure he was dead or whether it would be better to keep him alive to tell what he knew. She decided, reluctantly, on the latter.

Thomas lay motionless on the ground, blood oozing from his ears, mouth, and somewhere on his chest. Jess froze in horror as she surveyed the scene. There was a big crowd now gathering around the prostrate body of Thomas as Jess tried to get to him. Then she heard the familiar voice of Sergeant Berry, the stock squad member, demanding space and inquiring about the incident. Several people were on mobiles, and already Jess could hear the siren of the nearby ambulance in the distance as it rapidly approached. She knelt down beside Thomas, who was at least still breathing, but unconscious. Shortly after, the ambulance arrived, followed by a police car and then another. In the melee, Jess handed the cotton bag to Sergeant Berry surreptitiously and whispered to him that it contained a gun, and would he ensure it got to the Integrity Commission and no one else. He nodded his agreement. He still did not know who this woman was, but he realised she had some serious connections and he would comply with her request.

The ambulance men spent many minutes attending to Thomas and stabilising him before removing him to the Cooma hospital. He was not there long before they realised that he needed intensive care attention in Canberra or Sydney. Jess asked that he be transferred to Sydney so that New South Wales had jurisdiction over the inevitably complicated events that were sure to flow from this incident. He was flown there that evening. Meantime, Jess spent hours with the police describing her ordeal. The truck remained a crime scene for some time and Jess was unable to remove it. A bulletin was issued for the red BMW and road blocks were set up on all the highways leading out of Cooma. When Jess got a moment, she rang John and Livinia and informed them that there had been a serious accident at the saleyards where Thomas had fallen from the truck.

Jess also found a moment to contact the Integrity people and advise them of the event. She requested that Thomas be protected on his arrival in Sydney. The assailant had also been transported to Sydney in the same helicopter and he was to be guarded too.

Eventually, Jess was allowed to return to Auvergne in the truck. She advised Warren that there had been an accident and prepared for him to run the place with the help of the two girls and Samuel while she attended to Thomas. She spent some time on the telephone to the police in Sydney and then prepared herself for the long trip up.

Next day, Jess drove herself to Sydney in her Discovery and John and Livinia went in his Holden WD Statesman to visit Thomas in the hospital. He was still in intensive care suffering head injuries and a bullet wound to the chest. Jess still had not mentioned this latter fact to John and Livinia. John invited Jess to stay over at the unit in Manly but Jess responded that she would stay closer to the hospital. They were unaware that she owned an apartment in Rushcutters Bay.

John and Livinia went over to the hospital that evening soon after they had settled in at the unit in Manly and tried to visit Thomas. That was when they got their next shock. They were advised that he was comatose and dangerously ill and that there was no point in seeing him as such. Besides, at present, no one was permitted to pass the entrance to the ward. They could not understand why there was a police guard outside his room and why no one was allowed in. They waited outside after being told that the only authorised person allowed in was Mrs Summers. When they informed the guard that he was not married, he just replied that those were his orders and no one was allowed in.

It was three days before Jess contacted them and arranged to meet them at the cafeteria of the hospital. John was getting incensed that no information was forthcoming about Thomas or his condition. Even Thomas's mother, Audrey, was unable to see him. Jessie arrived in the afternoon and went straight down to the cafeteria to meet John and Livinia.

'It's nice of you to come up to see Thomas,' John said on meeting her.

'Why would I not?' she replied, a little surprised.

'Well,' he stammered, 'it's still good of you to come.'

They shuffled over to a vacant table and unwrapped the bundles of items they bought from the counter. Both John and Livinia showed the strain of the accident on their stressed faces and in their quiet demeanour.

'We can't get near Thomas,' said Livinia. 'Not even his mother.'

Jess said nothing. She looked at them sadly. If only she had not married him. If only they had supported her in her desire to persuade Thomas how wrong it was to do so. She tried to remain calm for the ordeal she was about to go through. She could not delay that for much longer. Jess steeled herself for the conversation about to unfold.

'I'm afraid I have something to tell you.'

They both turned their heads to look at Jessie, both with a pained look in their eyes.

'Thomas is not only suffering head damage. He's been shot.'

John and Livinia stared at her incredulously.

'What!' John exclaimed.

'Thomas has been shot in the chest. That's why he fell from the truck.'

'But how?'

'Someone was trying to abduct me from the saleyards and Thomas ran up to the truck to check. That's all.'

Jess spent some time explaining to them the circumstances to date. During this discourse, things arose that began to startle John and sow the seeds of mild panic in his mind. Jessie mentioned that firstly there was a suspect and that it was yet again the despicable Geoffrey Bales or his associates. She intimated to them that he had already been implicated in the mysterious death of the unfortunate Percy Pavilon on a bush track near Cooma. But more startling to him was the suggestion that all his sources of income may be investigated. He suddenly had the horrible thought that they just might delve into Audrey's income from the very successful Summers family company. His assets would not stand up to too much scrutiny if the authorities researched his formative years of acquiring assets. A sudden coldness came over him at the mere thought, despite Jessie's assurances previously.

Secondly, there arose in his mind the possibility that, if Thomas were so precariously clinging to life as Jessie suggested, then a replacement may have to be found for the management of Auvergne. That in itself would raise all sorts of complications, as Ethan always wanted to run that place and not Dave Quiggin's old farm behind Bridgehead. John felt it was unwise to try to ascertain Jessie's probable movements following this disaster.

While John was deep in these thoughts, he was interrupted by Jessie's mobile ringing. John and Livinia quickly excused themselves and went up to the floor where Thomas was located to wait for a while outside his ward.

An hour later, Jess arrived at the door to greet them. The

guard greeted her knowingly and prepared to admit her. There was no point in any of them entering, however, as he was comatose. John was very disturbed by all this news. He sat there contemplating the situation in a daze of confusion and dejection. Shortly after, he announced to Jess that he had been giving the situation some preliminary thought and had decided that he might have to send Ethan over to manage the property while they determined what was to become of Thomas, as the prognosis was so unsure at this stage. Jess looked at John and then at Livinia. She then suggested to John that that would not be advisable or even necessary at this point in time. She reminded John that Warren was more than capable of managing the housed sheep and she would be able to maintain the cattle with the help of the two girls whom the family had sent there for training, plus Samuel. She realised that once Ethan got a foot in the door, he would be very difficult to dislodge. John was slightly taken aback by the firmness of her tone and the manner in which she had expressed her desire to maintain the status quo.

The next afternoon trouble was brewing. Jess had strictly requested that Thomas's mother, and especially Geoffrey Bales, not be admitted under any circumstances. When Jess arrived this time, John and Livinia were there as expected, but so was Audrey, demanding to be let in to see her son and demanding an explanation from the guards. Jess, the anger in her being quickly aroused by what she saw, marched over to them and said in a severe and menacing tone, 'What are you doing here?'

Audrey tried to reply to a threatening Jess but was prevented by her from doing so as Jess continued on, 'Get out of here. Now! And don't come back. If I catch you here again, you'll be in real trouble.'

Audrey protested and spluttered. Jess looked at the guard and demanded that he remove her immediately. This he did, much to the amazement of John and Livinia, who looked on in thorough confusion.

Meantime, investigations had begun to escalate outside the hospital. The red BMW had been intercepted on the highway near Goulburn and the occupant detained. He was proving useful. The assailant in the truck was conscious but unable to speak, thanks mostly to the efforts of Jess. But she had managed to ensure that Judge Bales was thoroughly interrogated and informed that he was squarely in the picture for this attempted abduction and probable murder of the one person who could ruin him. The seriousness of the whole situation was slowly being revealed to an unbelieving John and Livinia.

The other issue that Livinia and John were keen to clear up was the expression 'Mrs Summers'. Livinia assumed that was an erroneous appellation bestowed on Jess in a moment of thorough confusion at the time of the accident. It seemed to have been perpetuated, however, and was causing concern for those legally entitled to bear that tag, at least at this early stage. Jess had ensured that Thomas's mother was forbidden to be anywhere near her son on the threat of arrest. She had, however, ensured the opposite with Livinia, encouraging her attendance as often as she wished. But legal niceties aside, there was the ever-present possibility of the death of Thomas and the right to decide his outcome. Audrey assumed she had that right and Livinia also pressed for some say in any matters pertaining to that issue. Livinia attempted to clarify it, but each time it was raised, she was informed that the patient had a legal guardian, and that was his 'wife', Mrs Summers.

On the third day of the waiting game, Livinia approached Jess while they were alone outside the wards and enquired diplomatically, 'Jess, I'm sorry to raise this matter, but I keep getting told that Thomas has a wife, and that she is making all the decisions about his health. Is that you making all the decisions?'

Jess had never anticipated that this delicate subject would ever arise, as she had planned to carry out the wedding as intended in September. It was not foreseen that Thomas would be in this position, forcing Jess to consider her place in the family – at least not so soon.

Jess carefully considered her reply and just answered, 'Yes.'

'You mean you are making all the decisions?'

'Yes,' she simply replied.

'But others have the right to be doing that, don't they?'

'Actually, no,' responded Jess.

'How come?' demanded Livinia. 'Surely you're not married to Thomas, are you?'

Jess looked at Livinia and paused for a long time before answering. Then she replied, after a big intake of audible breath, 'Livinia. It was all my idea. Thomas had no part in the scheme. I was slightly uncomfortable with the "arrangements", so persuaded him to marry me secretly in Melbourne a few months ago. We still intend to go ahead with the wedding as planned and no one should have ever found out. Have I offended you very badly by this? It was not intended that way.'

Livinia was dumbstruck. She was bitterly disappointed and saddened that she had been denied the excitement of the long-awaited wedding, and that they would get married without telling her and have a ceremony that she did not attend. On the other hand, it did reinforce her opinion of Jess as a very respectable woman. In fact, she was secretly impressed with her new granddaughter-in-law and conceded to herself that she would probably have done something similar if she were in her shoes. Livinia tried to show the barest modicum of annoyance, which she sincerely felt, without displaying total discontent with the news. She answered coolly, 'Of course not, dear.'

Jess detected the hurt and disappointment in Livinia and felt mildly ashamed, not only for herself, but for Thomas too.

'We still plan to have the wedding in September. We did until this happened. And no one needs to find out now, either,' she said hopefully.

Livinia just sat there in uncomfortable silence. At the first opportunity, she informed an incredulous John. For him, this really threw a brand-new spanner in the works. It was the third disturbing and completely unexpected piece of news. Now he began to understand why she had been so adamant about Ethan not taking over the running of the station. An even more disturbing thought for him was the implications regarding property rights of the wife of Thomas *vis-à-vis* Thomas's shares in the company and the station itself. John began to see Jessie as nothing but trouble for him and his family. *Maybe I should have sided with Jess and dissuaded Thomas from pursuing her.*

About a fortnight later, all hell broke out in the media. Jess had contacted the editor of the local Monaro Post newspaper one afternoon and met her in town. There she gave the editor a small package of papers and spoke to her at length about the case. Jess revealed to the editor, in confidence at this stage, who she was and that, while her address was now in Sydney, she was assisting a friend on a local property and had been attacked. She also advised her that there was a link between this attack and the death on the deserted Lochinvar Lane months earlier. She intimated that the same person was behind both incidents and that the death was no accident but retribution for failure to reveal Jess's whereabouts. Jess told her that a famous judicial family was involved – this the police knew because of telephone records tying it all up.

Jess had purchased a new laptop and a new printer and copied all the papers she possessed on Judge Bales, including some unconnected entries in her diaries. She also concocted, or rather, embellished, a few of the information scraps that she recalled from her days in Newtown and from comments that Don had made to her about Judge Bales Senior and a couple of other judges. Jess knew that this story would reach the big city media from there.

In addition, she enlarged considerably on the incident in Lochinvar Lane, insinuating that the paparazzi had failed in their attempt to expose the object of that exercise and that he was subsequently eliminated for that failure. Jess wrote: *It had been no accident that day on the lonely lane.* Jess also wrote in her package that the victim was associated with Judge Bales through mobile telephone records, information not released by the police. Jess knew that the whole thing was explosive and would cause a huge stir. Then she destroyed the new laptop and printer.

There were many consequences emanating from this affair. Jessie turned more bitter and vengeful, and regretful. She regretted that Livinia had to discover that they were married. Jess had hoped to keep that deceit quiet. Jess conducted most of her life in the Kimberleys in deception and as a fraud, lying and hiding her actions from her dearest, and now, even before she began a new life on the Monaro, she had been discovered doing it all again.

Before his possible recovery became more evident, the implications of Thomas's potential death slowly began to dawn on Jess. The repercussions affected more than just herself. She was now legally married to him, but the main concern for her was John and his property. A few days later, while they were all at the hospital, Jess decided she had better try to assuage any worries John might have.

Next to Thomas was a small quiet alcove that was private and behind where the guard was seated. A few days later, while Livinia was otherwise occupied, Jess asked John if he would like to speak to her for a moment. They entered behind the curtained alcove and sat on the hard plain chairs. There was a long silence. Finally, Jess asked, 'John, if Thomas dies, what would you wish me to do?'

He sat looking at the floor, deep in thought. He knew exactly what he wanted her to do but also wished not to be too undiplomatic. He sucked in an audible breath. Then he replied, 'Well, what would you like to do?'

Jess stared at him with her deep-set eyes. 'I feel you would wish me gone,' she answered. 'But I am open to your suggestions, especially in connection with the management of Auvergne till you can arrange something.'

They sat in deep silence, oblivious of their surroundings. In a rather conciliatory tone, John finally responded, 'Can I think about it? Anyway, he might still pull through.'

'Even if he does,' said Jess, 'things have changed somewhat. You can see what I'm up against. This sort of thing will probably never end.'

They sat in silence again. All that needed to be said was said for the moment.

The next day, Jess suggested that she might return to Auvergne briefly to ensure all was well as Thomas was not expected to have any change in the near future. John and Livinia would be staying for the duration of Thomas's hospitalisation. Jess returned to Rushcutters Bay and prepared to return to Auvergne.

It was a long drive from Rushcutters Bay to Auvergne. Jess had plenty of time to contemplate her dilemma. Once past Cooma, the road wound its way over undulating, gentle country until the station turnoff. Jess turned into the gravel track that was the entrance and, after only a short way, stopped to look at the scene. For the first time she actually looked deeply at the vista. She had been so immersed in her own turmoil about the offer of marriage that she had neglected the other aspects of the deal. Now that she stood to lose all of this, she looked at it all with different eyes.

Jess drove the short distance to the extensive compound that comprised the disparate collection of gardens, arbours and buildings, and crossed the ornate cattle grid that kept out all the extraneous and inappropriate happenings from the outer world. She parked under the portico and just sat. Not long after, she alighted from the vehicle and began to roam through the previously intimidating conglomeration that was once prized gardens and arboreta. She thought that if she had a chance, she would take much more interest in this collection and maybe even attempt to revive it. Deep in her heart, Jess felt this might be unattainable, as every time she found happiness, or at least contentment, it was often dragged away from her.

The other person Jess wanted to consult was Warren Costello, who ran the technical side of the profitable prime fine micron sheep that were shedded in the immediate vicinity of the homestead. Jess knew that this was the main game for the property but she and Thomas knew very little about. The cattle were just an adjunct to this main enterprise and although profitable, not essential.

Warren needed delicate handling. He was a devout Christian and a very decent person. Jess knew that her moving in with Thomas would not have been looked on favourably by the Costellos. Her dilemma was that she was torn between assuaging his feelings on that matter and keeping the marriage a secret until they could be officially wed at the church. She felt telling him alone would not guarantee her secret, especially from the women. The other issue was that she did not want Warren to feel left out of the information loop regarding all matters personal and farming.

Jess hurried over to the main shed where she knew Warren would be working. He seemed anxious to see her and enquired quickly after Thomas. They had a long conversation about administrative matters and whether he could cope on his own with the two girls and Samuel. Jess knew they were of little assistance in the technical aspects of this enterprise. They could, however, run the rest of the place on their own.

Jess leaned back on the heavy wooden pen railing and watched Warren for many minutes.

'Warren, what are your plans for the future?'

He stared sullenly at the prized animal he was attending, then slowly straightened himself and turned to face her. He appeared to Jess to permanently possess a black mood and taciturn, distant eyes. He rarely smiled. 'I have no plans for the future, lass.' He always called her lass for some reason. She supposed it was to do with her obscure and doubtful past, and her aloofness. He maintained his deep stare.

'You will stay on here, then?' asked Jess.

'That's the plan. Unless I'm released.'

'You know you are invaluable to Thomas here, Warren.'

He did not respond.

'Can others learn from you what you do, or do they need technical training?' she asked.

He was slow to answer. 'It is possible to learn the procedures without the college learning, but it is not recommended.'

As he moved along the line of valuable animals, Jess slowly followed him, trying to note what he did. Finally, he asked, 'Are you thinking of letting me go?'

'You've got to be joking Warren!' she blurted out. 'Ultimately, it's up to John, but he knows even less than we do about this operation. He's hardly going to ditch the only man who knows what he's doing here.'

After many minutes shuffling along the board, he asked her, 'What if Thomas dies?'

There was a long silence as Jess contemplated a response. 'Warren,' she said, 'can I tell you something in the strictest confidence?'

'Sure, lass,' he replied, still shuffling along the boards.

'I mean it, Warren. It is to go no further. Not even your wife.'

He stopped and turned to face her. He said nothing, his countenance said it all. He was all seriousness.

'Thomas is very ill and we do not know the prognosis with any certainty. John is thinking what he might have to do to maintain this place. After all, he bought it solely with the intention of it being for Thomas. If Thomas were to die, I'm not sure what will happen. But …Warren there is something else you need to know that no one else knows about yet and I want to keep it that way.'

He looked at her slightly concerned. She stared at him with her penetrating, mesmerising glare and said, 'There has been a development that was not intended to be revealed at this time but circumstances have necessitated that it surface. It has considerable impact on the whole situation.'

Warren stood expectantly, awaiting this revelation of such import.

'As you know, Thomas and I are engaged. We planned to marry in September, but that will probably now not occur.'

'Yes,' he replied.

'Well, Thomas and I are actually already married.' She said no more for a moment to let that sink in. He was perplexed. He was not sure what he had just heard.

'You mean…' was all he could say.

'Yes, Warren, we are already married.'

His facial expression changed. She thought she detected the barest glimmer of a smile. He stared at her, deep in thought. 'But how? I mean…' was all he could mumble.

'I'm sorry this had to come out in this fashion, it was not planned to be so,' she continued. He was becoming more animated as the news sank in. It almost seemed to Jess that it was news of great relief. Finally, he did smile, faintly, and shook his head. 'Well, that is good news.'

'It changes everything, Warren. All we can do now is wait

and see what happens next. Please keep this to yourself for the moment.'

He nodded contentedly, returning to the job in hand, a little happier than he was before.

CHAPTER TWELVE

As Thomas remained in hospital, things moved slowly. But gradually his brain functions returned to normal and it appeared that with a lot of attention he might fully recover. His chest wound was quite serious but, given the time he lay comatose, that allowed for its uninterrupted mending. He was going to require time to return to the physical condition he possessed prior to the incident.

The perpetrators of this crime took some effort to determine. Geoff Bales was implicated, but only indirectly. It appeared he had been scouting around for information on Jessie MacIntyre, and there were still many who wished her ill.

Thomas was in hospital for some time. Eventually it was determined that his recovery would be hastened if he could recuperate at home at Auvergne. Livinia suggested he be brought back to Bridgehead where she could devote twenty-four-hour care to him. Jessie acknowledged that that would be the best course but both she and Thomas determined that a preferred option, all considered, would be to return to Auvergne. There he would be in his own home, with his new wife, though most would not know that information, able still to be involved with the management of the property.

Jess was no Livinia when it came to catering and attention to an invalid, she had had no experience of that, but she was no slouch either. Thomas was inundated with love and care from Jess, and he was able to have input into the day to day running of the place. He received constant visitations from Livinia and Warren and other members of the family. Gradually, Thomas was able to tentatively walk about the sadly neglected and large former garden. He and Jess, and sometimes Livinia, would wander about the accessible parts of the almost abandoned overgrown former parklands. Samuel mowed the grass but he was no horticulturist and did not know one plant from another and could not care less about the appearance of the grounds. For that matter, sadly, nor did Thomas.

Livinia in particular was saddened by the state of the place. Slowly, the idea of restoring the grounds was thought of as a form of occupation that might be beneficial to Thomas's recovery. It occurred to Livinia that one of the grandchildren, Andrew, was studying amenity horticulture and might be of assistance in rehabilitating such a large area, especially as neither Jess nor Thomas had any inclination or ability in that field. In fact, Andrew was running a small part-time garden maintenance business on the side as he studied, and he worked on the Bridgehead and Quiggin's properties. Finding work on these properties for the ever-expanding Summers family was becoming a challenge. This might assist in the successful divesting of at least one of them.

Jess was ambivalent at the suggestion as she still had little interest in superficiality. How the grounds appeared was of little importance in her eyes and she was unconcerned about family members being employed on the property. The success of the rural enterprise bore no relationship to the appearance of the homestead. Livinia was quite struck at the depth of Jess's lack of interest in the grounds as she herself was a keen gardener.

Nevertheless, Livinia persevered gently, and eventually got them to at least agree to meet Andrew and see if he had any suggestions. One cool sunny afternoon, Andrew came out in his work vehicle to wander the grounds with Jess and Thomas. Andrew was a tall lad, about eighteen, quiet and well mannered. The three of them meandered about the large compound as Andrew pointed out this aspect and that aspect of the once magnificent vista. He enthused rather exuberantly and appeared to be very knowledgeable about his subject. His enthusiasm had quite an impact on Jess as he pointed out things and ideas that she simply did not see. It reminded her instantly of Henry and his portrayal of the Gibb River Road that she bought from him a few years ago. Despite driving countless times along that road in the Kimberleys, Henry's depiction had something in it that she had totally missed. *Maybe*, she thought, *this was another case of that.*

Jess and Thomas suggested to Andrew that he draw up a plan of attack and they would think about it. *After all*, thought Jess, *it might give Thomas another interest to aid in his recovery and take his mind off himself.* Andrew was very excited at the prospect of having the chance to restore the gardens. He spent a lot of time designing a plan, and a programme of restoration. Jess was impressed with the submission and together with Thomas agreed to let Andrew loose on the site. Within a month he was living in one of the workers quarters along with the two girls that had joined the workforce much earlier on.

Andrew began by cleaning up the site, mowing grass that had long returned to scrub, and resurrecting garden beds that had also long ago disappeared.

Over the next few years, he returned the compound back to its former glory and rehabilitated the neglected ancient trees. Jess was surprisingly delighted with the results.

Jess had successfully resisted John's efforts to assist Thomas with any additional management assistance from Bridgehead, Quiggins or Templemore, where Damien had his lucerne farm. She, along with Warren and increasingly Thomas, managed the place admirably and there was no interruption to the smooth operation of the property.

Slowly, Thomas improved. He would always suffer from periodic bouts of re-occurring pain, discomfort and restriction related to the chest wound, but essentially, he made a full recovery. Many months later, Jess again raised the issue of the postponed marriage. They had managed to keep that little secret, and only Warren, Livinia and John knew that they were already married.

Jess decided to leave all the arrangements to Livinia. This was for two reasons. One, Jess never forgave herself for inflicting such unintentional pain on Livinia by deceitfully marrying Thomas in secret, thus depriving Livinia of that pleasure; and secondly, she had no idea how to go about such an event herself. It was all to take place at the little church that held so much history for the Summers clan on the dusty road leading back to Cooma from Bridgehead. Suffice it to say, it was a sumptuous affair, well attended and dignified. Jess was nervous and slightly embarrassed by the whole affair, as she felt strange to be going through all this when she was already married. The pretence was something she detested immensely.

Despite the trauma of Thomas's accident and the time needed to devote to his recovery and the management of the disparate areas of the enterprise, Jess did not wish to neglect the one thing that was her real passion, her authorship. Jane Ransom as an author was now dead. George Norman Thaler was now dead. Kimberley West was still working but her output was taking a backseat to the quickly evolving Catherine Holbrook Seymour. Joe Scacci was now dead. She decided that after the disaster at the Cooma stockyards, he was possibly too dangerous to be let loose on the world. *Besides, he had to some extent achieved my aim by exposing what I knew to anybody that was prepared to read those novels. No, now all my efforts would henceforth be devoted solely to Catherine Holbrook Seymour.*

Keeping anonymity was always going to be a challenge, especially now that she was married and more permanently domiciled. Her change of name to Summers would assist enormously in that enterprise. However, she realised that one day, no doubt, her charade would collapse about her. Until then, she would take pleasure in her subterfuge. Moreover, her unbridled burning need to create was gradually diminishing, as she was becoming more fulfilled and occupied with her new situation. She was also ageing, maybe that was an influence as well as her priorities altered. She was becoming more contented. She looked back at her improbable life and its previous incarnations as if she were looking back at a complete stranger.

Several years after Jessie and Thomas were married, many changes occurred. Over that time, the family had come to accept Jess as she was – a complex, aloof and often distant person from whom none of her secrets from her previous life could ever be prised if she was unwilling to do so. She was private, reticent and unwilling to divulge anything of her previous disrepute. She found her fame and notoriety a slight embarrassment and rather burdensome. In fact, one of the greatest benefits to her of marrying Thomas was gaining the anonymity that the Summers name gave to her, and she accepted that new epithet with alacrity, in public anyway. She willingly, though sadly, disposed of the infamous Jessie

MacIntyre, and reluctantly, the secretive and mysterious Jane Ransom, and serenely bathed in the vagueness and elusiveness of her new married name. She had little in common with the herd, though Damien, who lived opposite John on his lucerne property, and she, could talk at length on esoteric topics.

John grew to like her, and her contribution to the family company, but he always had an underlying general uneasiness about her and her connections. She was the one person he knew who could rummage into his murky past, the only known person who possibly had any knowledge of his secret. To the Summers women other than Livinia, she was an enigma, a complete stranger; almost foreign.

As he aged, John occasionally fell ill with respiratory troubles, probably associated with the rigours accompanying the long bitter winters on the Southern Tablelands. He began to dread the cold and the infirmities it now invariably seemed to engender.

Recuperating slowly on one of these occasions, John was anxious to assuage his guilty mind, if possible, by delving into what Jess might know of him. He sat in his study in the expansive modern homestead, as he often did, all alone. It was deathly quiet; only the ticking of the long-case clock penetrated any silence, exuding a reassurance that was of immense comfort and familiarity to him. In here, he was surrounded by the tangible signs of his success. If any other sound penetrated the silence of his study, it was the sound of his stock or birds.

John had only one regret in his life and only one fear. His

only regret was the death of his twin boy, Brendan, at age ten. He blamed himself entirely for that event and often wondered what sort of man he would have grown into had he lived. He was proud of all his children, though less so of Audrey. He wondered where she had been infected with the 'disease', as he saw it, of hippy socialism. He knew it began when she attended university.

John could be sadly philosophical about his regrets, but he was plagued by his one fear. It was a constant, though diminishing, nagging dread that the manner of his acquisition of his enormous wealth and security would one day be unearthed. On this occasion, as he convalesced, he decided to invite Thomas and Jess to Bridgehead for a mid-week lunch, just on their own – an unusual occurrence.

Jess was always uncomfortable at social gatherings as she was not a good mixer. John was not a man to trivialise a gathering merely as a social assembly, so she suspected he had a more serious reason for the invitation. Jess found individual meetings difficult as she was a poor communicator of the spoken word and, simply found conversation boring. She detested large soirees even more as she harboured an inbuilt dread of people. Their incessant and inane nonsense drove her to distraction. She essentially displayed mild psychopathic tendencies. Her dread was further exacerbated by her soft voice, one which did not project well, and she would soon get stressed with her inability to engage in lengthy conversations. She also harboured an inbuilt fear of alcohol and never drank, therefore that avenue of stress relief was also denied to her.

Thomas loved and adored his grandparents and enjoyed being in their presence at every opportunity. Livinia was a garrulous, almost compulsive conversationalist, and thrived on the little she was able to engage in out in the wilds of the Monaro. John was a taciturn man, not given to outward displays, and tended to be secretive and guarded. A gathering of so disparate and small a group of personalities alerted Jess that it might entail considerable effort to navigate the day, a consideration that filled her with misgivings. *Besides, John did not normally invite people there just for company.*

They arrived at Bridgehead late in the morning and made for the casual sunroom off the kitchen end of the large house. They chattered idly throughout the morning, not delving deeply into anything much. Livinia had gone to a lot of trouble preparing a meal for just four people, but Jess knew that Livinia would do nothing less. They adjourned to the formal dining room for a disproportionately sumptuous lunch amid the incongruously splendid surrounds of the Victorian-like dining room. Amid much clanking and clinking, little was discussed, but Jess had time to thoroughly admire the sumptuous décor. Her mind was cast back to the deprivations under which the rural folks she had grown up with in the Kimberleys endured, and felt a tinge of guilt and envy. Slowly, Jessie's disquiet subsided as the afternoon wore on and she became more comfortable in their presence. Nothing untoward arose and nothing controversial crept into the calmness of the gathering.

As it was still winter, the days drew in quite early and Thomas and Jess would need to return soon if they were to get home in any light. Jess's mind slowly began to wander, engrossed in her latest creative thoughts and enterprises associated with her trade, an occurrence she realised was rather disrespectful to the Summers. Suddenly, breaking one of his more frequently occurring pauses, and with quiet deliberation, John said to her, 'Jess, would you like to come with me to the shed, there is something I'd like to show you. It won't take long.'

Jess snapped out of her half-idyll and muttered agreement. They both arose from their seats and Jess followed John out the back and over to the huge shed, part of which she knew was actually once his home. She assumed he was going to show her one of his many vehicles as this was one topic about which they both shared an enormous passion. The shed was now usually kept closed against the weather and he opened the small door that allowed entry to the building. It was dark as it was all closed up, and the late winter afternoon was well advanced, putting the sun low on the western hills already. John moved confidently in the dark over to the door that allowed entry to his former living quarters and opened it with a creaking slow swing, which enabled Jess to see better as there were windows in the old living quarters that released light into that part of the building, sufficient for her to see clearly.

Jess had never been into the old living quarters before. She had heard about it and certainly been into the vehicular part many times, but not into here. She was amazed to find it so elegantly furnished and seemingly still operational. She followed a determined John into one of the separate rooms further down the hall. She was slightly stunned to find an equally graceful room furnished in the fashion of an operating study or office. To her it was obviously still functioning.

John moved directly behind the large desk and sat in the old chair. He beckoned her to sit in the chair at the front of the desk. He sat silently for some time thinking and looking at her. Jess just sat there waiting, her hands clasped into her lap, staring at him with her disconcerting, severe and penetrating gaze that always seemed to alarm him slightly. He started, 'Jess, I read your latest book. I'm not much of a reader – in fact, to be honest, I haven't really read many of your books at all. I read very little.'

Jess nodded in agreement.

'I'm getting on now, Jessie, and I realise my health is failing also,' he said with a tinge of resignation and sadness.

'I have only two real regrets that worry me in this life.' He paused again, looking sternly at her. 'One is the death of Brendan.' Again, he paused, looking at a small framed picture to one side of the desk top. Jess knew very little about his dead son, except that it happened a long time ago. She said nothing, waiting for him to continue, staring blankly at him as he turned back to firmly face her. Then he continued, 'Jess, I know we both have secrets that we wish to keep hidden. Mine are not for public scrutiny as yours are, and my only other worry is that something adverse to my family may come up in the circles that you move in. I'd like to ask you what you know of me as I understand things have been said.'

There was a long pause as she stared at him in inner discomfort. She did not move in her chair as she finished listening and was deep in thought. She was rather taken aback by the question. She was now recalling in her mind the conversation she had years ago in Woy Woy with Ian Knuckey about the Summers name. The long pause continued. He sat just staring at her mute unmoving face.

Finally, she said to him, 'John, I know nothing of your family affairs and have made it a condition not to do so.'

'My name has not cropped up in any of your investigations?' he asked, rather pointedly.

'No John,' she replied. 'The only mention I've heard of your name was in connection with your father and his death in 1939.'

'What do you know of that?' he asked, suddenly a lot more animated now.

'Nothing, nothing at all. All we know was that he, and your mother, were killed in a car accident after leaving the race track. He was a very wealthy man, but then you would have known that.'

'No!' John blurted out suddenly. Then he realised he had better be very careful about what he said. 'No, not really,' he continued more calmly. 'I mean, I didn't really know how rich he had been. You see ...' He stopped talking mid-sentence.

There was a silence, then Jess continued, 'As I mentioned before, he had applied to join the AJC. You need big bickies to join that.'

'What is the AJC again? And what happened to the money?'

Jess stared at him. She was not sure whether he was bluffing or genuinely did not know.

'The Australian Jockey Club. You don't know?' she asked.

'No,' he said firmly, 'but I heard rumours when I was a child.'

'About what?'

'Well. When I was young, my grandmother spoke of going to the track and the money my father made there.' He leant over slightly to his right and opened a drawer of the desk and reached in to retrieve something. He withdrew a small item and toyed with it in his hands. He passed it over to Jess and said, 'Does any of this make sense to you?'

She reached over to accept the proffered item and examined it thoroughly – for a long time. John sat silently as she read and re-read the card. It was a sallow piece of thin, cardboard-like paper only about four inches by three. It consisted of several individual pieces unpicked from a once entire piece. There was also a small clipping from the personal columns of a newspaper. Jess read it all carefully. The cardboard piece simply read, 'Today discovered H secret. Money belongs John. There is C £120 grand in folding 4 AJC Already spent lot put this away for J. WTS died no will car to pars H nicked dosh.'

Jess thought about it. Then she turned over what was once the other outside piece. In the dull light of the office, she was able to discern some faint pencil weaving itself in the soft surface. She could not read it. John fumbled in his top drawer and retrieved a strong magnifying glass he used when mending instruments. Jess tried to make sense of the faint writing.

Jess stared at the bluish pencil scrawl that weakly covered the paper. It was almost too faint to decipher. She would return to this shortly, but first, to the clipping. It read, 'The death occurred yesterday of the well-known racing figure, Mr Wesley Thomas Summers. He was killed, along with his wife, in a car accident on Anzac Parade near the corner of Alison Road. The AJC has expressed its regrets at the loss as Mr Summers had only recently been awarded his Bookmakers licence to operate at Randwick Racecourse. Mr Summers is believed to have left a considerable estate, following some large and controversial betting plunges on races at both Randwick and Harold Park.'

Jess placed the clipping on the table. She returned to the faint bluish scrawl on the yellowing cardboard. She began to see the words in a certain light and to decipher one or two. She would return to this later.

She looked up at John seated on the other side of the large neat desk. She held the pieces in her left hand. After a pause, she said to him, 'What is it you want?'

'Does any of that make sense to you?'

She rummaged through the pieces and retrieved the first bit. She began, 'Well, this one is pretty clear. It states, *Today, whenever that was that someone discovered H secret.* Who is H and what is his secret?'

John shrugged his shoulders and looked blank. Jess continued, 'It goes on, *Money belongs John.* There is some money that belongs to a John. Is that you? *There is C £120 grand in folding 4 AJC.* There is about one hundred and twenty thousand pounds in cash, folding money, for the AJC.'

'What does that mean, exactly?' he interrupted.

'It means, according to me, that there is approximately one hundred and twenty thousand pounds, that is pounds not dollars, in ready folding cash available for use for the AJC. Probably as surety. You need a lot of moolah to be a bookie. Your father must have had a lot of money available to join up.'

'So, where is it then?' he asked.

'Good question. You never saw any of it then?'

'No,' he lied.

Jess sat deep in thought. Again, she recalled Ian Knuckey hinting that John was a very wealthy man with a lot of expensive assets that they would have liked to have known how he accumulated. Apparently not from any known inheritance. Jess thought, *There appears to be no criminal connection – nevertheless, they were intrigued. I'm not.*

'Let me continue then,' she responded. 'It goes on to say *already spent lot put this away for J. WTS died no will car to pars H nicked dosh.* I think that means, a lot of this cash has already been spent, probably by this H person. Do you know any Hs in your life?'

John thought for a while, or pretended to, as he assumed that this H could only be Henry Merritt. Then he replied, 'No, not really.'

He suddenly realised that he did not want anyone connecting the Merritts with his funding. Then there was another potential problem area; his wayward daughter and her husband Geoff Bales. John knew there were issues between Bales and Jessie and a connection that had the prospective ability to impact on him as well. If investigations into Bales led to too close a scrutiny of his finances, he might have trouble explaining his accumulated wealth, or more to the point, its genesis. He changed tack a little by asking Jess, 'Are there any problems with Bales?'

Jess looked at him queerly, then said, 'No. Not that I know.'

'I mean, is he a problem?'

'No. Not as far as I know. I do know that he is implicated in many bad things, but I think he will be too closely watched now to worry us, hopefully.'

John sat back deeply into the old chair and looked at her. He had grown to like her in a very wary and cautious way, maybe more to deeply respect her. Her knowledge of his affairs, or her potential knowledge of them were always a concern to him. He looked steadily at her for some time. Then he offered, 'Jess, I have been an exceptionally lucky man. My fortune has been accumulated with some amount of chance. I'd hate for it to be at risk now because of something someone else has done. Do you understand?'

Jess was not entirely sure what he meant or where this was going, or for that matter why he confided in her so. She looked at him. She detected a vulnerability she had not previously seen. *Was he seeking some form of assurance from me?*

Finally, she said, 'Look John, as far as I know, there is absolutely nothing about you personally that the commissions are investigating. Your father was suspected of shady dealings with horse racing, but nothing could ever be found, that is all.'

Jess was thinking about a comment that Ian Knuckey had made some time ago in Woy Woy. She gathered her thoughts and then said, 'John, Ian Knuckey told me that as far as he knows or has been able to ascertain, he surmised that, at your father's death, one of your relatives collected all the loot from the bank safe deposit box and kept it in abeyance privately for you into the future. Maybe passing it on to you outside the banking system? Is that not a possibility?'

John was not sure whether this was a genuine assumption or a hint of an explanation or excuse he could promulgate as an explanation of his early unaccountable wealth. It certainly gave him a huge clue to a good justification for his method. He was rather grateful for this brief interlude. It afforded him some considerable comfort. He was deep in these thoughts, and contemplating that any of the original miscreants were now all dead, so he could surely concoct a suitable rationalisation.

John was pensive, gazing mutely at Jess over the desk, neither speaking or moving. She was an amazing woman, he concluded. He was very grateful for her insight. Suddenly, he realised he was staring at her. He jumped slightly in his chair and leaned forward. He thanked her profusely for her candour. She merely smiled slightly and remained immobile. Then they wandered slowly back to Livinia and Thomas in the main house.

Over the next few years, life progressed in its inevitable way. Jessie and Thomas eked out a relatively uneventful existence together. They finally let Andrew loose on the original formal garden and, over time, he restored it to a state resembling its former glory. Warren began training the two girls from the family, who had first been sent as workers there, in his trade and they also both began tertiary studies in that field. Thomas kept the cattle on as both he and Jess rather enjoyed that aspect of farming, despite the main activity being sheep.

Jess and Thomas occasionally used her Rushcutters Bay apartment for holidays and minor business visits, but Thomas was not all that enamoured of city life. He was, however, much more interested in her hidden and remote bush block set high up in the distant ranges on the high plains. They spent much time there and allowed any of the younger family members access if they were truly keen. Jess still wrote novels but they were becoming much less frequent. The need, and passion, to create slowly dissipated as she aged and her sense of contentment increased in her life with Thomas and living at Auvergne. They visited Bridgehead very often as the family gatherings were mandatory for the clan while Livinia was able to maintain her health.

The issue of Livinia's failing health finally arose a few years after Jess and Thomas's wedding. She had maintained reasonable health most of her life, but, inevitably, as they aged, John and Livinia succumbed to ailments. Then, one day out of the blue, Livinia suddenly announced that she had been diagnosed with a nasty terminal disease that would run its inevitable and quickish course to a disconcerting and difficult end. John was exceedingly attentive to her as she deteriorated into a completely bedridden and finally immobile state. She died at home in some comfort. This left John alone, so to speak, as he remained in the big house.

This was not particularly abhorrent to him as he had always been in his younger days of a solitary mindset. Despite his now large family, John spent much time contemplating his life in solitude. If he had asked Livinia what was the highlight of her life, he knew that she would have replied unhesitatingly: meeting John; marrying John; being married to him and having the family – no more, no less. In reality, she had openly told him so many times during her life. Not so John. It pained him enormously that that was not the case with him. If he were asked that question, he would answer differently.

John used the analogy for his life of that of a child: *We are born; we are a child; we are a youth; we are a young adult, and finally a mature committed adult. The progression is inexorable. On reflection however, we may view any one of these stages as our favourite.*

John always viewed as the highlight of his life, the period from when he first purchased Bridgehead up until the time that he first met Livinia. That was his beloved time, a time of unbounded pleasure: buying things, accumulating assets and not a worry. It did aggrieve and distress him that this was his honest analysis.

John viewed that period as a form of early schooling, a form of childhood, preparing him for the real meaning of life and adulthood – family responsibility. The burden of accountability and stress was tempered by the memory of the previous nirvana. He wallowed in the satisfaction of his assets, all acquired before the onset of real duty.

Now he surveyed his domain with mature and reflective eyes. He had been assured by Ethan that he would maintain the status quo as much as possible. He would not interfere with Thomas; he would not interfere with Damien and his lucerne enterprise; and he would try to keep the family off-farm assets intact as a backup. His leading hand, Neil Brody, had long retired, so that irritant had gone. Most of his progeny who wished to be employed on the properties were catered for and all seemed in order.

As he neared the end of his life, John realised that all his worldly possessions did not mean that much to him. He was immensely grateful that Livinia had preceded him in death. She would not have coped being alone half as well as he was able to. He was rather grateful also that he now had this twilight time to reconsider his life. He often recalled a sermon of the long-retired pastor, Robert Meagher. He did not miss attending the small church the way Livinia did – she needing that outlet, he not so.

However, of all the words that the minister sprayed to that little flock, only a couple stayed with John. The one that gave him the most impact was this story: a wealthy man died and at his funeral a man said to the bishop, 'I believe he was very rich. How much did he leave?' The bishop replied simply, 'All of it.'

That tale resonated immensely with John. In some ways, the story gave him great comfort. He was very grateful for fate to allow him to live long enough to recognise these facts and endure the full extent of all of life's experiences – something that he would have missed if it were not for Livinia. He believed that he would have remained an incomplete human if he had not shared most of his life with her.

He received one more solace from the words of the reverend – that with his death, he would be leaving behind any sinful debts he may have incurred in the manner in which he acquired his wealth, at least in this world. With his death, he hoped that all evidence, and any chance of investigation of his life, would stay with him in his grave.

www.ingramcontent.com/pod-product-compliance
Lightning Source LLC
Chambersburg PA
CBHW020345120726
47904CB00002B/465